'Are you angry about something, Alexa?'

'You know I am—and you know why!' she flung back.

'I assure you I do not. Luc and I have spent a great deal of time together over the past few years. We enjoy each other's company and I have no intention of that changing simply because he has taken himself a young wife who demands all his attention. It is a little late to play the worried wife, don't you think, Alexa? Considering the engagements you are dragging the poor man to all this year—bad health or not.'

The insult robbed her of speech. Nothing could have been further from the truth, but she had no intention of arguing with Alain about it. It was none of his business.

'Are you jealous, *monsieur*, now that he prefers my company to yours?' she flung back with a toss of her fair curls. 'A wife's privileges come before those of a friend, even someone who thinks himself of special importance—as you do!'

Valentina Luellen was born in London in 1938, and educated in Gloucestershire and London. She began writing at school—mainly because she loathed maths! It took her twelve years of writing before she had a book accepted, but she has now had over forty-seven stories published. Historical romances are her favourite to write, because she loves researching into so many different countries, learning about customs and costumes and the way people lived hundreds of years ago.

Valentina Luellen and her husband moved to Portugal ten years ago when he became seriously ill. There his health began to improve and now they live in a farmhouse, still under renovation which they are doing themselves, located in a hillside village near Faro on the Algarve, with their son, fourteen cats and two Portuguese dogs and around 100 trees—almonds, olives, figs, plums, lemons and oranges.

Whenevere there is any spare time, Valentina Luellen's hobbies are restoring antique furniture, decorating, cooking and dressmaking.

THE WEB OF LOVE

The Sequel to Love and Pride

Valentina Luellen

MILLS & BOON LIMITED
ETON HOUSE   18-24 PARADISE ROAD
RICHMOND   SURREY   TW9 1SR

First published in Great Britain 1989
by Mills & Boon Limited

© Valentina Luellen 1989

Australian copyright 1989
Philippine copyright 1989
This edition 1989

ISBN 0 263 76643 8

Set in Times Roman 10 on 10¼ pt.
04-8911-91287 C

Made and printed in Great Britain

CHAPTER ONE

ALEXANDRINE dragged her eyes away from the clear
waters of the ornamental pool where she had briefly
paused during her walk in the gardens of the Château
d'Etoiles—away from the handsome features which had
suddenly become mirrored there, obliterating the brightly
coloured fish gliding beneath the surface. Mirrored there
to pierce her heart as clearly as if the man himself were
standing at her side. He had plagued her thoughts day
and night, no matter how hard she had tried to rid her
mind of him, since she had arrived at this beautifully
secluded place which was meant to be a retreat for her
husband, a chance to rest and recover his health after
the terrible nightmare in which they had both been engulfed at the hands of his own son. An embittered, vindictive young man who sought to destroy not only his
father, but also the stepmother who would inherit all his
riches upon his death, leaving him penniless—an outcast
from the glittering court at Versailles, the gaming tables,
the easy life-style to which he had become accustomed,
due to his father's money and influence in Paris.

Luc Boussières, Marquis de Mezière, had, as
Alexandrine had hoped, found the peace needed to restore tranquillity to his shattered brain. And for her too
the long weeks had brought a certain contentment—but
only when she was with her husband. Alone at night—
for he had never once attempted to lay claim to her in
any way, save that she look pretty for him at all times
and never bring shame upon his name by taking a lover
before he was in his grave—there was only ever one man
in her thoughts. The same who had insulted her the very
first night Luc took her to his home in Paris, the Hôtel
Boussières, and introduced her to his son—a son, she
had discovered, only a few years older than she was

5

herself! And the Marquis was older than her father had
been when he had died of the dreaded plague a few
months before!

The shame of those first few hectic weeks, when she,
a simple country girl, had come to realise the role being
thrust upon her! Alexandrine d'Albret was now the wife
of the Marquis de Mezière. *She* was a marquise, with
servants of her own, her own carriage and coat of arms.
She had been gowned and adorned with fabulous jewels
and shown off at Versailles and had been noticed by the
King himself, yet those dark eyes that had stirred the
hearts of so many women failed to stir any feeling in
hers. Her heart belonged to one man only.

Alain Ratan, Duc de Belaincourt, her husband's
closest friend—and the man she loved with all her heart
and soul. He was wealthy, arrogant and one of the
favoured élite whom the King often selected to have close
at his side. Disillusioned by the betrayal of the beautiful
wife he had loved—and lost through a tragic accident
after her many affairs had provoked sufficient gossip to
keep the whole of Paris chattering for a year—he had
sworn never to love again.

He would never love her, Alexandrine acknowledged.
He was too proud to allow himself that all-consuming
passion a second time. Yet it did not matter. Before she
had left Paris at Christmas she had given him not only
her heart—but her body!

I shall never let you go, Alexa—you are mine. The
words he had whispered as he held her in his arms before
they parted the next morning tormented her mind like
the fires of hell. As they should! She had been weak! It
was unforgivable to have betrayed her husband as she
did. It would never happen again. Alain's words had
meant nothing. Perhaps he had hoped they would ease
her mind so that she did not gather enough courage to
go to her husband and confess what had taken place.
For so long she had fought against the attraction growing
inside her, the need to be loved which he had aroused,
and then in one wild moment of madness his soul-
searching kisses had destroyed the last barriers.

She would never lie in his arms again. Never allow herself the pleasure of his passionate kisses. She was the wife of the Marquis de Mezière, a kind-hearted man who cared for her in a way she would never quite understand, but he cared—and Alain Ratan did not!

Luc was her husband—Alain a man who had seduced her with soft endearments and tender kisses. Nay! The truth of it was she had fallen in love. Cupid had loosed his arrow and she had been helpless against the barb which pierced her heart. The truth of it was, she had been weak! Never having known love before, she had succumbed to its temptations.

With a soft sigh Alexandrine picked up her skirts and turned back towards the house. The country château of her close friend, Jeanne d'Etoiles, was large, very comfortably furnished and set in pleasant, uncluttered surroundings—and managed by a staff of efficient servants who made every guest feel like royalty.

Her husband loved the intellectual atmosphere which prevailed here, for Jeanne was widely known throughout Paris for her patronage of poets and writers, and entertained them often both there and in the country. The mingling of keen minds eager to explore new theories, discuss books most people had never heard of—most of all to listen and learn. Luc's mind was once more awakened to the living world.

For the first two weeks he had taken little interest in anyone or anything, but then slowly he began to take part in the conversations, challenged a theory, put forward one of his own, and Alexandrine knew that day that he had not, as she was beginning to fear, lost his sanity.

Now he could walk with the aid of a stick and the strong arm of his constant companion and personal physician, the Moor Selim, but no matter how much he ate he never seemed to put on weight, and he tired so easily... Alexandrine was fortunate if she saw him for more than three or four hours a day, and that was usually in the evenings when he came together with the other guests.

A slight improvement took place at the beginning of February, but she doubted if he would ever again lead the active life he had once had in society and at Court. She did not care! He was well again, and the hours they shared, however short, were full of interest. She had begun to improve her own limited knowledge of books and had purchased some from Paris to be brought to Etoiles for her husband. When he had perused them he read to her, her fascination with distant lands and strange cultures satiated by his colourful rhetoric, which she knew very often came not from the book open on his lap but from his vast experience of other lands that he had travelled during his lifetime.

Alexandrine had grown comfortable and relaxed at Etoiles and did not want to leave, but leave she knew they must, to return to the city. To Paris—to Versailles— to the hatred of her stepson and more threats that she would never live to inherit his father's wealth!

As he watched his wife enter the pleasant sitting-room where he sat talking with Jeanne d'Etoiles, Luc Boussières thought how much the country air agreed with them both. His wife's cheeks glowed with health, bright pink from the sharp wind which swept the gardens. She wore a gown of saffron velvet, trimmed at the sleeves and hemline with three rows of intricately woven gold thread. It was the perfect colour to set off the fair curls which surrounded the young face. The little girl from Noyen had grown up. She had accepted with a serenity which touched Luc's heart all the unpleasantness and troubles which had plagued their lives since they married. She never complained when he grew tired and irritable, or reproached him when at times he snapped at her. She was perfect in every way, and he thanked God for allowing him to possess her.

'What are the two of you being so secretive about?' Alexandrine asked, her hazel eyes flecked with amusement as she bent to kiss a lined cheek and sat beside her husband on the couch.

'I have been explaining to Madame that we must leave at the end of next week. I shall send word to the house today, to warn them of our impending arrival,' Luc told her.

'Of course, if that is what you wish.' Alexandrine hid her disappointment at the news. 'I shall miss this place, even though Jeanne will probably be glad to see the back of us.'

'You know you are welcome to stay as long as you like,' Jeanne replied. 'What is there to go back to the city for? For me it is different, but life in the country seems to suit the two of you. How I wish everyone who came here were as interesting—or as pretty. Luc enthrals them with his tales of distant countries and if they grow bored—not that I have noticed anyone being so—they can look at Alexandrine all evening. Look at her! Married for six whole months and she can still blush at a compliment.'

'The sign of an unspoilt woman,' Luc said, patting his wife's slender hand. 'Your kindness will not be forgotten, *madame*. Our house will always be open to you also. However, I feel I have deprived Alexandrine too long of a little excitement in her life with this wretched health of mine.'

'I do not miss Paris at all,' Alexandrine protested. In Paris there was his son Paul to wreak havoc on their lives again. She had not forgotten the terrible threats he had made against them both! There was Versailles, and all those awful people who gossiped about her and her marriage to a man of sixty-two in ill health. She had been reduced to tears when she had first realised what they believed her to be—an adventuress, a scheming nobody from the country who had married for money. How different the truth was! But she had been too proud to confide in anyone but Jeanne d'Etoiles, who had befriended her soon after her arrival in Paris.

Worst of all in Paris—there was Alain Ratan! He was a frequent visitor to the house, making it impossible for her to avoid him. But if she did not...

'Perhaps we could go to the country for the summer,' Luc said thoughtfully. 'I have been considering opening up your old house in Noyen for some time now. Would you like that?'

'Oh, Luc, that would be wonderful.' She seized on the idea instantly as a way out of her dilemma. Perhaps, once there, she could persuade him to stay. 'And Jeanne can visit us.'

'An excellent idea.' She helped him to his feet, but he waved her back to her seat when she would have followed him to the door. 'I shall go and rest for a while, my dear. Stay and chatter with Madame.' For a moment his fingers lightly touched her cheek. 'You do look radiant. Quite radiant.'

'I am so relieved he is better,' Alexandrine said as she sank back into a cushioned seat. 'You have been marvellous to us, Jeanne. I will never be able to thank you enough.'

'You needed to get away from Paris as much as your husband did.' Jeanne's blue eyes studied her friend curiously. 'I think you also need to confide in someone, Alexandrine. You were a nervous wreck a month ago. And a moment ago, when Luc mentioned returning home, there was a look in your eyes which indicated to me that you may be reduced to that state again. What frightens you so about returning to Paris? Is that wretched son of his still planning to make trouble for you? We are friends, are we not? Surely you can tell me.'

Alexandrine hesitated. She had not wanted to involve Jeanne in her troubles, despite the close friendship which had developed between them since their first meeting. What a monumental day in her life that had been, Alexandrine thought. To learn that her companion's stars—as forecast by a fortune-teller in the poor Beggars' Quarter of the city—had decreed she would sit at the side of the King and, as his mistress, would become the most powerful woman in France. The very same woman who studied Alexandrine's hand and announced there would be two men in her life who would love her! She had not believed either story, but then, as the months passed, Jeanne Poisson d'Etoiles, born of the same humble background as she herself, had been noticed by the monarch of France—and into *her* life had come Alain Ratan!

'I—I don't know where to start . . . the last six months have been the strangest of my life . . .' she confessed, embarrassed colour staining her cheeks. Strange and frightening.

'Try the beginning,' Jeanne murmured, settling herself more comfortably into her chair. Once again Alexandrine found herself thinking how terribly fragile—and vulnerable—she always looked. A fragile doll, with skin like porcelain, a perfect figure and an alert mind which often confounded her critics. But would she have the stamina to hold a man as worldly as King Louis, whose wandering eyes were forever seeking new diversions? Or to combat the fierce possessiveness of his present mistress, the Duchesse de Châteauroux who, together with her close confidant the Duc de Richelieu, schemed to dominate Louis completely? It seemed so unlikely—yet Jeanne believed with all her heart that she would become the King's mistress. She had followed the hunt in her phaeton—been seen at many of the haunts frequented by the King—her patience inexhaustible as she waited to be noticed. As a bourgeoise, not born noble, she was not permitted to attend Versailles unless it was by invitation of the King himself, but she believed it would happen—one day.

'The beginning,' Alexandrine murmured. 'It seems an eternity away. Luc came to our village, Noyen, thinking he was coming to my wedding . . .' How strange. When she tried to remember the face of the young man to whom she had been betrothed since the age of fourteen, she could not remember it. 'I told you how close he was to my family. My parents had known him for years and he always brought presents for them and myself and my brother and sister when he came back from his travels— and the stories he told us . . .' She was silent for a long moment as memories of that terrible time came crowding back into her mind. 'A week before I was to have been married, plague struck Noyen. Half the village died within a week including my betrothed. It took my father, my brother and then my sister. I nursed them all. Finally my mother. I don't remember very much after she died except feeling very alone and frightened. And then one morning I opened my eyes and Luc was at my bedside, and Selim. How the first sight of his black face terrified me—he looked so fierce. By some miracle I had not caught the disease, but had collapsed from exhaustion.'

'And no wonder.'

A servant brought them light refreshment, placed the tray on the table between them and left the room as noiselessly as he had entered.

'As soon as I was strong enough to travel, Luc closed up the house, we were married in the village church and then he brought me to Paris,' Alexandrine went on.

'For a marriage of convenience it has certainly turned out to be a happy one,' Jeanne remarked, helping herself to a large almond truffle soaked in wine.

'When he said he only wanted to take care of me, I did not believe him. But he has been so wonderful to me and has asked nothing in return.'

'Nothing?' Jeanne queried, one slender eyebrow arching.

'Nothing at all—except that I always look pretty for him, do nothing to dishonour his name—and . . .'

'And?' Jeanne had no intention of allowing her to avoid the issue.

'And he made me promise not to take a lover until after he was dead. As if I would! Everything I have he has given me. I would never hurt him!'

But she *had* taken a lover. The shameful secret would remain locked in her heart. She would share her burden of guilt with no other.

'I swear he has grown ten years younger since he wed you,' Jeanne declared. 'Everyone can see he is happy.'

'Except his son Paul. That man is a monster, Jeanne.' The words began to flow fast and furious as Alexandrine described how she had been insulted the very first night she set foot in the Hôtel Boussières, and most days after that until heated arguments between Luc and his son resulted in the latter being barred from the house. And

that had not been the end of it. At Versailles she had
been subjected to the stares and lewd comments of Paul's
friends, every word meant to humiliate and goad her.
Had it not been for the calm demeanour of her husband,
she knew she would never have retained her temper.
Gradually she had learned to ignore the wicked tongues
and the insinuating glances, while the brief attention the
King had shown her had effectively silenced a few
tongues. If she had been noticed by the monarch himself,
then her friendship could be of value in the future, for
he did not show an interest in a woman and not pursue
her!

'Luc was quite right to disinherit the young man,'
Jeanne declared. She considered the plate of almond
truffles at her fingertips, thought of what another one
might do to her waistline—and accepted defeat with a
soft sigh and another mouthwatering delicacy. 'Without
money he cannot harm either of you—can he?'

'He hired men to kidnap Luc,' Alexandrine said in a
low tone. 'He was going to have him confined in the
Bastille until he died! That is the kind of wickedness Luc
has sired—and he is such a good man that I cannot
understand it. Paul broke into the house and forced me
to wait on him like a common servant... Oh, Jeanne,
the terrible things he said he would do to me after Luc
was dead! Had it not been for Alain Ratan, Luc would
have simply disappeared, and I——' She broke off, her
cheeks ashen. 'He was wonderful. Somehow he managed
to discover where Paul had hidden his father and ef-
fected a rescue...and you should have seen the way Paul
scuttled from the house when faced with a real man.'

'I should have liked that,' Jeanne murmured, her gaze
dwelling on Alexandrine. Alain Ratan and her friend!
She had suspected it for some while. 'No wonder the
two of you needed to get away from Paris. I hope you
will take precautions when you return home. You must
protect yourself against anything like this happening
again—especially with Luc's health the way it is. Hire
men as bodyguards.'

'Surely that will not be necessary? Paul has been exposed before his friends—people who knew and trusted him. No decent person will associate with him now, knowing he tried to kill his own father.'

'My dear Alexandrine, sometimes you are so naïve. There are those who would sell their souls for a handful of coins.'

'And there are those who still believe I am what he says,' Alexanderine returned bitterly.

'It is a pity you could not have a child. That would stop the gossip.'

'That will never happen. Luc has never shown the slightest interest in me—that way,' Alexandrine confessed, embarrassed.

'He has his reasons, I suppose. Now, when you return to Paris, I shall expect you to visit me often. Who knows?' Jeanne's eyes twinkled with sudden amusement. 'I may even see you at Versailles soon.'

She would say no more on the matter despite Alexandrine's entreaties. Like Alexandrine, she had a few secrets. She laughed as they parted, leaving Alexandrine to wonder if she had guessed how deeply she had become involved with Alain Ratan.

'It is so good to be home again,' Alexandrine said, linking her arm through Luc's as they entered the house. He looked down at her with a quizzing smile, prompting her to add, 'Truly, it is. I liked it at Etoiles, but I have grown to love this place.'

'I am glad. You were so carefree there—and to hear you laugh brought me such pleasure. I have neglected you these past months...'

'You have been ill.'

'And now I am better. In a week or two, I shall invite some people to the house—a token of my gratitude for your patience and understanding. This time *I* shall make all the arrangements and *you* shall enjoy the evening. I shall not ruin it for you the next time.'

'Luc! We are scarcely over the threshold and you talk of entertaining. I will not allow you to tax your strength.

You are not *that* well,' Alexandrine said firmly, looking to Selim for support. 'Tell him. He will listen to you.'

'If you think that, then you do not know me,' Luc returned, patting her hand.

'That is true.' The words were out before she had thought what reaction they might provoke. Six months a wife and she did *not* know him. It was the truth. His eyes became thoughtful as they rested on her face.

'Then I shall rectify that very shortly, my dear. You are right. It is time you knew the kind of man you have married.'

'Welcome home, Monsieur le Marquis. Madame... It is good to see you both looking so well.' Pierre met them in the hallway. For a moment shock registered in his eyes at the sight of the stooping figure supported between Alexandrine and the Moor. 'There have been many enquiries as to when you would return, and invitations by the score.'

'So, we are back in favour,' Luc remarked without humour. 'Give them to Madame; she shall deal with them. When you have looked through them, my dear, bring them to my room tomorrow morning and tell me which ones you think we should accept.'

'None,' Alexandrine said. 'At least—not for a while.'

'You will allow me to decide that—tomorrow,' came the answer, in a tone which brooked no further comment on the subject. 'Pierre, send someone to me within the hour. I want a message taken to the Duc de Belaincourt.'

Alexandrine opened her mouth to protest but closed it again without uttering a word, conscious of Selim's gaze on her. She would not see him when he came.

'The Duc has been here several times, *monsieur*. He was most concerned for you.'

'And my son? Not that I expect he will dare show his nose inside the door again.'

'I—I have heard nothing of Monsieur Paul since— since that night,' Pierre replied, and prayed the lie would not go against him on Judgement Day. He had heard unpleasant rumours, none of which he intended should

ever reach the ears of the Marquis. The house would not
be a battlefield again.

The look which passed between Luc and Selim puzzled
Alexandrine. Not a word was spoken to communicate
what was in his mind, yet a few moments after Luc had
retired to his bed to rest the Moor left the house.
Alexandrine watched his departure from the window of
her sitting-room, knowing instinctively that he had gone
in search of Paul. To effect a reconciliation? Surely that
was impossible? To gain information as to his whereabouts? That was more probable, but even that explanation deeply disturbed her. How could Luc want to
know where his son was after all that had happened?
Why did he still care? It was beyond her comprehension.

While Francine, her maid, unpacked she relaxed in
the pleasant room and went through the pile of correspondence which had been waiting for them. Pierre had
been right, there were many invitations, some from
people she hardly knew. Had they been prompted by
friendship—or curiosity? she wondered, as the pile of
rejects grew far larger than the acceptances. She had no
intention of allowing Luc to tax his strength, no matter
what he said to the contrary. Selim had warned her of
the devastating effects over-exertion could do to him.
They would live quietly, she told herself, as the last letter
was cast aside. There was no reason why they should
not entertain at home, but Versailles was out of the
question for a man in his ill health. She would present
herself there for appearance's sake only. She would have
Jeanne come to the house and bring her intellectual
friends. That would please Luc and enable him to continue the brilliant discussions which had taken place at
Etoiles.

She slept late the following morning and, when she
first awoke, was struck by the noise from the street
outside. At Etoiles, the first sound she heard was the
song of a bird. Instructing Francine that she would take
breakfast in her husband's room, she dressed in a casual
morning robe of pale saffron, gathered up the letters
and cards and went to see him.

He had slept well—that was her first thought as she found him propped up in bed, a sheaf of papers strewn across the coverlet in front of him. The eyes which surveyed her were once more clear and alert, and warmth crept into them as she kissed him on one cheek and pulled a chair close to the bed. His gaze lingered on her gown which left bare her arms and shoulders and curved tantalisingly across the rise of her breasts.

'The day has suddenly grown brighter,' he remarked cheerfully. 'Selim, get rid of these bills. Pay them all, but mark well those that have demanded payment more than once. We shall deal with them no more.'

'Would you like me to do it?' she asked, knowing full well that his last seizure had left him with a useless right hand. The fingers were so bent he would not hold a quill, even after four months.

'Selim has never had any trouble reproducing my signature before, my dear, and at the moment I prefer everyone to believe I am still capable of managing my own affairs. Come, now, show me what delights we have been offered by the cream of Parisian society. Where are we to go first?'

'Luc, I beg you, let us ignore these—all of them. No one will expect you to visit them after you have been so ill,' Alexandrine protested as crooked fingers flicked through the assortment of paper before him. 'None of them is really that important. I shall write to them all personally and explain.'

'You will do so in such cases as I dictate,' Luc returned. 'You will obey me in this, Alexandrine, and accept I know what I am doing. You have a position to maintain as my wife. Of course you will go out—and soon—and, as I have promised, we shall have a gathering here.'

Across the bed Alexandrine's eyes met those of Selim and saw the warning there, but what could she do? Luc was adamant and she knew better than to argue with him when there was such firmness in his tone. She would have to be more subtle, persuade him in another way of the folly of taxing his limited strength. She knew Selim would aid her in this. They had become as one in their determination to see Luc back on the road to good health. She smiled at the Moor.

'I am glad to see that the two of you are friends at last.' Her husband's pallid features broke into a faint smile. 'But do not attempt to conspire against my wishes. I know full well what I am about.'

'As always,' Selim said with a smile, and Luc glared at him, but not unkindly.

'And I will have no servile remarks from you, old friend, no more than from she who is the dearest thing to me.'

Alexandrine looked in astonishment at the Moor, unaccustomed to such familiarity between the three of them.

'Alexandrine, it is time you knew the kind of man you have married. Come, sit close beside me and place your hand in mine. I want to feel your warmth, your youth, you don't know what it means to me. There now... Where shall I begin? It is not pleasant, of that you should be forewarned. Selim, don't frown at me so. She has a right to know about me. Has she not turned out better than either of us ever thought possible?'

'Please, Luc,' Alexandrine protested, embarrassed. 'Don't talk as if I am not here. It makes me feel so—unnecessary.'

'Forgive me, my dear, force of habit.' He was interrupted by Francine, bringing Alexandrine's breakfast tray. Luc himself ate nothing and drank only the glass of white liquid which the Moor handed him, grimacing as he finished every drop and thrust it away from him.

'One day that concoction will be the death of me,' he said sourly. Selim said nothing as he took the empty glass and disappeared into the other room, but Alexandrine sensed he was lingering just inside the door, to listen to every word said. As if he feared what she might be told! What devastating secrets was Luc about to reveal to her?

'Well?' she asked with a smile. 'What terrible confessions are you about to unfold?'

'It is no laughing matter, child,' Luc returned gravely. 'I should never have married you. Indeed, I should not have married at all. I have sired a monster of a son who will one day, heaven protect him, become as I am now, know the agonies which I suffer and will continue to suffer until I draw my last breath. I wonder if he will have the courage to do as I shall do... No matter, that is for him alone to determine. He must be master of his own destiny as I am of mine. As you must now be mistress of yours. No, do not interrupt me. I shall answer all your questions,' he said, as Alexandrine opened her mouth to counter such a frightening statement.

'I was twelve years old before I fully realised how ill my poor mother was. I was an only child, thoroughly spoiled by my father, I confess. But I enjoyed every moment. I was told she was a frail woman and rarely ventured from her room lest the strain be too much for her. Sometimes I was allowed to sit with her, but there were days, nay, weeks when I did not see her at all, and so we were never close as a mother and son should be. But the love my father gave me more than made up for that.'

Until that moment Luc had been prepared to tell Alexandrine the whole truth, but as he saw the alarm which crept into her eyes he knew he could not cruelly destroy the safe world he himself had created about her. He must protect her as he had always done and, when he was gone, there would be another, more capable of doing so than he.

'I discovered, after her death, that the disease was hereditary. A wasting disease that eats at the bones and reduces the unfortunate victim to a mere vegetable in time.' Alexandrine's cheeks paled and the hand which lay in his trembled for a brief moment, but she did not speak. He was grateful for that. He knew Selim was hovering in the next room, listening to every word and condemning him for going even this far. 'That is to be my fate, my dear. I am prepared for it. I have been for many years, and I thought you should be too. It is no consolation to know I shall soon degenerate into a mindless idiot, but I believe you are strong enough to stand the strain which will be put upon you and survive it. Now do you understand why I wanted to marry you? I wanted my last few years upon this earth to be filled with beauty. You have not disappointed me. My days have been filled with the pleasure of watching you, listening to that lovely voice. You must continue to look as beautiful as you have in the past, continue to pander to this old man's foolish whims just a little longer.'

'Oh, Luc! Is there nothing that can be done?' Alexandrine cried, tears flooding into her eyes. She would have flung herself into his arms, but he held her back, his grave gaze intent on her distressed features.

'Nothing. I have accepted it and now so must you. And we will talk of it no more. I am in Selim's capable hands. He will do all that is necessary and you must never interfere with his wishes concerning me. Is that understood?'

'As you wish. I know now he will do nothing to harm you.'

'My dear child, he is all that stands between me and the fires of hell.' Luc chuckled softly, and his brave acceptance of his fate checked further tears. 'You will not discuss this matter with anyone, especially my son.'

'Do you not think he should know?' she questioned, appalled at the prospect which lay ahead for him.

'There is nothing to be done for him...for either of us,' Luc returned. 'Let him enjoy life as he chooses while he is still able.'

Alexandrine nodded. Now she understood Luc's preoccupation with finding Paul. It had been to assure himself the young man was still in good health. What a terrible secret to have kept locked inside him for all these years! How could he impart such a damning sentence to his son, even though they were no longer close— perhaps even hated each other after what had passed between them? He was too kind, too considerate to destroy his life. Paul had not been so particular when he had made plans to imprison his father and bring about his death by slow, tortuous means.

'Now, to these invitations. I see you have already decided to refuse most of them. Let me see them.' Luc held out his hand and reluctantly she gave the sheaf of papers to him. 'Grenville? St Cyr? Quite right to discard them both, my dear, they are utter bores. Perhaps the soirée at Madame Beauchamp's might prove interesting. Accept that.'

Alexandrine knew it would not be wise to argue further. Her husband would not waver from the lifestyle he had chosen. She must do as he said and accept the inevitable, and until that time came make life as pleasurable as possible for him. She could not imagine life without him! To live alone in the house—it was unthinkable. She would not remain in Paris. So lost was she in her thoughts that she did not hear the door open and Pierre announce a visitor.

'Alexandrine, you have not heard a word I have said. Stop dreaming, child, and welcome our guest.' Luc's reproving tone brought her back to reality—and the man who stood at the foot of the bed, regarding her with piercing green eyes that seared her very soul and brought fierce colour flooding into her cheeks as she became aware of her *déshabillé* state.

'There is no need to be embarrassed,' Luc murmured as she sprang to her feet with the excuse she should go and change into something more suitable. 'Alain is an old friend.'

And had seen her with fewer clothes than she now had on, his smile proclaimed as he inclined his head towards her.

'Good morning, *madame*. I trust you are well after your stay in the country?' he enquired politely.

'Quite well, *monsieur*, thank you. I really should go, Luc. Much of my unpacking is still to be done,' Alexandrine protested, desperate to leave the room and the gaze which probed her face questioningly. She had told herself that when next they met she would be distant—aloof—but one look had brought rushing back to her all that had taken place between them. Not that it was very far from her thoughts—the hours when she had lain in his arms and he had subjected her to the skill of his lovemaking, ardour and passion such as she had never known in her young life—and prayed never to know again with any man. Love destroyed! It had made her weak and vulnerable, unable to refuse him her body—unable to deny the need he had created in her with his kisses and scalding caresses. 'Please do excuse me,' she requested.

'For a little while, then. Come back before Alain leaves or he will begin to think he is no longer welcome here.'

Which he was not, Alexandrine thought as she left the room as calmly as she was able, a hand against her wildly beating heart. Little fool, she scolded as she turned towards her own apartment. Do not allow him to have this effect on you. He must never touch you again as he did that night, and you must learn to be strong and resist the weakness of your treacherous body.

'Alexa!' She spun about with a startled gasp as the form of her name that only he would dare use was called quietly behind her, and found Alain not two steps away. 'A moment before you rush away...'

'Are you mad to follow me? What will Luc think?' she began indignantly as he closed with her and his body effectively blocked her way ahead. He had no intention of allowing her to pass until he had said what he had come to say! How dared he presume to be so familiar with her beneath her own roof? Yet had he not been as far as any man could go—and in her own bed too! Did he think a few stolen hours had given him some special rights?

'I have told him I have brought the horses I promised before Christmas. You left so suddenly, I had no chance to bring them before, did I?' Alain reproved, his eyes sweeping her face. He sensed the disquiet in her, felt the way she trembled as he laid a hand upon her arm. 'Luc wants you to go and look at them and make sure they are to your liking—when you are more presentable, of course.' His lips deepened into a smile as his pale eyes considered the rise of her breasts above the silken robe.

The sweet fragrance of rose petals invaded his senses—in her hair or upon that petal-soft skin, he wondered?

How he had missed her! The weeks had been empty without his usual visits to the Hôtel Boussiéres. What had started as a challenge to his own will-power to resist this creature who was never out of his thoughts day or night, to be in her presence and assure himself she did not and never would affect him—had resulted in chaos in his orderly, uncomplicated life. No sight of her in three long, agonising months, and now he was with her again he ached to take her in his arms and explain what had driven him from her bed that night. She must suspect the worst of him, and he could not allow that to continue. No longer did he wish them to be adversaries—for him the game was over. He wanted a continuance of the wonder and reawakening she had brought about. 'Alexa, we must talk.'

'Talk?' Alexandrine had grown very stiff, her face cold, although she did not attempt to remove the hand laid purposefully upon her arm. 'We have nothing to discuss, Monsieur le Duc.' She forced the words through stiff lips, knowing she must destroy this moment of intimacy before it was too late. Destroy the last vestige of her feeling for this man before his soft words and her longing for him possessed her again.

'You deserve an explanation for the way I acted the night before you left for Etoiles. I owe you that,' Alain said. 'Wait for me in the stables...'

'I repeat, we have nothing to say to each other.' She was a stranger with eyes as hard as flints. 'I am well aware of the motives behind your actions that night, Monsieur le Duc.' She was deliberately formal, her tone as bleak as the eyes which stared at him. 'You succeeded, didn't you? Another conquest for the Duc de Belaincourt. More proof that all women are the same—shameless hussies who cheat on their husbands and therefore deserve your contempt, your scorn! I look on that night another way.' Inside, Alexandrine died with each word she uttered—each lie which tumbled out after another, intending to wound him as deeply as he had her. 'I consider what happened between us fair payment for the rescue of my husband. The debt is now paid in full. That is the way it is done in Paris, is it not?'

'Payment?' Alain repeated harshly, his fingers tightening about her wrist. 'Is that all it meant to you?'

'But of course. You followed me back to the *Hôtel* for that reason alone, did you not? To exact payment? Now I pray you will have the decency to leave me alone.'

'Payment,' he repeated again and the bitterness in his tone tore through her like a knife. 'I've been entertained better by tavern wenches. You're not a woman, you are a child, and an ignorant one at that. You don't know how to please a man—let alone satisfy him.' She gasped in horror and stepped back from him, only to find her back against the tapestried wall. His body came hard against hers, holding her immobile. He pushed his furious features close to hers and the glittering eyes made her feel sick with fear and shame. It had meant nothing to him! He had taken her innocence from her and now he unleashed insults upon her head which made her wish the floor would open and swallow her. 'You need additional instruction, *madame*, and I shall be happy to give it to you—free of charge.'

Her chin was cupped in fingers of steel, her mouth bruised by lips that had no pity for her futile struggles, the tiny whimperings of despair which broke from them. To add insult to injury, Alain's free hand pushed aside her robe and deliberately explored her breasts.

'Why, Madame la Marquise, I do believe you have missed me,' he mocked, raising his head to look down on her ashen cheeks. 'I shall not make you wait too long to be satisfied again.'

Alexandrine tore herself from his grasp and fled along the corridor, barely able to see for the huge tears which blinded her vision.

An hour elapsed before Alexandrine returned to Luc's room, and by then she was prepared for a second encounter with Alain Ratan. She had changed into a gown of pink silk, the delicate material sewn with a pattern of little rosebuds. Her hair had been brushed until it shone, and matching bows held it back from her ears, where diamonds sparkled. Her face had been sponged with cold water to get rid of the tell-tale redness her tears had caused. From beneath the hem of the gown peeped pink leather shoes with diamond buckles. She had taken great care with her toilette, as much to please her husband as to form some kind of defence against the man she knew awaited her return. When she regarded her appearance in the mirror, she was satisfied with the result. She looked elegant, full of confidence, in control. And that was how she intended to remain.

'How can I be annoyed with you for taking so long, when you come back to me looking like an angel?' Luc declared. 'Now you see what you are missing, Alain. You should marry again.'

'I hope that is meant as a joke,' Alain replied drily, dragging his gaze from the breathtakingly lovely vision that seated itself beside the bed and took Luc's hand. What a picture of domesticity! The devoted wife at the bedside of her sick husband. She had stated categorically that she loved him, and he had not believed her at the time. Now he was not sure—although she looked more as if she were about to meet a lover than stay to entertain an aging husband. How could she look upon him as anything more than a father figure, the man who had rescued her from a boring, lonely existence after the death of her own father and mother? Perhaps she felt gratitude, but love—never! Not the way she had lain in his arms and quivered beneath his caresses. He had fanned the fierce flames of dormant passion—something perhaps she had never been aware she possessed, but it was in her and he had awakened it. Then—and an hour ago when he had held her.

'Not at all. You are still human, Alain, although there are times when you try to prove otherwise. Find yourself a woman to brighten your life, as Alexandrine does mine. You will not regret it. Some women can be faithful, you know, to one man.'

'Then you possibly have taken the last one capable of such virtue,' came the barbed retort which brought a

faint flush of colour to Alexandrine's cheeks and a
chuckle from Luc as he saw it.

'Now you have made the child blush.'

'Your wife's capabilities are limitless.' Alain's pale eyes
were centred on Alexandrine, but she did not look at
him, intent on perusing the invitation cards which still
lay on the coverlet. She was suddenly a stranger, and
the deliberate attempt to ignore him provoked the devil
in him. He still smarted from the insults she had thrown
in his face. She had judged him without giving him a
chance to explain his conduct. He accepted she had every
reason to be angry at the way he had left her and had
been prepared to face it, but to be told that what they
had shared—what he had come to believe was the
opening of a door to a new life for him—was nothing
more than payment for his help had roused murderous
rage in him. Such a motive placed her in the same category as other women in his life—the painted whores
who frequented Versailles and nightly cuckolded their
husbands, their services paid for by favours received at
Court or by more jewels—women like his dead wife. 'But
then she has not long been in Paris. Time enough for
innocence to be corrupted.'

'One day I shall make you eat those words, you
damned insolent puppy,' Luc flared, and Alain wisely
acknowledged he had gone too far.

'I apologise, old friend. I meant no disrepect to the
Marquise, you know that. You see how difficult it is for
me to believe any woman can be such a paragon of virtue,
even when the proof is before my eyes? And you want
me to marry again? I should drive the poor woman to
her grave within six months. No, I shall stay with my
horses. Did you inspect the two mares I have brought,
madame? Are they to your liking?'

'They are fine-looking animals. I am sure Luc will be
as pleased with them as I am.'

'Lady Blue will be missed in my stables, but Luc
wanted the best for you, and that he has.'

'Lady Blue—the finest mare you possess! Alain, thank
you. I did not expect such generosity. We must settle

upon a fair sum for both mares.' Luc was clearly taken aback by the news.

'Consider them a belated wedding gift. I cannot wait to see the two of you in the Bois.'

'A pleasure I shall unfortunately have to delay for some considerable time,' Luc returned, 'but it will give Alexandrine an opportunity to take the air more often. And, of course, when she returns to Versailles, she will now be able to follow the King's hunt in style. The fine weather will be here soon—picnics in the grounds, plays performed under the stars, torchlit barges on the waters. I'd forgotten how active the Court could be. You will enjoy it, my dear.'

'I am sure I shall,' Alexandrine said, knowing she would hate every moment. It was obvious Luc would not be attending these functions with her. She would have to go alone, but this time she would be prepared for what awaited her. She would not be the easy, accessible target she had been before. If need be, she would fight fire with fire. She was resolved to do all that Luc asked of her, to please him in any way she was able, and if that meant returning to Versailles, being part of the world he was now forced to abandon, then she would do so. She prayed she had sufficient courage to sustain her through the months ahead.

'It is time I was leaving.' Alain rose to his feet. 'Remember, Luc, I shall accept no excuses for your not coming to Belaincourt next month.'

'Nothing could keep me away. And from what you have told me the festivities you plan should produce some interesting results. I am curious to see if they succeed.'

'When one is at the command of the King of France, dare one fail?' Alain laughed softly. '*Madame*, I leave it to you to ensure your husband's health improves, so that you will both be able to enjoy the hospitality of Belaincourt. I can promise you will not be bored.'

Alexandrine absorbed the shock of his words without emotion. Belaincourt! What had possessed Luc to accept an invitation to go there, of all places? He knew how full their social calendar had become. She saw the mockery which lurked in the green depths as Alain touched her fingers to his lips, a perfect gentleman— except for the silent challenge which accompanied that mockery. Did he expect her to make a fuss? Try to change Luc's mind?

'Bored, Monsieur le Duc...in Paris! Is that possible?' With a frozen smile she withdrew her hand from his and replaced it in that of her husband. 'I am sure I shall always find something—or someone—to amuse me. As you have so correctly observed, I have not been here very long.'

The implication was not lost on Alain; she had made it too pointed. If she wanted company other than that of Luc, she would not turn to him!

'I am relieved to hear it. Boredom is so often the downfall of a pretty young woman.'

After he had left them, Luc settled comfortably back amid the pillows, with a deep sigh.

'Despite all I say, I fear that young man grows more cynical every time we meet.'

'The Duc de Belaincourt will go to hell in his own way and probably enjoy every moment,' Alexandrine declared without thinking, and her husband's eyes grew amused at the candid remark.

'I am sure you are right. He is his own man. He will not be dictated to by any woman—or man. A pity. Sometimes I feel towards him as I might to my own son...more so, for he is always there when I need him. Has he ever spoken to you of his marriage—his wife?'

'Never,' Alexandrine said, wishing Luc would change the subject.

'She was a beauty. She possessed the kind of face to haunt a man's dreams. Alain may never totally forget her or the pain she brought him. It will be a rare woman who obliterates the past for him.'

'He has admitted he would drive the poor woman to her grave,' Alexandrine said. 'Rare or not.'

She spent most of the day in Luc's room, listening to him making plans for the coming year. How brave he was, she thought, as he listed those functions they would attend together and then others she would attend alone, for he knew full well he might not complete the adventurous programme. Yet he seemed pleased, even excited, at the prospect ahead, and the months they would spend together at Noyen. He would begin renovations on the old house immediately, he told her, to make it ready to receive them. She was to let him know of any special alterations she herself required, and they would be taken care of. It would be nice to have a summer residence. It would be as much a quiet retreat from the heat and noise of the city as it would be a sanctuary for Alexandrine when she was alone again.

A bride of less than a year, and soon to become a widow! There were days when her mind still refused to accept what was to happen, but she was careful never to allow Luc to sense her disquiet.

One of the first visitors to come to the house was Jeanne d'Etoiles, brimming over with excitement at the forthcoming ball at Belaincourt.

'I believe it is well over a year since the Duc has entertained on such a grand scale,' she said to Alexandrine as they sat in the garden one afternoon. 'When his wife was alive the house was always full of guests. Unfortunately, I believe she used the occasions to have assignations with her many lovers. Perhaps that is why Monsieur Ratan has been so reluctant to open up Belaincourt again. Have you been there? A beautiful old place...but far too large and lonely for one man. Do you not agree?'

'What is the occasion?' Alexandrine asked curiously, wisely ignoring the question in Jeanne's bright eyes. 'The Duc spoke of being at the command of the King, as if something very special—perhaps secretive—is being planned.'

'The King is to be at Belaincourt,' Jeanne declared. 'Of course no one is supposed to know, and as it is a *bal masqué* he will be able to attend incognito, but when Monsieur Ratan came to visit me the other day to deliver an invitation personally, I knew...' She broke off and laid her head back amid a mound of soft cushions. 'Oh, Alexandrine, think of it! At last I am to fulfil my destiny.'

'Go on, before I die of curiosity,' Alexandrine urged, surprised by the news. Was Alain playing matchmaker on the orders of the King? A man who despised women, arranging for his monarch to meet a woman to whom he was attracted and who, if she were right to believe in Fate, would reside in the royal bed!

'The occasion is Monsieur Ratan's birthday. He has invited a select few to celebrate with him. At least, that is what he calls them. Over a hundred people from the best families in the country and I hear there has not been one single refusal. I would, of course, have accepted his invitation anyway, but when he indicated that the request for my presence came from another source—from one who has admired me from afar, but is too shy to approach me openly—I knew at once this was what I had been waiting for all my life.'

'The King, shy!' Alexandrine echoed. It was common knowledge that, during the seventeen years he had been married to Marie Leszczynska, by whom he had so far fathered ten children, he had taken at least five mistresses, four of them from among the same family.

The first had been one of the Queen's own *dames du palais*, Louise de Nesle. They were together for five years while the Queen—always pregnant, always having babies, as someone once described her—retired to her own southern corner of the palace where she entertained her own friends, played cards, wove tapestries, ate—and grew fat.

Louis was also to be enchanted by Louise's sister, fresh from a convent, but the liaison did not last. She died bringing into the world a son who so resembled his father he would be forever known as the demi-Louis.

Marie-Ann de Nesle was the fifth sister in the family—and the prettiest. Also the most ambitious. She was just twenty-four when she was introduced to the King. Widowed a year earlier, she had ambitions which far surpassed those of her sisters. When she became the acknowledged mistress of Louis, she was given her own apartments above his. Any children born as a result of the liaison were to be legitimised, and she was created the Duchesse de Châteauroux with an income of eighty thousand *livres* a year. And her power over the King alarmed many who watched from afar.

And this iron-willed, cold-hearted woman was the one to be ousted before Jeanne d'Etoiles could fulfil her destiny. A daunting task, Alexandrine thought, but in her heart she somehow knew her friend would succeed. One day Jeanne Poisson d'Etoiles would sit at the side of the King of France.

'Come in and close the door, Jules,' Alain said. He sat back in his chair behind the large mahogany desk inlaid with delicate scrollwork, and studied the man who approached. He knew the man to be a product of the back alleys of the quarter across the river, but since he had first engaged him, over five months ago, he had had no cause for complaint. Nothing in Alain's expression betrayed the devastating shock he was about to deliver.

'I was told the matter was of the utmost importance,' Jules said, not liking the way those green eyes surveyed him. Sometimes aware of them watching him as he worked, he felt as if every thought in his mind was on open display. The Duc was an unusual man, too shrewd by far, but a fair one. Jules had never had cause to complain about his treatment since he came to Belaincourt. On the contrary, he was finding the work quite easy and pleasant—and his sideline very lucrative.

'It is, if you value your neck,' Alain returned.

The look of surprise which spread across Jules's face at the remark would probably have convinced most people that he knew nothing of what was to come. Alain, however, was well aware of the man's ability to conceal his feelings. The night they had rescued Luc he had seen the animal surface, the quiet, servile manner disappear and known then the manner of man he had in his employ. If he were concerned, his back against a wall, he would kill to escape. Alain knew and accepted this—and was prepared.

'I'm afraid I do not understand what you mean, Monsieur le Duc.'

'Then in a moment I will enlighten you. First, however, I am sure you are aware that Daniel, my head groom, is leaving me next month. He is past seventy and should have retired years ago, but until now he has never found a suitable man to take his place. He has recommended you, Jules. Would you like the position?' Alain asked casually. 'With it comes a smallholding—a house and land enough, if cultivated carefully, to provide you with all you need. Daniel will no longer require it, as he is going to live with his widowed sister in Leon.'

'I—I don't know what to say, Monsieur le Duc.' Want it! It meant he could marry Francine at once! And still be wealthy... He had planned to buy a place, miles from Paris and Versailles and the countless victims he had deprived of their money and jewels. Dared he risk settling in this place?

'You are a good man with my horses and I reward those who deserve it—and deal harshly with those who betray my trust.' There was a sudden menacing note in Alain's voice that caused Jules to stiffen.

'I shall serve you faithfully, *monsieur*. As I have done since the first day you gave me work. The house is really to be mine?'

'It is in need of repair; Daniel was content with few comforts—a good roof over his head and food in his stomach. But you, I suspect will want more. You may do as you wish with the place, in your own time. There is one condition, however. If you cannot fulfil it, then...' Alain shrugged his shoulders, and muscles rippled beneath the silk shirt to remind Jules that this man, like himself, had another side to his character.

'A condition,' he echoed slowly, his instincts warning him his run of luck might well be over.

Alain opened a drawer at his fingertips, reached inside and took out a leather pouch which he dropped on to the desk in front of him.

'Don't bother to deny that you recognise this. I took it from the place where you had hidden it, in the stables. And don't tell me you don't know what it contains.' He tipped a shimmering mass of rings, bracelets and necklaces out on to the leather, toyed momentarily with a gold snuff-box studded with diamonds. 'This belonged to the Duchesss de Mallen. I've often seen her use it. The rest of this stuff has come from many of my neighbours. You will return it. Every last piece here.'

'Return it!' He had taken leave of his senses, Jules thought, weighing his chances of grabbing up his hoard of wealth and fleeing the room.

Alain removed the dagger from the sheath at his waist and laid it to one side of him. 'If you run, I shall pin you by your ear to the door,' he threatened, 'and leave you there until a constable comes to take you away. Consider the alternatives, Jules. I can use a man like you. I shall pay you well for any—*additional* services you may perform for me, as I did once before. I am offering you all you have ever wanted, plus a steady job for the rest of your life. All you have to do is return these items to their rightful owners. I am sure such a task will not prove too difficult for you. If I ask too much, then you can leave Belaincourt this minute.'

Never had Jules been faced with such an outrageous proposal. Give up his life of crime? The excitement of pitting his wits against his fellow thieves? He was the best! No one could move as stealthily as he did; he was like a shadow as he silently flitted through darkened houses. Sometimes he had found it amusing to steal when they were full of people. He was the cleverest pickpocket in all France . . . and no lock could withstand the talents of his persuasive fingers. Give it all up?

He had no weapon himself, yet for a full moment he contemplated throwing himself at Alain Ratan and snatching what he could before taking to his heels. He could go back to the Beggars' Quarter and lose himself. No one would dare follow him there, and he would be free. But without Francine. She would never marry him if she discovered he was still keeping to his old ways...and he wanted *her* more than he wanted the jewels. He could take what was offered him—why not? Marry her and try to be a respectable man. If it failed, he could always return to a more profitable way of life...without her knowing. The next time he stole anything, it would be well away from Belaincourt. That had been his mistake.

'*Monsieur* gives me no choice.'

'On the contrary; you can walk out of this room— without the jewels, of course—and go your own way,' Alain returned, sensing that victory was his. He was not fool enough to believe the man would change overnight, if at all, but he also knew the opportunity he was offering was too good to be rejected out of hand. 'In a week's time, I shall be entertaining here at Belaincourt. It will be a good opportunity for you to return these items. I have ensured that everyone who has been robbed recently in these parts will be here, and I have drawn up a list of their property so that you do not make any mistakes. Do we understand each other, Jules?'

'Perfectly, *monsieur*. I shall do as you wish,' Jules answered, tight-lipped, as he held out his hand.

With a laugh Alain dropped the jewels back into the pouch, secured it and returned it to the drawer.

'On the night of the twelfth, you shall have it. If you are thinking how easy it would be to take them and never come back, I should warn you how foolish that would be.'

'I am no more a fool than you are, Monsieur le Duc,' Jules said humourlessly. 'They will be returned and I shall come back.'

Alain rose, returning the knife to its sheath. He would not have hesitated to use it, and Jules was aware of the fact. A mutual respect was born from that knowledge as Alain stood surveying him, a slight smile playing at the corners of the lean mouth, the pale eyes alight with mockery.

'One last thing. None of my guests is to lose any valuable item. Is that understood?'

'I am a reformed man, *monsieur*.' And, besides, there were plenty of wealthy people in Paris. He would just have to go further afield and be more careful.

'And you will not involve the Marquis de Mezière's maid in any of this.'

'This was all for her, *monsieur*!'

'Do your work for me well and remain loyal and she will never know what has passed between us,' Alain told him. 'But no scandal shall touch my name or this place. I have plans of my own.'

CHAPTER TWO

FOR the three weeks after Alexandrine returned to the house, her life was a whirl of soirées, dinner parties and fittings for the new gowns Luc insisted she should have made for the visit to Belaincourt. She protested in vain that she had not yet had a chance to wear the wardrobe he had had made for her after they were married, but then gave in to his determined requests that she should have a ballgown created for her that would make her the most dazzling woman at Alain's party—and him the most envied husband. The design he left to her. It was a surprising decision, for he was always so critical about what she wore, and yet it secretly pleased her that he now trusted her judgement in such matters.

For days she sketched and threw away designs, en-listed Jeanne's help and finally, with several to choose from, went to Madame Héloïse. The final choice took another two days, and quite took the seamstress by surprise.

'Every woman who is at Belaincourt will be trying to outdo her companion, especially when they believe the King might be present,' she told Jeanne when the latter queried the simplicity of the gown. 'You know how ru-mours send them into a frenzy. I don't want to look like everyone else. I want to be different.'

'You are a remarkable woman despite your tender years,' Jeanne remarked, watching an assistant help Alexandrine out of a gown she had been fitting. 'And that waist is still the envy of many at Versailles. They are waiting for the day you become fat and are no longer attractive to their men. Do you think you may yet have a child, Alexandrine? Or am I prying?'

'Of course not ... but with Luc's health as it is ...' She lifted slender shoulders. 'I do not think it will happen now.'

'He still does not come to you?'

'Nothing has changed since we last talked, Jeanne.'

Alexandrine did not mind being frank with her friend, for she knew Jeanne would keep her secret. Knew, in fact, that she gave everyone the impression that Alexandrine and Luc were a happily married couple. A powerful weapon against Paul Boussières, should he ever again decide to try and disrupt their lives. Madame d'Etoiles was fast becoming the most talked-about woman in Paris. Her salon was always a hive of activity, frequented by the most talented minds in France as well as by the aristocracy, who came perhaps at first out of curiosity, to stare at this woman whose mother's notoriety had kept her out of their circle for so long, and found themselves returning again and again because they found her not only intelligent, but witty, amusing and talented.

Alexandrine had been appalled at how little she could do. She had no great talent for any one thing in particular. She supposed she was a moderate hostess, but not exceptional. She was not a brilliant horsewoman, although she had promised herself, now she was the proud owner of such a fine animal as Lady Blue, that that would soon change. Nor could she drive a phaeton, sing, perform before a critical audience, or play the clavichord. Jeanne could do all these things and did them well! She had been noticed by Madame de Mailly, who had been instrumental in precipitating the King's liaison's with her own sisters, the Nesles, and upon whom he still relied a great deal for information. A fact which did not go unnoticed among the inhabitants of Versailles. Tongues began to wag, rumours ran rife through the corridors of the royal palace. When would the King openly declare his growing interest in Madame d'Etoiles, and when he did, what would the Duchesse de Châteauroux do about it?

'Then there is still hope. Or perhaps the prospect of motherhood is too daunting for you. After all, you have only just been launched into society.'

'I should have liked to give Luc a son, to love as he has never been able to love Paul,' Alexandrine replied truthfully. 'He has made me so happy and yet I seem to do so little for him in return.'

'Have you been troubled by that young rogue since your return?'

'No, not really. He wrote to Luc asking to be allowed to visit the house, but the request was refused. The next day there came another message demanding to see his father. Luc never replied to that one and we have not heard from him again. I expect he was in need of money.'

'And if he accosts you at Versailles?' Jeanne asked, and Alexandrine shrugged.

'He will be dealt with. I will not allow him to disrupt our lives any more. Luc is too ill. And I have not forgotten what he forced me to endure...' She broke off with a shaky laugh. The memory of that night was still vivid in her mind. Would she ever be able to forget Selim unconscious at her feet? Wine being forced down her throat until she almost choked. The crude comments and searching fingers which thrust their way into her bodice! 'I spoil a beautiful afternoon with such talk. Let us discuss nicer things.'

And so, once again, the conversation turned back to the gowns which Madame Héloise was making for each of them for the ball at Belaincourt, but long after her friend had left the house, Alexandrine found that her thoughts still dwelled on that hateful night. She had discovered the extent to which Paul Boussières would go to have his father's money, and she could not believe he had given up so easily.

'The apartments are to your satisfaction, Madame la Marquise?' asked Gaston, the head of the Duc de Belaincourt's household, as Alexandrine stood in the middle of the huge sitting-room, absorbing the new surroundings. The tapestries and hangings and the comfortably padded bergère chairs were all yellow velvet, a

deep, rich colour that competed with the warmth of the
brilliant spring sunshine flooding through the open
french window to bathe her in its golden glow. 'Allow
me to show you the bedroom,' he added when she did
not reply.

Alexandrine followed him in silence. The rooms had
the distinct touch of a woman's hand about them. Had
Alain dared to install her in rooms he maintained for his
women? Had Claudia de la Fontaine walked on these
same thick sunflower-coloured rugs, slept in the
enormous fourposter bed with its delicate silken
hangings—shared it with him? The thought appalled her.
He was trying to humiliate her for the way she had deliberately snubbed him! Had she had her own way she
would never have set foot inside Belaincourt again, but
Luc had insisted, quite excited at the prospect of spending
some time with an old friend.

The furniture was quite small and mostly of oak or
pine, the latter matching the panelled walls, quite bare
of tapestries or ornaments. A simple room, yet containing everything a woman might require, with a small
table beneath the window-seats, scattered with tasselled
cushions, upon which rested an embroidery box and,
beside that, an unfinished sampler, depicting the garden
outside as seen from that spot. Tiny glass and silver-
topped perfume and powder boxes were displayed on
the dressing-table, in front of an oval mirror. Against a
far wall a marble-topped washstand held a porcelain jug
and bowl. Embroidered towels were folded beside them.

'Thank you...Gaston.' It took Alexandrine a moment
to recall the steward's name. 'I shall be quite comfortable here. What is that lovely aroma? These flowers?'
She bent to inhale the perfume of the wild flowers arranged in a tall vase in front of her. 'No. I can smell
lavender.'

'I think possibly it is the herbs, *madame*. I had one
of the maids prepare a pot-pourri for each of the rooms.
They have not been used for quite some time and I was
afraid they would not be fresh enough by the time you
arrived.'

'Not used?' she echoed, turning to look at the man curiously. There was not a speck of dust to be seen. Everything was clean and immaculate, as if they were cared for every day.

'Not since Madame la Duchesse, the master's sainted mother, passed away.'

'Oh. I thought perhaps they might have belonged to his wife,' Alexandrine answered tactfully. His mother! She recalled the warmth in his voice when he had mentioned her, and a sadness in the eyes which had betrayed the great love he had felt for her.

'No, *madame*. Those are on the far side of the house and used by the various guests which come here. Not that we have received many these past years. The old Duchesse and the Duc's wife died within months of each other and he does not receive many people now.'

An equally tactful comment, she thought.

While Francine completed the long process of unpacking her trunks, Alexandrine made herself comfortable on one of the window-seats, her face upturned to the warm sun. She had brought enough clothes for a month, although they were to stay but a few days. She would have a dress for every day—more than one, she mused, watching the maid carefully hang the garments in the pale golden closets. How peaceful this room was, like the drawing-room below where she had sat that day and waited for Alain Ratan to return to the house. She decided his mother must have been a quiet, yet sensitive person—so different from her arrogant, over-confident son! Had he inherited none of the gentle qualities she must surely have possessed?

Angrily she tried to dismiss him from her thoughts, but it was difficult. He seemed to fill them every hour. It would take every bit of courage and determination she possessed to remain aloof from him for the next few days. Yet she knew she must—not for her sake, but Luc's. For that last remaining time he had left, she would allow no breath of scandal to touch his name—or her reputation. And after he was gone from her life and she returned to Noyen, life there would soon erase the shameful things she had done in the name of love! Time would heal her wounds...but would it erase the memories...?

The months ahead were to be full of social activities, but she discovered her heart no longer fluttered nervously at the thought of Versailles or the bold eyes of the King upon her. Her friendship with Jeanne d'Etoiles was proving beneficial to them both, for they were received in many houses, where the doors had previously been closed against them. It no longer seemed to matter that Jeanne's mother's past had brought the name of Poisson into disrepute or that Alexandrine was a country girl, before she took her husband's rank. And there were moments when the latter actually found she was enjoying herself.

Her attention arrested by the sound of voices, she looked down into the garden. Luc and Alain Ratan were walking along one of the narrow pathways, bordered with young orange trees just coming into blossom. Her husband was listening intently to something being said by his companion, and then he threw back his head and laughed aloud. She had not seen him give way to such mirth in a long time. Whatever antagonism was between herself and the the Duc de Belaincourt, she could not deny that his company was good for Luc. He thrived on it as he did on the intellectual throng which surrounded Madame d'Etoiles at her salon. His body was tired and weakening day by day, but his mind was still active, his rhetoric still as witty—or as cutting—as he chose.

'Selim is here, *madame*. Will you see him?'

'Yes, Francine. Show him in here. I am enjoying the sun too much to move.' When the maid left them, Alexandrine beckoned the Moor to her side and indicated the two men in the garden below. 'My lord is much improved. You have done well.'

'He does not take easily to his bed, but he knew if he did not rest he would never have the strength to make this trip and return to Versailles,' Selim returned, as he gazed thoughtfully at them. 'Even now, however, I question the wisdom of his decision. Sometimes I think it is his intention to hasten the end.'

'Do you blame him? For a man who has led such a rich, full life to slowly wither and waste away... I want what he wants. Whatever will make him happy.'

'I accept that now. There was a time when I would not have believed you,' the man returned candidly. 'We are both helpless to stop him doing exactly what he wants, for we love him too much... even if it kills him. I told him not to bring the horses, but he insists he will ride with the Duc each day and perhaps even join the King's hunt.'

'I knew nothing of this,' Alexandrine declared. 'It was my hope that he would relax at Belaincourt.'

'Even from the grave there will be those of us who will yet experience the power of his will and lead the lives he has planned for us,' Selim said, slipping his hands inside the wide sleeves of the long embroidered robe he wore. He was never at ease in tight-fitting Parisian clothes and preferred the loose, flowing oriental robes from his past. And when she saw him in them, Alexandrine did not find it difficult to think of him as a man of rank and importance. They imparted a grandeur which was quite beyond words, and the magnificence of the fabrics sometimes took her breath away.

'At least I shall not fall off my horse, thanks to you,' she replied smilingly. The Moor had been secretly teaching her to ride. She wanted to surprise Luc when they first rode together—and impress him. It had not been as difficult as she had imagined, but had proved nothing like the experience at Noyen when she had ridden astride—and bareback when dared to do so by her brother. Now she was a lady and must ride side-saddle, the skirts of her gown carefully arranged to look at their best upon the horse's back.

'You are a good pupil; a woman who listens when she is being instructed and does not answer back.'

She would not have dared, she thought, for she had not forgotten that where Selim came from the tongue of a chattering woman was cut out to silence her.

'Luc has told me much of his background, but he has never mentioned how you met. Is it some great secret I should not know?' she asked boldly. There were times lately, such as now, when she found him easy to talk to and did not mind his black eyes watching her.

'There is nothing to tell. The Marquis and I encountered each other when there was much unrest in my country. My brother wished for more power—my rightful inheritance—and, goaded on by one of my wives, he bribed men to help him take it from me. But he would not kill me—one does not shed the blood of a brother.' Only of women, because they were unimportant, Alexandrine thought, but wisely did not interrupt. 'I was left to die in the desert with neither food nor water. It was my brother's contention that if Allah wished me to live, I would do so.'

'What a terrible man. But it was Allah's will that you survived.'

'The Marquis found me after four days. Had he not been a man of great learning he would not have been able to save my life. It is written that, if a life is saved through compassion and wisdom, then that life belongs to whomever restored breath to it, for as long as that man lives. *Inshal'lah.*' Selim lifted broad shoulders in a shrug of acceptance. 'That is my fate. I shall serve him for as long as he lives.'

'But it is more than just—servitude,' Alexandrine said quietly. 'You still have your freedom, your dignity. You stay because you want to. It is out of love.'

'Yes, out of love.' Such a love as he had never known with anyone before. Luc Boussières had taught him everything he knew, and the Moor's quick mind had absorbed every detail and found for himself a new vocation, a new reason to live. One day, he always told himself, he would return and reclaim what was rightfully his and take revenge upon the brother who had sentenced him to death—and the woman who had been instrumental in planning it all—but it could wait. He knew it would come in time. His rescuer was now the one needing to be saved, to be protected, and he would not leave his side until death decreed his services were no longer required.

'So this is where the two of you are closeted together,' Luc declared, coming into the room unannounced with Alain behind him. 'What a pleasant room. Are you comfortable here, Alexandrine?'

'Perfectly, Luc.'

'I thought the Marquise would like a view of the gardens,' Alain said cordially.

'And what kind of view do I have?' Luc chuckled.

'I have given you somewhere quiet, and private, where you will not be disturbed if any of my guests decide they need to stay overnight and sleep off their celebrating—or continue with it! I took the liberty of having Gaston leave several bottles of Madeira and claret for you to sample. You will not find them up to the standards of your cellar, but I would be interested to have your opinion of them. The Clement brothers are going to retire to the country and have just sold me their entire stock of wines, so we shall have plenty to enjoy during your stay.' Alain laughed, a friendly hand upon Luc's shoulder.

'We are only here for a few days, Monsieur Ratan.' Alexandrine rose to her feet, knowing it would not be wise openly to criticise the gesture. Alain knew nothing of Luc's true condition and, if he chose, her husband would drink himself insensible—a not uncommon occurrence, she had discovered from Pierre, the major-domo. Selim would never have told her, but she knew, from the way he was staring at Luc, it was the truth.

'Haven't I told you our change of plan?' Luc exclaimed. 'Of course not; Alain and I have only just this moment been discussing it. Dear me, I don't think I should have tried that brandy, Alain. Alain has suggested that we stay here, Alexandrine, and not return to Paris. Is that not a good idea? Think of all these tedious journeys back and forth from Versailles! And the thought of sleeping more than one night in those ghastly, cramped little rooms given to us is a nightmare.'

'Here?' Alexandrine echoed in a hollow tone. 'For how long? Luc, we cannot impose on the Duc's hospitality this way. You know you are not that well and you always prefer to be in your own bed...' She was aghast at the news.

'Nonsense. Selim is here with me, and I shall have all the rest I need—when I think it necessary. We are here to enjoy ourselves, my dear, and I intend to do just that. Alain has offered to teach you to ride Lady Blue...'

'That will not be necessary. Selim has already given me the benefit of his experience.' It was almost impossible to keep the hostility from her voice, and she did not fail to catch the gleam of mockery which entered Alain's pale eyes, challenging the annoyance she dared not give way to.

He was manipulating Luc—but for what purpose?

'You are full of surprises these days, my dear. I look forward to seeing what you have learned—perhaps tomorrow. I am tired now, Selim. I shall rest for the afternoon.'

Alain rang for a servant to escort Luc to his rooms, but he did not depart with them and Alexandrine's expression now proclaimed her hostility as she faced him in the sitting-room.

'Are you angry about something, Alexa?' he enquired, watching the colour mount in her cheeks as she sought words with which to berate him.

'You know I am—and you know why!' she flung back.

'I assure you I do not. Luc and I have spent a great deal of time together over the past few years. We enjoy each other's company and I have no intention of that changing simply because he has taken himself a young wife who demands all his attention. It is a little late to play the worried wife, don't you think, Alexa? Considering the engagements you are dragging the poor man to all this year—bad health or not.'

The insult robbed her of speech. Nothing could have been further from the truth, but she had no intention of arguing with him about it. It was none of his business.

'Are you jealous, *monsieur*, that he now prefers my company to yours?' she flung back with a toss of her fair curls. 'A wife's privileges come before those of a friend, even someone who thinks himself of special importance—as you do!'

'At last I begin to understand.' Alain was no longer smiling. His features were taut with anger. 'You are afraid I shall persuade him as to the true nature of the supposed little innocent he has wed.'

'I have nothing to fear from you. He will not believe a word against me, even from you. He knows I—I love him,' Alexandrine challenged defiantly, and the words brought a chilling look to those green depths.

'In a few short hours I destroyed that pose of innocence, so why bother with it now? We both know this talk of payment was but an excuse to be yourself. You were tired of being a doting wife—and an unsatisfied one, from the way you were in my arms,' Alain snapped. 'Perhaps such subterfuge was not necessary when you rolled in the hay with your village boys—but you have learned quickly.'

Alexandrine recoiled from the words lashing her. He was blaming *her* for what had taken place! His way of absolving himself from all blame.

'You forget how far you went to have me! Pretending Luc's friendship was the only thing important to you! Pretending to be my friend, sympathising with me.' She spoke scathingly, her eyes flashing.

'All cats are the same in the dark, *madame*! And Luc is my friend and always will be. Never forget that!'

'No, Monsieur le Duc de Belaincourt, I will forget—nothing.'

'I must get back, or my lady will be wondering where I am,' Francine protested as Jules pulled her back into the straw.

'Another kiss. Just one, and then I'll tell you my good news,' he said with a wicked grin.

She allowed him one long, searching kiss and then jumped to her feet, fastening the front of her blouse and picking the straw from her tousled skirts.

'What a mess I look.' She hated these stolen moments, their love-making too swift and often unsatisfactory, for she was always afraid someone would come upon them and report what they had seen. How different it was now from that night at the Hôtel Boussières when her mistress had entertained the Duc de Belaincourt. 'What news is this? And don't ask me to marry you again, Jules. I won't. Not until we have saved enough for a place of our own. It is too important to me.'

'We have—a place of our own. As from next month I shall be promoted to head stableman, and with the job goes a cottage. I've had a look at it and, I tell you now, it isn't much, but when I've finished with it...' Jules's thin face grew quite thoughtful. Such a price he was going to pay to give her what she wanted, but the look on her face as she absorbed the words was reward enough. Later, when things were a little more settled, he could take up where he left off and the Duc would be no wiser. 'Well, girl, can't you say anything? Isn't it what you want?'

'A promotion...a cottage...' Francine was not sure which of the two made her the more excited. 'Oh, Jules, the Duc thinks *that* highly of you! But—that will mean I shall have to leave my lady?'

'So? Looking after my needs and running your own home will be better than waiting on her! Besides, when that husband of hers dies, I wouldn't be at all surprised if she didn't remarry—and quickly...you know who,' Jules said reaching for her, but she quickly moved back out of reach and, with a scowl, he clambered to his feet. He was growing as impatient as she to have more time together.

'If you mean the Duc de Belaincourt, you are wrong,' Francine declared. 'She doesn't like him.'

'He stayed the night at that house of hers with her, didn't he? And sent you out of the way? They were not sitting upstairs playing cards, you know!'

'Whatever happened, I don't think she wanted it.' Francine came instantly to the defence of the mistress who had taken her away from all she hated and given her a new life. She had pretty clothes now, a full stomach and a soft bed to sleep in. And, even though she loved Jules, the thought of leaving the Marquise's house made her sad. 'Since that night she has never spoken to me about him, and when I hear them together... Always he is goading her—as if he hates her—and at night I have heard her crying, and I know it is because of him.'

'Perhaps she won't cry at Belaincourt,' Jules murmured with a smile and she looked at him questioningly. 'Don't you know he is next-door to her?' He laughed at the horrified look on her face. 'If you ever want to know anything that goes on here, sit down with the cook and have a glass with him. *Mon Dieu!* How that man talks when his tongue is loosened. I know all about the bitch the Duc was married to—led him a merry dance, she did, until she died. Good riddance, the cook says, no one here liked her. But the old Duchesse, his mother, seems to have led a sainted life. Always doing good work with the poor and the sick. Never took a lover after her husband died. What a boring person she must have been.'

'Jules, that is not fair. Not everyone lives life as you do,' Francine reproved.

'The Duc does. Now there is a man I can respect. He's master of sword and pistol, rides like the wind, has the stealth of an alley-cat when he chooses, and in a fight...I would not like to go against that one, I can tell you. He will always get what he wants out of life—like me. Shall I see you tonight? You can slip away while the ball is going on. I can't see the Marquise retiring until the early hours—and then, I'll take a bet, it won't be to her own room. I'll meet you here about midnight.'

'I could be here earlier,' Francine said hopefully.

'I have—an errand to do for the Duc first. I'll try and be back by eleven. Wait for me.'

He caught her to him, pressing her thin body against his in the way he knew always aroused her and some time elapsed before Francine managed to slip out of the stables and back into the house.

* * *

'Mix the powders for me, damn you!' Luc commanded, staring across the room to where the Moor stood beside a table on which was an empty glass and a pitcher of water. The man looked at him without speaking and continued slowly to grind with a wooden pestle what was in the bowl he held. 'Now! Do you want me to be a gibbering idiot by tonight?'

'I warned you not to go riding this morning,' Selim returned. 'For the past three days you have been acting like a fool. A man of your age cavorting across the countryside like a boy. Who are you trying to impress?'

'Still your tongue.'

'I will not. You will not listen to *her*—or to me...but I shall say it just the same. Don't you know how it hurts her to see you playing this charade?'

'It is for her benefit—and those who think I am at death's door.'

'Which you are,' the Moor answered, a momentary flicker of emotion passing across his ebony features.

'I must protect her to the last,' Luc insisted, his eyes riveted on the mixture being tipped into the glass and mixed with fresh water. Would it be strong enough to hold back the fire in his brain? 'Do you think Paul will give up his attempts to dispose of me?' He gave a harsh laugh and Selim frowned, relieved that they were alone so that no one else heard the unnatural sound. 'We are of the same blood, remember—he will shed every tainted drop to inherit when I die and he cares not what that will entail. Only when Alexandrine has the power that my wealth will give her will she be safe from him. No one must know how ill I am. No one must suspect she has never bedded with me. My God, Selim, how I want that woman...'

'Drink!' Selim thrust the glass out to him, disturbed by the passion in his last words. 'And put such thoughts from your mind. Would you destroy her too?'

'Destroy? I love her! I worship her! But I am a man and I have needs. Rather you took the dagger from your belt and killed me.' Luc drained the glass and fell back on to the bed. 'I cannot touch that which I desire most in this world—but perhaps I can dream...'

The Château de Belaincourt had been built in the early fourteenth century and over the decades had housed many kings and princes of royal blood. The House of Ratan was an old and noble family, proud of their association with the rulers of France, and more than once, it was boasted, the ties had become much closer, more binding. In an age when kings did so much more than just rule and had learned to enjoy life to the full, a pretty face at Court was a relief from boredom and perhaps a failing marriage—a challenge to the masculinity of that ruler. And the Ratan women had always been pretty— and many had been ambitious.

The men had been soldiers, going off to wars for months on end, leaving the château to be defended by women and the personal army the family was never without. Alain's own father had been no different—but his mother had. She had never looked at another man during her husband's absence, never stopped loving him, utterly devoted to him even when she discovered he had been unfaithful to her. It was the nature of men to be unfaithful, she had once told Alain, when he had questioned her acceptance of what he had found abhorrent. The reverence of a twelve-year-old boy for his father had been destroyed by the sight of him making love to another woman—a servant girl young enough to be his daughter. He had never felt the same love for his father again. Respect he had always maintained for Gervais Philippe Claude Maridot Ratan, as a soldier, a skilled veteran fighter whose knowledge had been passed on to the son who would one day inherit his name and estates. But love had died in him that day, never to be rekindled.

Alain had drunk and fought at the old Duc's side, had nursed him on the battlefield when he was wounded, but had stood dry-eyed beside his tomb on the day he was buried, his grief borne deep within him, the loss he felt for the father he had been unable to know as he would have liked. With his mother he had found it possible to talk of things other than war and weapons, or the latest female conquest who would be discarded as casually as all the rest. Together they had brought new life to the château after his father's death as Henriette Ratan found herself able, for the first time in thirty years, to share herself fully with her son, without the eyes of her dominating husband boring into her back.

The renovations and alterations she had brought about transformed the gaunt, grey stone château into a place of charm and beauty. She had carefully watched the transformation of Versailles from a hunting lodge to a magnificent palace, and, like so many other nobles who could afford the expense, she had copied many of the designs for furniture and lighting and the landscaping of the gardens. Flowers and trees and evergreen shrubs bloomed in profusion all around the house. The terraces had been enlarged and paved, the walkways broken by cascading fountains.

Even now, when he stood at the window and surveyed the wonders she had performed, Alain felt a tug at his heartstrings. She had been dead just over five years, but the emptiness inside him had not gone away. He swore she had saved him from madness in the months after the death of his wife where he had been plunged into an abyss of despair. Not through his loss, but through anger. Anger at himself for allowing her to use him the way she had, for allowing himself to be deceived by the emotion so laughingly known as love! Fury at her for being so beautiful. It had taken him so long to accept that she was no more than a whore who would go to the bed of anyone who attracted her—and paid her! He had given her clothes, jewels, carriages, a country house, which he had promptly disposed of a week after she died. She had wanted more. Even his love had not held her— and in the last few nightmarish months of her life she had openly displayed her wantonness at Court, forcing him into more than one duel with men who had uttered a careless remark about his wife's morals.

And then one day she was gone and he had been free again...a freedom without pleasure...only blackness which swallowed him up day and night. He was like an enraged bull in those days, he remembered, full of hate and bitterness which he had not then learned to control. Now it was different. He did not give way to his feelings, nor wear his heart on his sleeve for all to see and snicker at behind his back.

And then, without warning, his mother took to her bed one day. Within three she was dead and he was totally alone. No one could share in that loneliness. He bore it by himself in silence, grief eating away at him until he felt there was nothing left inside him, no emotion, no decency, nothing! He drank too much, rode the stallion Midnight Blue about the countryside without track of day or time, knowing he must return to the château and collapse into his bed too weary to do anything but fall asleep—or *she*, the unfaithful bitch whose face would not leave his memory, would haunt him throughout the hours of darkness...and now there was no gentle woman to comfort him, no soft voice to soothe the frayed temper and ragged nerves. He was quite alone.

One morning he awoke with a heavy head which throbbed from too much wine, and came to terms with his life. It was going to be different from what he had planned, but it was the only one he had and he must learn to live it the best way he could. And he did...until that day at the Hôtel Boussières, when he had come across a dripping wet, naked nymph, and a pair of sparkling eyes and a mouth like sweet rose petals had once more turned his world upside down.

He hated her. He hated himself. He had betrayed the trust of a friend who had helped him over many a difficult moment, who, in many ways, had become the father he had always wanted. He could talk to Luc Boussières...and now he coveted his wife! To have touched her was the most dishonourable thing Alain Ratan considered he had ever done. He had not even made love to his wife before their wedding night—but now, when he thought about it, neither had he been driven to do so with her as he had been with Alexandrine. He had fought against the desire to go to her...had weighed the consequences and still known he would do so.

Nonsense! She was only a woman. Flesh and blood. There was nothing special about her. He had allowed himself to be blinded to her true nature by the pose of innocence. If it had taken in Luc, a man of the world, with twice as many years in which to have become knowledgeable about women, then what chance had he stood?

Alain turned away from the window as Gaston announced from the doorway that the first of the carriages was drawing up outside. The guests were arriving for the ball. He was making excuses again, and the plain fact was that not one was honest. He had wanted her as no other woman he had ever met. He had played a cat-and-mouse game with her, determined to prove she was exactly what he thought she was, but he had been beaten at his own game—by a child! Like his wife, she had cleverly concealed the trollop in her until it was too late. The trap had been baited and set, and he, for all his cynicism, had walked into it like a naïve boy!

How many more had she deceived? Luc, himself... More than just two, he suspected. And what relationship did she share with the Moor? Luc, as trusting as always, had apparently thought nothing of finding them together. Not so Alain, whose sharp ears had overheard the last of their conversation. 'You stay because you want to. It is out of love,' Alexandrine had said. And she had been so casual in her attitude towards him, reclining on the window-seat completely at ease in his company. And Selim's answer... could it mean anything other than he thought? 'Yes—out of love.' Love for her! Cold rage rose inside Alain. Would she sink so low as to amuse herself with Luc's servant? For the last few hours he had been unable to get the scene out of his mind. It had forced him into reappraising her relationship with Paul. On the surface they had always appeared antagonists, at each other's throats, and she seemed always the injured party. But was that really how it was?

Out of sight of Luc, of everyone, how did she really treat Paul Boussières? Had she tried to use him, and then, realising he would never accept her in the house as its mistress or his own, repulsed him, thus bringing about the act of revenge Alain had come upon the night he rescued Luc and brought him home? He knew Paul was capable of great cruelty when he chose. What was Alexandrine capable of?

Alain swore and Gaston startled, stepped back from the door in alarm at the sudden, vehement expletive.

'Something is wrong, my lord?'

'On the contrary, all is well. I have just come to my senses.'

The game they had played was over and, as he had predicted, never for one moment believing it would become reality, they had become lovers! Now a new game was about to begin between them, but the rules would all be of his making—and this one she would lose! So he promised himself with a grim smile as he went to greet his guests. And before it was over, she would want him!

'This is such a comfortable old place,' Jeanne remarked later as she and Alexandrine wandered in the gardens before the last light faded. 'I feel at ease here, as if I were at Etoiles. Don't you?'

She found it *too* comfortable, *too* accommodating, Alexandrine mused smilingly as she nodded agreement. There was always a liveried servant outside her door to carry out the slightest request, and Francine herself had remarked on how pleasant the other members of the household were to her, and how the maids stopped to chat with her. It seemed nothing was too much trouble for the Marquise de Mezière. There was always hot water. The towels were clean and there was perfumed soap, with oils to soften the water. Fresh flowers were placed in her rooms each day. Just as it had been when the old Duchesse was alive, she had heard someone remark.

Alexandrine paused to inhale the sweet, heady fragrance of blossom on one of the orange trees bordering the path. It filled the air all about them.

'I have a clever little woman who crushes these petals and makes me the most exquisite perfume. She refuses to tell me her recipe, but has promised never to sell it to anyone else. I shall send you some when I return to Paris,' Jeanne said. She looked stunning in one of her favourite colours—pink—diamonds sparkling at her throat, a velvet mask of the same delicate colour, edged with lace, hiding her features. But against her friend she felt insignificant. Already Alexandrine's gown had aroused great speculation as to who the wearer could be…she had even heard it whispered that Jeanne herself was hiding behind the mask of dyed ostrich feathers, which covered all her features and folded behind the fair curls perched high on her head, to be secured with jewelled pins. The gown was cut daringly low, which had caused still more comment, curved seductively over rounded breasts, nipped into the small, envied waist, before billowing out into a wide, full skirt, which used an accumulation of tiered petticoats to give it the desired fullness without the hindrance of the cumbersome, obstructive panniers used by most fashionable women.

Alexandrine glided rather than walked, her identity safe behind the mask. Even Luc had not recognised her at first, and she had waited apprehensively as his gaze scanned her appearance. Then with a broad smile he had kissed her, not on the cheek as he usually did, but on the mouth. She had felt a different apprehension at the action.

'You will be the envy of every woman here tonight, my dear. I am relieved that Madame d'Etoiles is here to distract the King's attention from the most beautiful woman who has graced Belaincourt in many a long day. Perhaps the most beautiful ever. I must ask Alain.'

'You must do no such thing,' Alexandrine had protested. 'What is the use of wearing a mask if you tell everyone who I am? Where is yours?' Alain was the last person she wanted to know her identity!

'I am too old to participate in such games. But I shall enjoy watching you and the young men who try to flirt with you.'

As she left him, Alexandrine had thought she would
never understand how a husband could find it amusing
to have his wife ogled by other men, to know that secret
invitations were whispered in her ear, propositions for
a clandestine meeting—perhaps an affair. He was so sure
of her that he did not believe she would ever betray him!
Nor had she in her heart—only with her body, and the
pleasure had been over too quickly... and the realisation that she had been used to slake a man's desire,
nothing more, deepened her bitterness.

'I wonder if the King has arrived yet?' Alexandrine
murmured as she and Jeanne returned to the crowded
salon where most of the guests were assembled. There
were many tall, distinguished-looking men who could
have been the monarch, and by the little groups of ladies
huddled together, fans fluttering or pointing to one individual after the other, there was great discussion as to
which masked man was indeed Louis.

'No, he is not here yet,' Jeanne remarked after only
a brief look into the room. 'Let us remain out here a
while longer where it is cool.'

'How can you be so sure?' Alexandrine asked, mystified by her companion's confident answer.

'When you see him, you will know why,' she said with
a soft laugh. 'Have you not seen how he stands out in
a crowd? His bearing? The way he moves? And that
huskiness in his voice... why, I shall be able to recognise
him at once, even without hearing him speak. I shall
place a wager with you if you like? A small one only—
ten *louis d'or*—that I recognise him before you do.'

'Very well,' Alexandrine returned boldly. 'It is a
wager.'

She knew gambling took place every night at Versailles
and in most of the wealthy Parisian homes, but she had
never indulged in what she considered a precarious and
unsatisfactory occupation. At the turn of a card for-
tunes were won—and lost, men suddenly achieved their
dreams or had them cruelly dashed. But it was the
fashion. Both the King and the Queen indulged in the

pastime and that was enough for others to follow suit, regardless of the consequences.

'Have you thought any more about opening a salon of your own?' Jeanne asked as they sat down on one of the stone seats outside the long terrace.

'I have,' Alexandrine confessed, 'but I can do so little. I am not accomplished like you. I have little to offer.'

'My dear Alexandrine, you must begin to think more positively. You are an excellent hostess. There was not one person who came to the Hôtel Boussières who did not enjoy themselves. And wanted to come again, I might add. Not everyone has a flair for organisation as you do. I was inundated with questions about the new décor, and when I explained you had chosen the designs and the colour schemes...well...you could do worse than advise some of those old fuddy-duddies with too much money how to brighten their homes. Who knows? It might help to keep their husbands around a little more. Most men I know are only too glad to get out of the house, and the same boring routine.'

'It is the men who make that routine,' Alexandrine protested.

'But it doesn't have to be boring—or dull,' Jeanne said, with a shrug of bare shoulders. 'If you want to keep a man you must make life interesting for him, and in sharing many varied interests you will not be dull to him—that is to be my quest in life. To make—and keep— the King happy...and I do not mean in the way that all the others have tried. There is more to our existence than being mere playthings. Open your salon, Alexandrine, excel at what you are good at...organisation! I shall bring all my friends, and soon people will be clamouring for your company. Everyone will forget the unpleasant- ness with Paul Boussières. You will have friends you can turn to in times of need.'

A subtle hint that perhaps Luc's son was still a problem to be reckoned with, Alexandrine thought. It was tempting, and Alexandrine wavered no more on the brink of a decision.

'Yes, I shall do it,' she exclaimed enthusiastically.

'Bravo!' Jeanne clapped pink-gloved hands in delight. 'Come and see me next week. I would come to you, but my mother is not in the best of health and I do not like to leave her when she is in pain. The doctors say they can do nothing more. Poor thing, life has not been easy for her.' When she paused Alexandrine did not speak. She knew very little about Jeanne's background and did not want to press for details she might wish to keep to herself, but after a moment Jeanne continued.

'My father was forced to flee Paris when I was four years of age, did you know that? I thought everyone did. He was agent to the Pâris brothers, the bankers whom the Duc de Bourbon used when he was managing the young King's affairs many years ago. Scoundrels! You would not remember the terrible bread famine of 1725, you could only have been a year old then . . . I was four, and when the price of bread tripled in six months my father was unjustly accused of selling wheat on the black market for an exorbitant price. The Pâris brothers abandoned him to the mob, and he barely escaped with his life. For eight years he lived alone in Germany. Our house in the rue Richelieu was seized with all its contents, we were left with nothing. Had it not been for the intervention of Monsieur Le Normant de Tournehem, a family friend, we would have been destitute. He took care of my mother and my brother and I until my father was able to return and clear his name. Those were terrible years . . .'

Jeanne's small mouth tightened visibly. The pain of the infamy which clung to her mother long after the return of her husband and the resumption of normal family life had etched a deep scar on her heart. Not even her marriage to Le Tournehem's nephew had stilled the vicious tongues. Doors were firmly closed against her mother and herself until just recently when the latter's illness confined her to bed. Alone, Jeanne Poisson d'Etoiles, a friend of the Marquis and Marquise de Mezière, was, in some circles, acceptable.

She had a position in life now, a husband and money, a lovely château and the salon where she could be herself and excel in the things she had been trained to do. She had her mother to thank for all the accomplishments which now brought her such compliments...and yet that mother could not share in her daughter's glory by being by her side.

'Oh, Jeanne, you have such strength of purpose. You believe in your destiny and intend to fight anyone or anything that stands in the way of its becoming reality. I am not like that. I am afraid to believe, for I know if I accept what Solange told me...' Alexandrine broke off, afraid to continue.

'The day I took you to see her, she looked into your very soul, Alexandrine. You were a stranger to Paris, yet she knew you had just suffered the loss of your family, that you were a bride of only a few weeks. And when she retained your fan to help her cast a more detailed horoscope you did not object. You wanted to know the future as much as I. You never did tell me what she predicted. Was it so terrible?'

'Terrible? No—unbelievable. I shall never forget her words. She said that the signs were favourable, but before I would find happiness I would know pain and sorrow. My life would not be without danger but there would be one man who would stand by me, risk death for me...wish himself dead because of me.' As Luc's wife she knew both pain and sorrow. As a victim of his son Paul's insane vendetta, she was constantly in danger. Solange had seen it all.

'That was all?' Jeanne queried, one slender eyebrow rising at her companion's reluctance to continue. 'Solange is usually very explicit.'

'She told me there would be more than one man in my life. One was known to me—I suppose by that she meant Luc. Both men were of strong character, but one would soon die...' She heard Jeanne suck in her breath sharply. 'Yes, I believe she meant Luc again. But she has promised me happiness. I see little chance of that! My husband is an invalid, and his son will lose no opportunity to malign my name and drive me from Paris. Well, he shall have his way as soon as his father is dead.

I have made up my mind to return to Noyen for good.
I do not belong in this fashionable world.'

'Alone? That cannot be, my dear friend. If Solange
has told you there is another man for you, then you
cannot avoid him. Why do you try? Accept what must
be. Perhaps he is the one to bring you happiness. Remember her words, Alexandrine. Always be happy. Let
no one know when you ache, when you cry inside, lest
that weakness be your downfall.'

'You sound like my husband.'

'A very wise man. I am proud to know him. He has
enriched my life.'

'He is dying. He has told me so himself. There is
nothing to be done!' The words tumbled out and she
heard her companion catch her breath.

'Oh, Alexandrine . . . I am so sorry.'

'Please, tell no one. Until—until it happens, Luc
wishes everyone to believe his health is returning; that
is why he has accepted so many invitations for the season.
It is his way of proving to others that our marriage is
quite . . . normal, and that we are happy together.'

'He is a good and caring man.' Jeanne suddenly sprang
to her feet and began to smooth down the skirts of her
gown. 'Is my mask straight? Do I look all right?' Her
gaze was riveted on two men who had just stepped out
from some trees to their right and were walking slowly
towards the house. Both were tall, one clad in rich burgundy, the other in white and gold, but in the fading
light, their features masked, Alexandrine found it impossible to guess their identities.

The hand that was laid on her arm trembled and,
looking at her friend in surprise, she saw the mouth curve
into an impish smile.

'You owe me ten gold *louis*, Alexandrine. Here comes
the King!'

CHAPTER THREE

IF IT was indeed the King, his approach towards them was deliberate, Alexandrine realised, as the two men ascended the steps to the terrace. And that left her in little doubt as to the identity of his companion. It could only be the Duc de Belaincourt, his host. Resplendent in burgundy silk, slashed with grey, the dark features hidden behind a black velvet mask, he seemed totally at ease with his royal guest as they approached, his deep laughter reaching her ears to quicken her heartbeats. She had avoided him thus far and had every intention of continuing to do so.

'Courage,' Jeanne hissed from behind her fan. 'He is only a man...and I do not speak of the King. Do not run from him, Alexandrine.'

It was too late, even though every fibre of her being screamed to do so. Alexandrine still smarted from Alain's earlier comments and did not wish a time of enjoyment to be spoiled for her by more unfair criticisms of her morals.

Jeanne lifted her skirts, just enough for a pair of dainty little satin-clad feet to be seen, and then dropped into a low curtsy. Above the fan her eyes lifted momentarily to lock with those of the man in white and gold, the curls of his long wig falling about broad shoulders, and then she lowered them demurely.

'Did I not promise some of the most beautiful women in Paris would grace Belaincourt with their presence tonight?' Alain murmured, as the men bowed courteously before the two women, and Alexandrine followed her friend's example and sank to the ground.

'You have more than kept your promise, Monsieur Ratan. Here I have not even stepped foot inside the house

61

and I swear we have been met by the two most fascinating creatures we could ever hope to encounter.'

Jeanne was right, Alexandrine thought, startled. It was
the King. Even she recognised those deep, vibrant tones,
with an undercurrent of huskiness in them that had
probably won many a lady's heart.

'From one who is surrounded by beauty that is the
greatest compliment I have ever received. You are most
gracious, sire,' Jeanne answered, as Louis took her hand
and touched it briefly to his lips.

'Fie, *madame*! Am I to understand I am no longer
incognito...?'

'Your secret is safe with me—with us.' Jeanne looked
significantly at her companion as the King extended his
hand and lifted Alexandrine to her feet also. 'Not even
the rack could drag it from me.'

'I can assure you, *madame*, I would not subject anyone
so young and lovely to such a fate—even for love of my
country.' Louis looked past them into the salon and, beneath the mask, Alexandrine sensed the smile fading, as
he gazed at the crowded room and listened to the noise.
'Not yet...I wish to enjoy this tranquillity—this love-
liness—a while longer. *Madame*, you shall show me the
Duc's gardens.'

What a perfect pair they made, Alexandrine thought
to herself as they moved away. He—so tall and grand.
She—petite, fragile, in need of that masculine protection, the comfort of that strong arm on which her
little fingers rested. At last Jeanne's dreams were to
become reality. She was with the King!

She turned to find the pale green eyes of Alain Ratan
gleaming as he considered her appearance from head to
toe. Torches and lanterns were being brought out on to
the terrace by liveried servants and, in the blaze of sudden
light, the brilliance of Alexandrine's turquoise gown was
stunning. He had known it was she the moment he saw
her, for he had had Jules find out from Francine what
her mistress would be wearing. When she had refused
to divulge any information Jules had peeped into the
bedroom as he held her in his arms, and promised again

to meet her in the stables later on that evening, and he had seen the magnificent creation spread out over a chair.

Alain had watched Alexandrine moving about the room chatting to his guests, so sure of herself that he was quite taken aback. At Versailles she had given him the impression she wanted to run away from the probing stares and endless questions. But, of course, that had been in the beginning, when it had been her intention to impress everyone with her shyness, her timidity. There was no need to continue with that now she had been received in so many places—and had caught the eye of the King. Nothing would ever come of it, not with Jeanne d'Etoiles on hand—willing and available to climb into the bed of the King of France. Most women did so from ambition, and a few because they were paid, but—what were her motives?

'Would you care for some refreshment, Alexa? Or perhaps you would prefer to dance?' Alain watched her lips purse in annoyance at the realisation he knew her identity. 'Come now, how could I not fail to know you? Your gown is a masterpiece. Simplicity coupled with seduction. I suspect Luc did not design this one.'

'Save your flattering words for those here tonight foolish enough to be taken in by them,' Alexandrine returned coldly.

'The only man any of the women here tonight are interested in is the King,' he said. 'Each one of them has tried to outdo every other in the hope she will be noticed. We have two Dianas, hunting for a royal lover, several Fairy Princesses, no doubt hoping to become the Queen in Fairyland, and the rest are so laden down with jewelled gowns they would be unable to get out of them even if Louis did take a fancy to one of them. And there is no chance of that, is there, Alexa? Not now he has seen Madame d'Etoiles close to. Do you condone what is in her mind? Betrayal of her husband? Her marriage vows?'

'Jeanne is old enough to know what she is doing.' Alexandrine did not like the sardonic note creeping into his voice. She sensed the words were meant for her also.

'I am her friend, not her keeper. Besides, how could she refuse him? He is the King. He can command her.'

'If a woman is virtuous enough, she will refuse, over and over again. Nothing would make her submit to something she would find abhorrent,' Alain flung back cuttingly. 'I am surprised you are not in competition with her. You have a talent for the unexpected. Have you no wish to end up in the King's bed? Most women dream of it. Is that why you had such an alluring gown made?'

'Not his, and not yours!' Alexandrine flung back. Picking up her skirts, she swung away from him towards the salon, but the doorway was blocked by a group of people just coming out. His soft laughter followed her down the steps and into the garden as she hurried along a path towards another entrance.

How dared he suggest she had set herself up to be noticed, like all the others! He knew it was not true. He was going to make life as unpleasant as he could for her during her stay at Belaincourt. Why? Because she had refused his advances a second time? Did he not have enough women to amuse him, on whom to inflict his bitterness and irony? She had carefully scrutinised the women she saw, seeking one that in some way resembled Claudia de la Fontaine, but had been unable to find her. Perhaps the rumours that she and Alain were no longer together were true, after all. Jeanne had been sure they had parted before Christmas, and Claudia had then begun a liaison with Paul Boussières. A weak man and a strong, possibly jealous, woman. Not the best of matches.

She paused beneath the low, overhanging branches of an oak to drink in the heady perfume of orange-blossom. Alain had spoiled the evening for her as he would spoil the remainder of her days here if she allowed it. She took a deep breath and fanned herself slowly while she composed herself. She had almost lost her temper, but not quite. And the fact that he had failed to rouse her would bring him no satisfaction. It was a comforting thought.

A shadow came out from the bushes ahead of her. For a moment she thought he had cut through the gardens to waylay her, and then realised the masked man before her was smaller in stature and dressed in dark clothes.

'Good evening, Madame la Marquise. I have brought you a message—from Monsieur Boussières.' The unemotional voice sent a chill of fear through her, momentarily rooting her to the spot.

'A—a message?' Her fan snapped shut as the man took a step forward. 'We have nothing to say to each other, Monsieur Boussières and I. I do not want to hear it.'

Paul was trying to communicate with her now, having failed to gain a favourable response from his father, she surmised, but she would not listen.

'It is not a—verbal message, *madame*. He knew words would be wasted on you as they have been on the Marquis. He wanted you to know his patience is at an end.'

Muted light from the terrace behind him glinted on something taken from an inside pocket. A scream rose in Alexandrine's throat as the gleaming blade of a knife flashed upwards. She knew she could not escape it…she was going to die! Even as the thought flashed through her mind, the breath was knocked from her body as something or someone collided with her, knocking her to the ground. Before her horrified gaze, she saw her would-be assailant struggling with another man and, catching a glimpse of the thin, weasel features, gave a glad cry. Jules!

Her senses were reeling, but somehow she managed to drag herself to her feet where she stood swaying as the two men rolled on the ground before her. She must fetch help! Jules was of even slighter build than his opponent—he would be killed, she thought wildly, as they fought for possession of the knife.

Her skirts trailing behind her across the flowerbeds, she stumbled to the terrace, past a man and woman embracing on one of the seats who took one look at the breathless, dishevelled creature coming towards them and made some comment on the amorous effect Belaincourt seemed to have on people. Fools! Alexandrine stalking past them scornfully. Useless fools! Selim would soon deal with the problem.

'Are you in need of assistance?' Alain asked, stepping out from a sheltered arbour, a glass of wine in one hand. His eyes swept over her, missing nothing, and narrowed sharply. 'Are you afraid of the dark, Alexa, or running from an over-enthusiastic friend? You have only yourself to blame, you know...that gown has attracted more than the eyes of the King.'

'Save your breath, *monsieur*. Your servant Jules is being murdered in the garden!' she cried and then, spurred to a recklessness that had lain dormant in her since childhood and unable to withstand the hateful taunts a second time, Alexandrine drew back her hand and, with all the force she could muster, dashed the glass from his grasp. Then she swept past him into the salon.

She did not care that her appearance caused a stir. She saw no one but her husband and Selim as she pushed her way through the crowd to their sides.

'Selim—quickly! Outside. A man tried to kill me!' Her words were for the ears of no one else and too quietly spoken to reach the people watching them with curious faces. But the urgency in her tone conveyed to both men her fear and horror at what had taken place.

'Go!' Luc commanded, and a pathway opened up before Selim as he lunged towards the open french windows, with a surprising agility for a man of his height and build. Or perhaps it was the cold fury on the ebony features that caused the sudden upsurge of conversation. A hand went beneath Alexandrine's elbow as she swayed slightly. 'Compose yourself, my dear. Let us go outside for some air. Selim will deal with the man, never fear.'

How calm he sounded, as if she had just declared it to be a fine day. Had he understood fully what she had said? One look into the bleak eyes which surveyed those about them as he led her out again on to the terrace told her that he did. She leaned weakly against a pillar, a hand pressed against her fiercely beating heart.

'He had a knife.' Her voice shook as she recalled how close she had come to death. 'Paul sent a man to kill me!'

'Paul? My son was mentioned by name? Tell me everything said to you,' Luc insisted gently, drawing her against his chest. She trembled as she did so, and felt his hand stroking her shoulder comfortingly.

'Is she hurt?' Alain appeared out of the darkness beside them, Selim and Jules close on his heels. The latter's face was bruised and bleeding, and he muttered fiercely under his breath as he touched a swollen jaw.

'No, just badly shaken,' Luc returned. 'You have the man? Bring him to me, Alain. I want to question him…'

'He is dead. It could not be helped. In the struggle Jules turned the knife on him.'

'Is this true, Selim?'

'Do you doubt my word?' Alain flung back as the Moor nodded confirmation of the statement, and Luc rounded on him instantly.

'An attempt has just been made on Alexandrine's life. To have had proof from that man's own lips that his orders had come from Paul——'

'That is what you were told?' Alain looked questioningly at Alexandrine, still standing within the circle of Luc's arms. Paul had gone mad to attempt such a thing. To send an assassin to Belaincourt! 'Tell me inside—we have an audience of eager ears.' He motioned sardonically towards the listening guests who had followed them outside.

A woman detached herself from the group and came close to Jules, peering at his injured face before asking, in a high-pitched voice, 'Do you have wild animals in your garden, Alain?'

'Only two-legged ones, *madame*, and no more dangerous than your companions,' came the dry retort which brought roars of laughter and relieved the growing tension in the air. 'Go back inside, everyone, the excitement is over. It is all a—misunderstanding.'

Alexandrine felt the colour rise in her cheeks as people filed past her, their eyes lingering on the hem of her gown which was covered in earth from her flight across the garden, or on the remnants of her fan, broken when Jules had flung her to the ground. Hesitantly she disengaged herself, and went to Jules, laying a hand on his arm.

'Thank you. You saved my life.'

'Go and have that face seen to, Jules,' Alain ordered. 'And tell the cook he is to give you a bottle of his wine. We will talk in the morning. And make sure all traces of our unwanted visitor are removed.'

'Yes, Monsieur le Duc.'

'If he had not been out there...' Alexandrine murmured, her eyes widening. She did not want to know what would be done with the body.

'I suspect he was on his way to the stables to keep a rendezvous with your maid. That is where they have been meeting since you arrived,' Alain replied. 'He is a resourceful little man, but, like you, Luc, I would have liked the opportunity to question this assassin of Paul's. You realise I have no choice but to call the young fool out? I cannot allow this to pass.'

'You would have my undying gratitude if you did let it pass, in fact,' Luc returned, and Alexandrine caught her breath in disbelief. She had almost been murdered and her husband did not want to pursue the matter! 'I shall deal with this in my own way. When I have proof that Paul was behind it——'

'Luc!' she gasped. 'You have my word! The man said Paul had lost patience with us. He is no longer resorting to threats. Now he plans murder. Have you forgotten he tried to kill you also?'

'I forget nothing, my dear. I am so sorry that this has happened. It has been a frightening experience for you, but you must allow me to do things my way. Had the man lived to testify against my son, then it would be a different matter and Paul would be arrested by morning. But there is no witness against him. He will say he was with a dozen other people and can prove it, and that he has never seen the man before.'

'You are right, of course, but to do nothing!' Alain growled. 'And the fact he sent him here—to Belaincourt! Either something has brought him new courage—or he has gone out of his mind.'

'I think I shall go upstairs . . . I do not feel very much like going back inside,' Alexandrine said, still unable to accept Luc's strange attitude. 'You do not mind, do you, Luc?'

'Of course not. Try to put this out of your mind, child. I shall ensure it never happens again.'

'It should not have happened in the first place,' Alain said cuttingly as Alexandrine left them. His eyes followed her to the edge of the terrace and lingered there long after she had disappeared round the corner. 'I told you to hire men for protection.'

'I do not need to be told that had I listened to you this could not have happened.' Luc leaned heavily on his stick, his face suddenly drawn in the light of the wall torches. 'I shall attend to it tomorrow. Perhaps you can suggest . . .'

'Allow me to arrange the matter. Jules has some strange friends, but they have proved advantageous to me in the past. Four of them will be sufficient, I think. Together with Selim, they will give you all the protection you both need.' Alain wondered if the man would have survived to be questioned if the Moor had come upon him first. He doubted it, remembering the carved oriental dagger he had seen. He remembered his earlier suspicion that Selim had become as susceptible to her as he himself had been.

'Thank you, Alain. Once again you are here when I need you,' Luc said, relieved by the offer of help.

'As you were once when I needed wise counsel and advice. I am your friend, Luc, never forget that.'

'Alexandrine, are you hurt? I have just heard the dreadful news?' Jeanne found her friend reclining on a day-bed in her sitting-room, her fair head supported by a thick cushion. The lovely mask of feathers lay dis-

carded on the floor alongside her shoes. Only one candle
burned in the room and Jeanne quickly lighted more on
the table beside Alexandrine and beneath the window.
'That's better. Goodness, you look terrible. What a
monstrous thing to have happened. Everyone is talking
about it. Where is your maid? You need something
stimulating to drink. Why is no one taking care of
you . . .?'

'Jeanne, please, I just wanted to be by myself,'
Alexandrine protested, lifting her aching head a fraction.
Jeanne frowned at her tear-streaked face. 'I didn't mean
to break down—after all, I am not hurt. But sitting here
in the darkness, it was all so horribly unreal. Paul sent
a man to kill me! I cannot believe it. How can he hate
me that much? I have done him no harm.'

'My poor Alexandrine!' Jeanne cried, dropping on to
the day-bed beside her. 'I shall stay with you until you
feel better. Would you like to undress and go to bed? I
shall not leave you until your maid comes. Where is the
girl? Her place is here with you.'

'With—with Jules, the Duc's stableman. They are
sweethearts. Oh, Jeanne, if he had not been going to
meet her tonight, he would never have come across me—
I would have been found . . .' She broke off, her face in
her hands.'

'Hush, now. I'm going to ring for someone to bring
you a warm drink and then I'll help you get undressed.
And, if you feel up to it, you can tell me all about it.
Madame du Clos said you had been attacked in the
garden and ravished by some mad village peasant. The
Duchesse de Villac suggested you had gone off with an
admirer who had wanted more than you were willing to
give. I soon put her in her place, the stupid woman! The
King was most concerned and wished to be assured that
you have come to no harm.'

'How kind.' Her own troubles were forgotten as she
looked into Jeanne's flushed face. The mention of the
King had brought a sparkle to her eyes. 'You—and he?'

'I have been invited—unofficially, of course—to follow
the royal hunt the day after tomorrow and again the fol-

lowing Monday. We talked of so many things,
Alexandrine. He is not only a King but a very special
man . . . so intelligent underneath all that formality. But
then I don't suppose he has many opportunities to be
himself. Really himself, I mean. We talked of music, of
my salon . . . he has promised to come and visit me one
day soon . . . of the arts, Versailles. In a short time I shared
so much with him we were no longer strangers.'

'I am pleased at your success . . .' Alexandrine did not
know quite what else to say.

'Success? Not yet . . . but it comes closer. I do hope
Charles-Guillaume—my husband—will not disapprove.
He loves me deeply and I care for him, we have been
happy together, but this is my destiny.' Her voice rang
with excitement. 'I shall send Solange a little present to
celebrate my success. What do you think of her predictions now?'

'I prefer not to think of them at all; they are too ludicrous,' Alexandrine answered, struggling out of her
dress. She was glad to relieve herself of the weight and
slip into a cool robe. While Jeanne rang for a servant
and ordered wine for herself and a spiced drink for
Alexandrine, she sat down and began to brush her hair.
She was still deeply agitated by what had taken place
and knew she would not be able to sleep for a very long
time. It would have been better to have stayed downstairs, but she could not have faced the questions, or the
insinuations. There would be no keeping the incident
quiet in face of the insatiable morbid curiosity of Alain's
friends. By tomorrow the whole of Versailles would
know. By the time the gossips had finished with it the
story would bear no resemblance to reality, she decided,
and she must accept that and not allow herself to be
further upset.

'Let me go! I want to go to my wife,' Luc insisted, vainly
trying to break free of Selim's grip. They were in the
corridor leading to her rooms. The Moor had watched
him drinking heavily for the past hour and had guessed
what was in his mind when he had slipped away from

the other guests, without even announcing his departure to anyone.

'No! You cannot. You know that.'

'I shall have her. She belongs to me...' Luc's face, blotched with the effects of the rich wine, contorted in anger. His long nails dug viciously into the back of Selim's hand, but the grip on him did not slacken—it increased. 'Damn you—you are hurting me!'

'If I must. Come to bed, Luc. I shall give you something to help you sleep...'

Alain reached the top of the staircase and watched the two of them at the far end of the corridor. Luc struggling against the determination of the Moor to drag him away from Alexandrine's door. Alain's footsteps quickened as his first instinct was to go to Luc's assistance, but then they slowed and he melted back into the shadows, listening to what passed between them. Luc was clearly drunk, but was the Moor's concern for him or for Alexandrine? Again the ugly suspicion that he was too close to her rose in his mind and he started after them, only to find they had reached the upstairs corridor and were out of view.

He turned back, hesitating outside Alexandrine's door. Then he knocked. It opened slightly, framing her in candlelight—a pale, slender figure with tousled hair the colour of sunlight, the magnificent ballgown replaced by a magenta-coloured silk robe which left bare her arms and shoulders, but which, to him, was equally seductive. How long would it be before he could look at her and honestly tell himself he no longer wanted her?

Her eyes widened at the sight of him and the soft lips he had enjoyed possessing trembled as she asked quietly, 'What is it, *monsieur*? I was about to retire.'

'The King needs to be assured you have suffered no ill effects from the unpleasantness in the garden,' Alain answered, his tone matching hers. It was the truth, but he had also come on his own account.

'Please thank His Majesty for his concern and tell him I am quite recovered now.'

'Is that the truth?' His finger went beneath her chin, tilting back her head so he could see her face more clearly. 'You are still exceedingly pale. Will you not accept that I too was worried about you? You are a guest in my house, Alexa...a very special guest.'

'Please, no more of this,' Alexandrine whispered. 'I am too tired to fence words with you now. Leave me in peace.'

'Would you not prefer some company? Luc unfortunately has been drinking, and Selim has had to use more than a little persuasion to make him understand you would not wish for his company tonight—but I am here, and sober...'

The figure who appeared in his view took him completely by surprise. The arm which had encircled Alexandrine's waist, pulling her close to him, fell away. A tight smile masked the anger which rose in him, and he acknowledged the presence of Jeanne d'Etoiles with a brief nod of his head.

'How touching of you to enquire after Alexandrine's condition, Monsieur le Duc. You have always been a perfect host. I shall stay with her for a while yet until her maid returns, so you may rest easy that she is being cared for.'

'I am pleased to hear it, *madame*.'

Jeanne moved back to the day-bed, a satisfied look flickering across her features. She surmised they would not be disturbed again tonight—by anyone!

'Goodnight, Alexa...' Alain's soft whisper, full of mockery, was to linger with Alexandrine long after she had climbed into bed and tried unsuccessfully to sleep. 'There will be another night to settle the balance of your account.'

Alexandrine did not awake until late the following morning. Declining anything to eat, she had Francine bring her some lemon tea in the hope it would revive her low spirits. She had slept surprisingly well, considering the turmoil her thoughts had been in when she had climbed into bed as Jeanne took her leave. Dear Jeanne. What a friend she was! The maid gave a gasp of horror when she came back into the bedroom and discovered her mistress examining a large bruise on one arm, just below the elbow.

'*Madame*, you were hurt after all! I shall kill Jules for not telling me the truth sooner,' she declared, two fierce spots of colour burning in her cheeks, and the hand holding the cup of lemon tea shook so violently Alexandrine was afraid it would spill all over the honey-coloured rug.

'Give that to me and calm yourself,' she said quickly. 'Madame d'Etoiles was with me until you came, and there was nothing you could do. He is a rogue, your Jules, I agree with that, but I owe him my life and so you will say nothing to him. Do you understand me?'

Jeanne had rounded on the girl the moment she had appeared last night, which was some considerable time after she had persuaded Alexandrine to go to bed, re-monstrating with her for abandoning her mistress when she was most needed to give her aid and comfort. After Jeanne had gone, Francine had broken down in tears, confessing that until a few moments before she had known nothing of what had happened. Jules had come to her in the stables in a terrible state, she said tearfully, his face cut and bruised. He had told her he had fought with another man and avoided any questions as to the man's identity or the reason. Avoided them most per-suasively, Alexandrine had thought, remembering the wisp of straw she had seen still clinging to Francine's hair. Only as she was returning upstairs, when one of the other servants had asked after the Marquise, had she discovered that the Marquise had been attacked.

'Do you understand me, Francine? This time I shall overlook not only your absence but these secret meetings you have been having with him since we arrived at Belaincourt. But they cannot continue. I have nothing against the young man, but I would prefer, for your own sake, that you remain close by me. It was Monsieur Boussières who sent that man to attack me.'

'Monsieur Boussières? Madame, can that be true?' the maid whispered.

'I believe it.' How she wished Luc did too, but it was in her mind that, if he had, he would have dealt with the situation far differently. Was this terrible sickness he possessed eating away at his mind as well as his body? Perhaps he had not fully understood the implications of what she had told him? Yet Luc must remember that his son Paul had once attempted to take the life of his father also! The questions brought back the ache to her head that had kept her awake half the night, and she drank the hot, sharp tea slowly, giving herself time to regain her composure. She would not help herself, or Luc, by making her nerves more ragged than they already were and descending on him pale and lifeless, demanding answers he could not supply.

'What time is it?' She stretched, wincing as her bruised arm brushed the coverlet.

'A little after eleven, *madame*. The Marquis and most of the guests who stayed last night are still in their rooms. There was so much food left over that the kitchen staff have prepared cold meals, so as not to spoil it. Madame d'Etoiles called earlier, but when I told her you were still sleeping she would not let me disturb you. She said she would leave a message with the Duc de Belaincourt. *Madame*, did she really meet the King here last night? You should hear what is being said.'

'I do not want to hear,' Alexandrine returned sternly. 'I know only too well what wagging tongues are like. Remember Madame d'Etoiles is my friend, and make that known to others who would speak against her!'

'Oh, it was nothing cruel. All the servants think she is far prettier than the King's mistress, Madame de Châteauroux—in fact, than all his mistresses. And the Queen is so dull, how could the King not fail to be interested in such a charming lady? And so accomplished. She played for the guests last night and sang. I have heard her voice compared to that of a lonely nightingale . . . and the King was supposed to be in the room, not a few feet away from where she sat. It is romantic...'

'Spoken through the eyes of love,' Alexandrine said with a faint smile. 'But she has a mother whose in-

famous reputation has cast the whole family into disrepute...and a husband! I fear the way ahead for her—
for them both—will not be a smooth one. Lay out a
gown for me. Something with long sleeves, to cover this
mark. I am not in the mood to be questioned about anything today. I shall go and see what my husband wishes
to do today.' As the girl turned away, Alexandrine caught
sight of a box on the table beside her, attractively
wrapped and tied with a dark red ribbon. 'Francine, what
is this?'

'I do not know, *madame*. A servant brought it an hour
ago.'

'There is no card.' The wrapping fell away without
bringing to light anything to tell her who had sent it.
'Oh, look! Is it not beautiful?'

She lifted out a small golden box, encrusted with precious stones. A large sapphire dominated the top of the
hinged lid, which lifted, to reveal a satin-covered cavity.
The moment it was raised... 'A musical box! How exquisite. Luc!' Of course. Something he had brought back
from his travels. A gift to apologise for drinking too
much, perhaps, or for his lack of action over the attack
on her? Either way, it did not matter. It was the most
delightful gift she had ever been given! She lost no time
in dressing and going to his rooms.

When Selim hesitated at the doorway, she said with a
bright smile, 'I know all about last night...Luc indulged a little too much with the wine. He was worried
about me, Selim. And how can I be angry with him when
he has sent me such an enchanting present?'

She held out the box for him to see, but he showed
no signs of recognising it.

'What are you chattering about over there? Come in
and let me look at you.' Luc's voice sounded from the
bedroom, and she quickly went to him. He took her by
the hand and drew her down beside him, his eyes
searching her face. She noticed at once how drawn he
was; he was beginning to look ill again. 'How are you
this morning?' Luc asked. 'Was it the truth you told

Alain? You have suffered no ill effects from that cowardly attack on you last night?'

'He—he told you he had been to my room?' The words were out before Alexandrine could stop them. Was he protecting himself as always, lest she said something to her husband?

'Why should he not? He came to you at the King's command, my dear. I am relieved to see you looking so bright and cheerful. I must admit I slept better for his comforting words.'

'And the wine you had consumed,' Alexandrine said with a smile. 'You know you should not drink so much, Luc. You will turn poor Selim's hair quite grey if you do! Anyway, I forgive you...how can I not, when you have sent me such a gift?'

'Gift? I know of no...' He looked sideways at the Moor, who shook his head. 'For a moment I thought I might have been giving orders in my sleep. What is it you speak of, child? I have sent you nothing, although, now I think on it, it is time I did. A little something to make you forget the horror of last night. Something pretty to grace that lovely neck...'

'I have so many things, I do not need more,' Alexandrine protested, but she knew he would not listen to her. She would receive another piece of jewellery, or a monogrammed trinket-box made from seasoned wood and polished until it shone. Or ivory combs for her hair...each time it was something different and exciting. Hesitantly she showed him the jewelled box and saw his eyes light up with appreciation as he examined it.

'A superb piece of workmanship. Italian, rather reminiscent of a box Lucrezia Borgia once owned. It was supposed to contain her poison phials.'

'Oh—how terrible! It cannot be the same.'

'I doubt it, but it is an excellent copy. I shall be interested to know which young gallant thinks so highly of you that he is willing to part with this little treasure.'

'If it is so valuable I shall discover who has sent it, and return it. I cannot accept it,' Alexandrine said, reluctantly retrieving the gift. She had fallen in love with it at first sight, but she could not take such an expensive item from any man but Luc. At least, she supposed it was a man. Luc did! Perhaps Jeanne... Yes, that was it. 'I think I know who has sent it. Madame d'Etoiles. She left before I was up.'

But why then was there no card with it? Yet she could not think of anyone else whom she knew well enough.

Alexandrine stayed with Luc for a while longer, and it was as she was about to leave that Gaston appeared, with a message that Alain Ratan was waiting downstairs. Luc clapped his hand to his head with a frown.

'I'd forgotten all about it. Sit a horse in my condition? Impossible. I am sure he will accept you in my place. Your safety is assured while you are with him, my dear, and Alain has promised to provide men to ensure no such occurrence happens again.'

'If that is what you wish,' she replied, conscious of Selim's gaze on her. What thoughts lay behind that bland stare? There were times, especially since they had arrived at Belaincourt, that she believed he knew about her relationship with Alain Ratan.

'It is a lovely day. Go and enjoy yourself. Show Alain what an accomplished horsewoman you have become. It will please him to see someone competent riding the fine horse he gave you,' Luc declared, and sent Gaston back to the Duc to tell him of the change in the arrangements, giving Alexandrine no chance to argue.

She returned to her room and changed into a gown of deep blue, a necklace of lapis-lazuli around her neck. The colour suited her, Alexandrine thought. She needed something to bolster her courage if she was to spend time alone with Alain. If he was obnoxious to her today, she would hit him, she thought, slapping the leather riding whip in her hand against the side of the door as she went out.

'Madame la Marquise, I trust Luc is merely over-tired and not ill again?' Alain was the perfect gentleman as he came to greet her at the bottom of the stairs, where late rising guests were wandering in search of food or more wine, with servants close on their heels to anticipate their wishes and ensure they did not stray somewhere they should not in the vastness of the sprawling house. He took her hand and lifted the ringed fingers to his lips. A gleam came into the eyes which candidly inspected her appearance as he murmured, 'Are you looking beautiful for me? I am flattered, Alexa.'

'I should have dressed this way if I were going riding with the King or the devil!' she retorted, snatching her hand free.

'I am not the King...' Alain chuckled, as he escorted her outside to where the horses waited. Lady Blue stood quietly beside his huge black stallion, occasionally turning to nuzzle his nose affectionately. Alain stroked her coat, and, with laughter in his voice, added, 'Can we not be friends, as they are?'

'No. You have made that impossible.' A groom came forward to help her to mount, but Alain waved him back and, before she could protest, had lifted her as if she weighed no more than a feather and set her on the saddle.

'I was hoping my peace offering might have stirred a little compassion in you.'

'Peace offering!' Alexandrine drew in her breath. '*You* sent it!'

'If you are referring to the casket, of course I did. Who else did you think?'

'Why, Luc, of course. I am not in the habit of accepting gifts from men, Monsieur Ratan.'

'My, how formal we are again. Did it not please you?' Alain enquired, turning his horse about. Lady Blue fell into step beside him without the need of an order.

'It is very pretty. Luc seemed to think it is a copy of a box once owned by Lucrezia Borgia.'

'He is correct—except that it is not a copy. My mother used to say perhaps she listened to the music while deciding what poison to use on her next victim.' He laughed at the look of horror on Alexandrine's face. 'I jest. The poor woman was unfairly maligned, and I doubt if she was capable of committing all those crimes attributed to her. She was a useful scapegoat in an age when poison was a way of life. Come to think of it, it still is. La Voisin, before they burned her, was said to have committed hundreds of murders, performed several thousand abortions and done away with as many unwanted babies. Madame de Montespan, the late King's mistress, barely escaped with her life for her association with such notoriety.'

'I prefer to think that a casket of such beauty was created to give pleasure, not pain and death,' Alexandrine returned. 'I cannot keep it, however.'

'You shall accept it, unless you wish me to give it to Luc to give back to you,' Alain threatened. 'It is a thing of beauty, to be owned by beauty, as my mother owned it before you. She used to lull me to sleep when I was a babe with it.'

'A scene I can hardly picture,' she said, forced to agree, and he chuckled wickedly.

'Contrary to what you think, I was once a decent human being. I possessed a heart. I loved my parents, and I was as chivalrous as the next man. And then I grew up. I discovered the world is full of cruelty and deception. Of lovely women falling over themselves to break a man's heart. Of men who will lie and cheat and who do not possess the scruples of an alley-cat.' For a moment the dark features were grim and unsmiling as Alain contemplated the black void from which he had emerged bitter and vindictive, seeking revenge. Then, as quickly as the mood had seized him, it passed and his face cleared.

'Very well, I have no choice but to accept your gift, but there it must end.' They left the gardens and orange groves behind them, allowing the horses to continue at a leisurely pace towards the forest of Sénart stretching ahead. This was where the King hunted regularly, she realised, wondering if it was merely chance they were heading in that direction.

'I do not trust this change of attitude, *monsieur*. You took me in once; you will not do so again. I know now that your sole purpose was to prove me as weak and fickle as other women in your life, unable to resist the charm of the Duc de Belaincourt.' Alain's lips twitched sardonically at the jibe, but he remained silent. 'And in that you succeeded. It is not something I am proud of, and it will haunt me for the rest of my days. But from that moment of weakness I have gained strength. Enough to withstand your—persuasive tongue, Monsieur le Duc!'

'If you believe that, then you have nothing to fear, have you?' he flung back. He did not dispute her accusation that he had used her, his silence condemning him in her eyes.

'No. Nothing!' Her bold gaze challenged his disbelief and the smile grew.

'Then let us enjoy our ride. But take care, Alexa. You may think yourself immune to seduction, but you are still riding with the devil!'

'A devil I know.' Alexandrine spurred her horse ahead, abandoning herself to the new sense of freedom she had discovered on horseback. Had she seen the strange look which entered Alain's eyes as he kneed Midnight Blue and followed her, she might have questioned the wisdom of those words. But at that moment she was lost to the complexity of the character of the man who rode with her, unaware of the bitter thoughts and black moods which dogged his existence, or of the emotional turmoil he had experienced the night he held her in his arms and which he relived—and fought against—whenever he was with her.

'Let us see what Selim has accomplished with you, country girl,' he challenged, and gave his stallion free rein. The animal surged away, with her in pursuit, into the forest.

CHAPTER FOUR

'If I did not know better, Alexandrine, I would believe
you were trying to make some young man jealous with
all this attention to me,' Luc remarked drily, as his young
wife found a seat for him at one of the gaming tables
after they had finished dancing, and bent to lay her lips
against a lined cheek before she drew back from him.

'Luc! How can you say such a thing to me?'
Alexandrine protested, as she seated herself beside him,
conscious of the other people at the table watching them
intently.

'A joke, child. Nothing more.'

It had not sounded so to her! For the past week, since
they had come to stay at Belaincourt, she had noticed
Luc's attitude towards her beginning to change. At first
the change was only slight: he would comment, with a
smile or a chuckle, on her long rides, mostly with Alain.
Or on the way she enjoyed dancing with whoever asked
her when they attended at Versailles. And she had begun
to gamble there, too, under the wing of Madame de
Mailly. Alexandrine sensed the latter was being friendly
to her so that she said and did nothing to prejudice the
King's so far secret attentions to Jeanne d'Etoiles. She
did not mind. At the side of the woman who was Louis's
close confidante she knew she had secured for herself a
place at Court envied by many. Her closeness and
friendship with the person who had failed to become the
King's mistress, yet still shared the secrets of his heart,
gave her a new and much favoured status. She discovered what it was to bask in the limelight which surrounded one of the King's chosen friends. It opened even
more doors for her, and invitations came flooding in
their direction.

At first she had thought Luc pleased by her unexpected success. She was no longer afraid to go to Versailles alone or to accept invitations without him. Few dared speak out against her in public. Even Paul, who had snubbed her when she had first appeared in the palace, now acknowledged her—with silent hatred in his eyes—openly, for everyone to see.

She considered she was doing everything Luc wanted of her. Being gracious to all, even those she did not like, while remaining a little reserved still, aloof from their intrigues. Luc insisted they remain at Balaincourt, but there Alain was happy that Alexandrine should entertain their friends. She planned to open her salon, too, an idea which had interested Luc at first. Now, whenever she mentioned it, something about the way he spoke told her he no longer considered it desirable, and this dulled her enthusiasm. His manner was growing more demanding, his touch more possessive. Was he growing jealous of the ease with which she now attended Court functions, entertained herself? She could not understand. He himself had groomed her for the part of hostess and perfect wife!

His drinking was becoming a constant worry to her. He behaved for days quite normally, indulging himself very little with the abundance of wines which flowed like water at Belaincourt. And then there were days when he would shut himself in his room and drink heavily, and she knew Selim was forced to sedate him to avoid his becoming violent. She was helpless at times like these, unable to be of assistance in any way. Alain's penetrating looks became more and more questioning as the days passed, and he too began to notice a change in his friend.

They had ridden many times together since that first day when he had extended an uneasy truce between them—a truce which was uneasy for both of them, for always she found herself wanting to relax in his company yet aware that to do so would be disastrous. He was always pleasant, though often his remarks cut, never allowing her to forget what they had briefly shared. Yet without those rides she did not know what she would have done on those days when Selim forbade her entry to Luc's rooms. And each time he emerged and returned to her and the gaiety of Versailles she sensed the gulf between them widening. If he knew of her liaison with Alain, surely he would have faced her with it? she reasoned. Something was eating at his heart—and it had nothing to do with his illness. Or did it?

Many a night she had lain awake, half expecting Luc to come to her. She could see no other reason for his manner than that he now regretted the terms of their marriage arrangement and sought to change them. Why else did his eyes always follow her? Why did he question her every move, need to know whom she had been with?

There had been a time when she would have welcomed him to her bed, accepted him as her husband... Now, in her heart, she knew if he came to claim what was rightfully his she would submit to him out of duty— and loathe every moment. To be used, even by the husband to whom she belonged by law, was something repulsive to her.

Now settled at the gaming table, Luc turned to the man behind them. 'Alain, why don't you take my wife away and dance with her?' he said, and Alexandrine stiffened as she sensed the presence behind her chair. 'I hate to be watched while I play cards. Besides, she is better at it than I. She wins and I invariably lose—like the Queen.'

His remark brought smiles to many faces at the table. The Queen gambled nightly in the Grand Appartement and nearly always lost. Three times a week she vowed her luck would change, but it never did. She was said to be as stupid about cards as she was about everything else. And cheating at Versailles, which had become known in the time of Louis XIV as *le tripot*—the gambling den—was rife among all the inhabitants. Most were shameless cheats and were never challenged. It was a way of life!

Alain appeared in her line of vision, extending his arm towards her. She rose and placed a ringed hand upon the pale honey-coloured sleeve. What else could she have done with so many eyes watching?

'How long has Luc been gaming in this manner?' Alain asked, as they joined the dancers in the room beyond. In another, the King was playing billiards with the Duchesse de Châteauroux and some close friends.

'This past week. I have never seen him show such a passion for cards before, but then he seems to do everything to excess these days,' Alexandrine returned, concerned for the casual way she had been abandoned to another man. Luc worried her more and more!

'Really?' A dark eyebrow rose quizzingly, accompanied by a brief, wicked smile which brought a rush of pink to her cheeks.

'I was referring to his drinking,' she returned icily. 'You know that. His pace of life has become almost frantic.' Because it would soon be over, she thought, but refrained from revealing that truth to her companion. The secret was hers, and Luc's and Selim's. No one else's! 'Even Selim cannot talk any sense into him these days.'

'Luc is his own man. He will do what pleases him.'

'He once said that about you.' She looked up into the handsome features and felt a tug at her heartstrings. Outwardly she had learned to control her emotions, but inside her the fire still burned when she looked at him and recalled that night. His touch was like a branding iron upon her flesh! Yet, for appearances' sake, she had to bear his company.

'Did he now? Would you like me to speak to him . . . suggest he take things more slowly?' he asked.

'No!'

There came a narrowing of his eyes at the swiftness of her answer. If he succeeded in persuading her husband to do that, Luc might encourage Alain and herself to spend more time together so that she would not be bored, and that was the very last thing she wanted! It was bad enough having to be polite to Alain at Versailles, conscious of all those speculating looks, and there was the additional burden of climbing into bed at night at

Belaincourt, wondering if he might appear without
warning in her rooms. 'I mean—thank you, but it will
not be necessary. We shall be returning home soon and
I shall be able to ensure he rests more.'

'Luc gave me the impression this morning that he is
in no hurry to return to Paris,' Alain drawled. 'I am
glad. He has always liked Belaincourt and I enjoy his
company. And yours, of course, Alexa. It is a pleasure
to see such a happily married couple—a devoted couple—
beneath my roof. My wife and I never shared such idyllic
moments as Luc leads me to believe the two of you share.
She sought her pleasures elsewhere. She found my love
of my home a bore, my lack of interest in her friends
unforgivable.'

'She was a fool.' Alexandrine said without thinking,
and the fingers gently holding her arm tightened as he
led her back towards the gaming-room. 'Any woman
who would throw away what she was offered could be
no less.'

'I am touched by your concern. No, she was anything
but a fool, Alexa. She was a beautiful, scheming little
slut whom I loved—nay, worshipped with every breath
in my body. She almost destroyed me as a man. She
succeeded in killing me as a human being. You yourself
have said I no longer have a heart—no true emotions—
and that is the truth. What are they but weakness to
plague the mind? I am better without them.'

Instead of returning her to the table where Luc sat,
engrossed in a game of hoca, staring moodily at the cards
which would ruin many a man that night, Alexandrine
thought, as she saw the expression on his face, Alain
halted beside the table where 'vingt-et-un' was being
played. For a moment he surveyed the faces there, and
then, as if deciding he would stand a fair chance of
winning here, Alain pulled out a vacant chair for her.

'Stay a moment and bring me luck.'

'I am the last person to do that,' she said in a low,
fierce whisper as she lowered herself into it and acknowledged the others at the table, Madame de Mailly
among them. The latter looked pleased by her arrival,

and Alexandrine knew she must stay for a few minutes at least or the woman would be offended, and she was too powerful at Court to risk that.

'Perhaps I should have left a few poison phials in your casket,' Alain returned with a smile, as he seated himself close beside her and cards were dealt to him.

'Perhaps you should.'

'*Madame*, how pleasant it is to see your husband so fit again...and ready to win, I'll warrant. That mind of his is working well tonight, I see,' Madame de Mailly remarked cheerfully, glancing across the room. Following her gaze, Alexandrine saw a broad smile light up Luc's face. He *was* winning. Thank goodness! He could afford to lose great sums of money, unlike many in the room, but he had always lectured her on the futility of gaming, astonishing her when he had suddenly taken it up as a pastime himself...and seemingly pleased that she too was indulging, albeit very gingerly, with Lady Luck.

Why had he chosen to play hoca, she wondered, knowing how crooked the game was? It had been banned in the time of the late King by La Reynie, the head of the Paris police, but here in Versailles every rule was broken when the monarch so decided! The King himself liked to play it but, as he disliked being still for too long, his favourite pastime was billiards, usually played in the Salle de Diane in the Grand Appartement.

Occasionally Louis would dispense with the enormous following which attended at Versailles—and which followed him from the moment he rose and went to Mass to the hour he retired to bed—and adjourn to Marly. Built by Louis XIV, who had also used it as a retreat from the lack of privacy his every day entailed, it was a haven of sweet blooming flowers and forests, of shimmering lakes, where balls and parties, and the inevitable gaming took place amid a strict circle of close friends. It was an honour to be received at Versailles. To accompany the King to Marly was an acclaim of friendship.

'Your luck is still with you,' the Duc de Blas remarked as he threw down his cards with a grimace. 'Dammit, Alain, that's the fourth hand in a row.'

'I make my own luck,' came the quiet reply. 'Stay with me and perhaps I shall throw some your way.'

'And have my wife come at me with a hairbrush? My jaw still aches from last night,' de Blas retorted ruefully. He was a young man in his early twenties, married only three months and the talk of the Court because he allowed his wife to berate him over trivialities such as gambling. He did not yet have a mistress and was utterly devoted to her. Alexandrine liked them both, and knew Alain did also. 'I've lost too much as it is.'

'Then go home to your wife before you lose more, foolish boy,' Madame de Mailly said. 'The Duc de Belaincourt and I want to do some serious playing.'

'Alain, will you take my note...until the end of the week?' De Blas's cheeks went a bright red as he came to stand beside Alain's chair. 'A momentary embarrassment, you understand.'

'Only too well, my young friend. I've been married too,' came the sardonic retort, and Alexandrine pretended not to notice the look which came her way, accompanied by a slightly raised eyebrow. 'At your convenience. Don't forget we are dining together next week. At Ricard's.'

'You are too good to the boy,' Madame de Mailly remarked as they began to play again. 'You do him no favours, you know. Others will not have your patience.'

'I shall give him the chance to win it all back after we dine together,' Alain chuckled. 'I don't want his money. We will play another hand, *madame*, before I too shall leave you and take the delightful company of Madame la Marquise with me...back to her husband.'

'And give me no chance to recoup my losses, *monsieur*?'

'I am giving you time to practise, *madame*, so that the next time you can take my money from me instead!'

'I am ready to leave, Alexandrine.' It was Luc's voice. He stood to one side of her, Selim behind her. As

Alexandrine looked up and, startled, found her husband's eyes were dark with anger, she saw the Moor give a slight shake of his head as if to indicate she should not argue. Not that she had any intention of doing so.

'I am sorry, I thought you were enjoying your game of hoca.' She quickly rose and said goodnight to the others at the table.

'I have been waiting for you for the past ten minutes, but you were otherwise occupied,' came the sarcastic reply, and Alain sat back in his chair, his expression growing guarded.

'The night is still young, Luc...'

'And I intend to enjoy what is left of it with my wife. Your hand, Alexandrine.'

She gave it to him, a smile hiding the puzzlement she felt at his manner. He had won at hoca and should have been pleased, yet was not. She had been sent away in the company of his friend, yet now she was rebuked for remaining with him. Luc had deliberately interrupted the vingt-et-un game to embarrass her, but she could not imagine why. He was in another of his strange moods; even Selim had realised that.

They did not speak until they were in the carriage returning them to Belaincourt, and then Luc suddenly said coldly, 'You are growing too friendly with Madame de Mailly. I like not her closeness to the King or yours to her.'

'But she has been very kind to me, Luc...and only good can come of having her as a friend. As you say, she is close to the King.'

'She can be of use to you only if you have a notion of catching his eye with a mind to sharing his bed,' came the brutal reply, and she gasped as if he had struck her and lifted a hand to cheeks that were suddenly ashen.

'Of what am I being accused? You have no right——'

'I have eyes. You smile at anyone who looks at you these days. Alain was right...you are becoming accustomed to the Parisian way of life!'

'No! The way of life *you* have chosen for me. I will not have such cruel and unjust words thrown in my face!'

Alexandrine cried, incensed by his words. 'If I am not the way you wish me to be, then the fault is yours—you have moulded me...'

The flat of Luc's hand caught her a stinging blow across one pale cheek as the carriage came to a halt. As a lackey opened the door she climbed quickly out and ran up the steps into the house, brushing past a startled Gaston, who followed her flight upstairs with astonished eyes and then saw the ascent of the Marquis, glowering like a black beast more slowly in her wake. Luc went directly to his own rooms. No one was allowed entry to his rooms that night to undress him, and when Gaston knocked on Alexandrine's door to enquire if there was anything she required he was told by her maid to go away.

'Did you and Luc argue last night?' Alain asked quietly, eyeing the pale-cheeked girl who sat beside him beneath a shady tree in the Forest of Sénart. They had been following the King's hunt all afternoon and were in need of a break from the hectic activities. Many others shared their view and had fallen back from the main group of enthusiastic hunters, to seek a few moments' peace in the pleasant surroundings of the forest. Those who had accompanied the hunt in their coaches reclined at leisure in their seats, and enjoyed the refreshments they had brought along, chattering incessantly of the King's good luck that afternoon.

Louis was in excellent spirits and had spoken of extra entertainments that evening—that could mean a play by Molière, which everyone still enjoyed, or a trip down one of the canals at Versailles in the gondolas which had been sent to the Sun King, Louis XIV, by the Venetian Republic. Soft music, torchlight on the water, a romantic setting which produced many secret assignations. With whom would the King sit tonight? His present mistress, the Duchesse de Châteauroux? Or was he growing tired of the domineering, jealous woman who ruled his life?

Was not Madame de Mailly showing a great deal of interest in the Marquise de Mezière these days? And although the King himself had on more than one occasion sent presents to the delightful little Madame d'Etoiles, she had not been invited to attend Court. Madame de Mezière was right under his nose and looking more enchanting every day. Even the Duc de Belaincourt was seen constantly in her company. She spent more hours with him than with her own husband...

Alexandrine was aware of the speculative eyes upon them, sensed the curiosity when Luc was absent from Versailles, or when she allowed Alain to accompany her. Better the devil she knew, although many times she had deliberately gone out of her way to seek the company of others, hoping to avoid the linking of her name with his.

'Argue? No, why should you ask such a question?' she returned, accepting the goblet of wine Jules held out to her. The man had spread a large cloth on the ground a few feet away and produced a container full of food and wine. If she drank more than one glass, she would never be able to sit on her horse for the rest of the afternoon, she thought, as the cool, sweet wine slid down her parched throat. How good it would be to sit beneath this tree until it was time to return to Belaincourt. Each day was as hectic as the one before. If she was not at Court, there were always invitations to fill out the day. Parties, soirées, Jeanne's salon. Belaincourt at this time was an open house for all who cared to call and enjoy its hospitality. Francine had told her how surprised the servants all were at the change in Alain Ratan, since she and the Marquis had taken up residence. It had been years since he had even invited anyone to stay for more than a few hours.

Alexandrine did not for one moment believe that she was the cause of his change of attitude. She sensed a deeper, more devious reason but could not imagine what it could be. He was not the kind of man to change his life-style overnight without very good reason.

She shook her head as a tempting plate of cold smoked ham and beef was offered to her. Alain helped himself with gusto, following the food down with a second goblet of wine. Then, relaxing against the gnarled trunk of the oak, he folded his hands behind his head and surveyed her through half-closed eyes.

'I don't believe you. Luc was in a foul mood last night, and drinking like a—like a bottomless barrel.' He smiled without humour. 'What have you been doing to him, Alexa?'

'I . . .!' She was speechless. Of what was she being accused? He knew of the quarrel! Of course, Gaston had seen them return last night and would have told his master. She doubted if any secrets at Belaincourt were kept from him. 'Whatever has passed between Luc and myself—and I assure you there has been nothing to make him act the way he has these past days—it has nothing to do with me. He has been gambling, perhaps he has lost more than he would like.'

'No, there is something else which is deeply troubling him. His way of life, perhaps. Since you arrived here, he has been acting half his age and I do not like it. No wonder he takes to his bed every so often—it is the only way he can get a little peace. He is not young any more, Alexa, and he is ill.'

'You dare to tell me that!' She bristled at his comment, and watched a familiar gleam enter the pale green eyes. He was deliberately baiting her—in the hope of what? That she would reveal some indiscretion to him—some titbit of information which would satisfy his curiosity? 'I did not want him to come to Belaincourt.'

'But for a purely selfish reason. You did not want to be near me again—to have to face temptation. A temptation you might not be able to resist.' Alain chuckled, and her cheeks flushed as he came too close to the truth.

'I have resisted you so far, *monsieur*. You have nothing I want.'

'And Luc does?' he countered. 'Could it be possible you could love him?'

'I do.' Deep fire burning in her eyes warned him of her growing anger, but it was ignored.

To her relief a man detached himself from a group of people nearby and came across to them, for it distracted

Alain's attention from her and, she suspected, prevented probing questions she had no intention of answering.

'Alain...have you heard the amazing news?'

'About what, Claude?' Alain drawled, annoyed at the interruption, but wise enough not to show it.

'Do you remember that a few weeks ago my house was broken into? Some of my wife's jewels were taken and a pretty little snuff-box that belonged to my mother-in-law.'

'The Duchesse de Mallen.' He nodded. He remembered it well, for it had been one of the many items in the bag he had retrieved from Jules. For some time now he had been listening to reports of the return of so many items to his neighbours. Claude Latour had a house not three miles from Belaincourt and was the last of those he had been waiting to hear from.

'My dear fellow, it's back again. What do you say to that! About a week ago...why, it was the same night we came to your birthday festivities. The next day when my wife went to put on her jewels...there were all the others, back in their place as if they had never been taken. What do you say of a thief that returns stolen property! The man has taken leave of his senses...though I thank heaven he did. It was costing me a small fortune to replace everything. And that snuff-box...I've never heard the last of its loss. The Duchesse is a veritable dragon, as you well know!'

'Perhaps your thief has seen the light—of religion,' Alain chuckled, with a shrug of broad shoulders. 'I am pleased for you, Latour.'

'I don't seem to recall whether you lost anything...?'

'Perhaps because I did not tell you. Give my regards to your wife and the Duchesse, won't you?'

The pointed dismissal was not lost on the man, who stared hard at Alexandrine before returning to his friends.

'You did not have to be so rude to him,' she said coldly. She lifted her eyes to where Jules stood beside the food. The thin face bore no expression, but he was extremely stiff and tense, she saw, as he stared across the space which separated them. Jules! Could it be? Francine had said he was the best thief in Paris. The best in France, she had boasted. No! It was too outrageous. If he had robbed all those houses, that could only mean he had been persuaded, or forced, to return his loot...and she knew of only one man who had the strength of character to do that. 'Did you...?' she began.

Alain jumped to his feet and helped her to rise, his fingers brushing across one cheek in an unexpected caress before he stepped back.

'Do not speak of it. Would you blight love's young dream?' As she looked at him, mystified, he laughed and slipped on his coat. 'Your maid is, I believe, a God-fearing, honest girl who would never marry a rogue. Let her keep her illusions while she can.'

'You did that for her! You amaze me, *monsieur*,' she breathed.

'And you credit me with qualities I do not possess. I did it for myself. Shall we return to the hunt, Madame la Marquise, before all those inquisitive eyes begin to wonder why you are gazing at me so starry-eyed?'

For the fourth night in a row, Luc sent word that he would not be accompanying Alexandrine to Versailles, but wished her to go and enjoy herself. Always the message came as they should have been leaving, as if it was his intention that she should have no time to argue that she should not go alone. Not that she was ever un-chaperoned. Alain had escorted her on those other nights, as she suspected he would tonight. She had been neglected by her husband for almost two weeks now. Was it some kind of punishment for the unkind words she had flung at him? If he truly believed her capable of flirting with every man who glanced her way, why did he allow Alain to be her constant companion? Or had he set his friend to watch the wife he suspected of infidelity?

She *had* been unfaithful that one time and it still haunted her, but it would not happen again, despite the temptation under her very nose night and day. She would resist Alain! She did not love him, she told herself resolutely, as she rode at his side each day, danced with him in the evenings, or sat at the gaming-tables, watching him indulge in various games. Her manner was always the same. She was never over-enthusiastic when he won, never over-sympathetic when he lost, which was rarely. She danced with many men, the same polite smile on her face, her conversation frivolous and light-hearted, never touching on her husband or her marriage, apart from answering questions about Luc's health, and then she assured everyone that he was well on the road to recovery.

If only she could believe that herself. How long would it be now? Months? Or weeks? Even days? Since Christmas her husband had become a stranger, two men in one, and she never knew which one she would face when they came together. The benevolent, kind-hearted man whom she had grown to love? Or the husband who accused her with recriminating reproaches, whose eyes condemned her? Luc did not know of the night she had spent with Alain, of that she was sure. It was as if sickness was turning his mind against her. No matter what she did these days she could never please him. She longed to be back at the Hôtel Boussières, for there at least they would have privacy. At Belaincourt she was always too aware of Alain's presence everywhere. What he did not see and hear, his steward Gaston or Jules, who followed him about like a shadow, would no doubt relate.

'Francine, go to the Marquis and tell him I wish to speak with him before I leave,' Alexandrine instructed. If his concern stemmed from the bold-eyed men at Versailles, then she would not go. If only the reason were as simple as that. In her heart she knew it was not.

She turned away towards the window. She had often stood in the same spot during the late afternoon, watching the sunshine dancing over the cascading water in the fountain directly below. Sometimes at night the gentle sound soothed her to sleep, but never so efficiently as the beautiful music-box Alain had given her. It sat on the table beside her bed and often was the last thing she saw before she drifted into sleep, relaxed and at peace. Sometimes just to lift the lid was sufficient to bring his unseen presence into the room with her. Comforting, yet disturbing.

'You wished to see me, Madame la Marquise?' Selim accompanied Francine on her return, but the latter retired immediately as she saw the look of annoyance which crossed her mistress's face.

'No, Selim. I want to see my husband.'

'He is sleeping...'

'He is drugged?' she interrupted and the Moor lifted his shoulders in a half-shrug.

'It was necessary. To calm him, you understand. Perhaps tomorrow—for a few minutes.'

'I think it advisable we return to the house as soon as possible,' she said, her eyes searching the implacable black features. 'Luc's health has been deteriorating since we arrived at Belaincourt. I no longer know how to act when we are together—what to say... There will be gossip at these prolonged absences from Court and we must prevent that.' Her anger dissolved as quickly as it had come. Selim was not at fault. 'Forgive my sharpness, I am so worried. Tell me what to do! I obey him and go to Versailles, pretend all is well between us, and he accuses me of—of flirting! Yet he will not allow me to remain with him. It is as if he no longer wants me. Is that it, Selim? Has he tired of his toy?'

'You are being foolish, *madame*. You know you have his love...'

'Love! Of a man who shuts me out of his life as often as he shuts me out of his room? But there is more than just a door between us, is there not? You know him better than I? Help me—please. I am so confused——'

'For the moment I can be of little help. You must continue to lead your life as you have been doing. It is what he wants.'

'There are those who have begun to question why I am without my husband, why it is that the Duc de Belaincourt is always my escort. He too knows there is something wrong, Selim.'

'I am sure you will be able to convince him to the contrary,' came the smooth reply.

'With a smile? I am fast running out of those. And I would not like the Duc to think I grow lonely—or bored by Luc's continued absences—as many would,' she added quickly.

'*Madame* has only to confide in me if anyone—anyone at all—gives her cause for concern,' Selim answered. 'You told me that the Marquis has told you of his background and I am aware that this also entailed confiding to you the true nature of his illness. He has placed a great burden on your shoulders, but he believes, as I do, that they are strong enough to carry the load. I shall pray to Allah that you be granted patience and under-standing to survive this exacting experience.' The Moor turned away from her. At the door he turned and *salaa'med* respectfully, before leaving her presence in a swish of silken robes.

Patience and understanding! She had one, but the other eluded her. She sought reasons and found only excuses. The only plausible explanation for the way Luc was acting towards her was that either the long years of the illness that now sapped his strength so drastically, or the continual drugs he was forced to take, were af-fecting his brain and so causing this transformation in his character. It was a chilling thought, and she found she had grown quite cold as she descended to the drawing-room where she knew Alain would be awaiting her—as he did every night.

He rose from a chair beneath the portrait of his mother, his searching gaze probing the cheeks she had fiercely pinched as she came downstairs, and it was only with a great effort that she withstood the unasked ques-tions she saw there—the lingering suspicion which darkened the pale glitter in those green eyes.

'As always, Marquise, you look radiant. The thought of spending another evening in my scintillating company, no doubt?' he mocked as he poured wine for them both. Out of earshot of the servants, and away from the house when they were alone, he was never so formal. His fingers brushed hers as she took a glass from him, aware of one eyebrow lifting slightly as she drank the contents a little too quickly. 'There was a time when I recall you did not like wine.'

'In time one becomes accustomed to so many things,' she returned lightly. 'You yourself told me that. Why should you care that I am adapting myself to my surroundings—exactly as everyone else does?'

'Care? I do not . . . I find it disappointing, that's all, that all women want to be the same. Each as boring as the next. A woman who does not conform can be a most exciting creature.'

'You forget I have been modelled in the image required of me by my husband,' Alexandrine flung back, furious at herself for rising to the taunt, but unable to hold her tongue. He was more provoking each day! If only he had been different . . . she could have confided in him, told him of her fears for Luc's sanity. Surely between them they could have found some solution to the problem? Perhaps not! She had paid a high price for Alain's rescue of her husband after his abduction; if she enlisted his help yet again, she had no doubt he would demand the same of her . . .

'Luc created something flawless, without imperfection . . . or so he thought,' Alain drawled. 'In his desire to achieve the impossible, he blindly ignored the obvious—that all women are faithless cats.'

'We are what men make us,' Alexandrine retorted, infuriated by the mockery on his voice.

'That has been the excuse since the beginning of time. No is a very simple word, but difficult to utter, I suspect, when there are so many advantages to saying yes!'

'I have noticed Madame de la Fontaine finds it a very easy word,' she said meaningfully, but the jibe didn't touch him. Was it true, she wondered, that he had indeed become interested in a certain attractive young woman called Caroline Bardot, newly arrived at court with her father, the Comte de Morrière? Alexandrine had been introduced to her and thought her a pleasant enough young girl, a little shy, but with a pleasing figure and a

witty turn of phrase which had already brought many
men flocking to her side. Much to her father's satisfaction, she had noticed, and had come to the conclusion that the poor child had been brought to Court
for one reason only—to find her a husband as quickly
as possible. The resources of the Comte de Morrière were
rumoured to be dwindling. A swift marriage would
enable him to supply a dowry for his daughter before
they were gone altogether.

She had seen her in the company of Alain several
times. As she gazed into his dark features now,
Alexandrine wondered if he had been attracted to the
new arrival. Why not? Another challenge for him. But
marriage would not be in his mind. Or would it? Perhaps
Caroline de Morrière would be the one to break down
the barriers of mistrust and cynicism he had erected
about himself.

'She is playing with fire,' Alain answered as he helped
her into the carriage which waited to take them to
Versailles. Tonight the King had planned a special
evening of entertainment, with fireworks and musicians
to play for them as the gondolas drifted slowly on the
water, and then a performance in the gardens.

'You—you do not think Paul would...harm her?'
Even though she did not like Claudia, she was appalled
to think harm might come to her at the hands of Luc's
unpredictable son.

'I believe him to be capable of—anything,' Alain said,
after a moment of silence. 'That is why I have Jules accompany us wherever we go. And you will probably have
noticed, he is never far behind you when you venture
out alone. I have arranged for more men—with Luc's
approval, of course—to guard you both when you return
to the house. Until we are sure there is no further danger.'

And to have her constantly under surveillance would
confirm or refute the ugly suspicion which had been
placed in his mind one afternoon when he had summoned Francine to the library to question her about her
mistress's movements. He had wanted to ensure neither
she nor Luc would be alone at any time when they left

the house. He had not bargained for the unexpected revelations which had set his brain seething.

The girl had been nervous, he thought, as she had hovered on the threshold until a firm push from Jules sent her unsteadily across the thick carpet towards the desk where he sat.

'Come and sit down, girl. I won't bite you.'

'Thank you, *monsieur*.' She lowered herself carefully into a chair, clasping her hands tightly together in her lap. He had instructed Jules to remain during the interview, and the man came into the room, closed the door and stood with his back against it.

'Do you accept that I have the best interests of the Marquis and the Marquise at heart?' Alain had asked quietly.

'I—I—yes, *monsieur*,' Francine said, somewhat surprised.

'Good. Then you must also accept that what I tell you is the truth. I believe their lives to be in danger. I shall not identify the source of that danger until I have more proof, and while I seek to secure such proof I need to know they will be adequately protected at all times. I have trusted Jules with that undertaking while they are here at Belaincourt. Others will take over from him when they return to Paris. But I also need your help.'

'Of course, *monsieur*. In any way I can,' Francine replied.

She had been more than a little agitated to be summoned into the presence of the Duc de Belaincourt, unsure what wrong she had done. She did not understand the strange relationship he shared with her mistress, nor why he had not taken advantage of the communicating door which separated their rooms. Not once since the Marquise arrived at Belaincourt had he attempted to go to her at night . . . and yet she had been sure they were still lovers.

'I need to have some questions answered so that I may better determine what course of action to take to prevent a recurrence of the incident which took place here. The attempt on the life of the Marquise. The man Jules killed came here with the intention of murdering your mistress. He was a paid assassin—and I fear there will be others who will come after him, hoping to succeed where he failed.'

'What can I do, *monsieur*? I rarely leave her side, except when she goes to Versailles. But she is safe there, is she not, with so many people about her, and you, Monsieur le Duc, to watch over her?' Francine said, wide eyed. 'And as for Monsieur Luc, he could have no better bodyguard than Selim. The man is like a shadow.'

'Unfortunately it would take only one moment when either of them is alone. As you say, the Moor is an able watchdog...but the Marquise—especially when she is at Versailles, or visiting friends in the city—could be most vulnerable. You say you are with her most times, but surely there are occasions when she is alone?'

'My mistress is not yet...happy.' The girl hesitated, loath to betray any secrets, even in the best of causes. 'At times she is still embarrassed by the attentions paid to her. Many times she has said to me, "Francine, Noyen was never like this. Sometimes I wonder where I belong."'

'I thought she was making the adjustment quite satisfactorily,' Alain drawled. 'Go on.'

'Sometimes she likes to walk—alone. Each evening, in fact, she will walk in the gardens, both here at Belaincourt...and at Versailles.'

'And you do not accompany her on these little excursions?' Alain demanded. Suddenly his eyes had narrowed to sharp, suspicious slits. Walks? Alone? Why should he doubt they were anything but an innocent attempt to be by herself? To elude a crowded room and chattering monkeys who pursued her asking for a dance, or for more than she was willing to give?

'No, *monsieur*. I wait upstairs, on the terrace.'

'And how long do these walks usually take?' End it here, a voice cried inside him. Ask no more questions lest you hear what you do not wish to hear. Begin to wonder, no doubt, to secure information which will denounce her.

'Not long, usually, but sometimes she has been gone as long as——' Francine looked over her shoulder at Jules. He frowned at her silence and gave a nod. Her voice considerably lower, she added, 'An hour. Have you not noticed, at Versailles, *monsieur*?'

'Yes, once I have,' Alain recalled. On that occasion she had been missing from the gaming-tables for some considerable time, but he had been too absorbed in the cards to read anything significant in her absence. Walks in the garden! By God—not alone! Secret assignations covered by a simple lie. No devious explanations for her. Simplicity was her trademark. It had fooled Luc into marrying her—deceived Alain for a time. Now they were both aware she was not the innocent she pretended. Was this why Luc had changed so drastically in his attitude towards her? Had he discovered some unsavoury relationship with another man? What other explanation could there be?

'So—your mistress likes to walk alone?'

'Yes, *monsieur*...but there is never anyone with her. I would swear to that,' she added, not knowing why she chose to defend her mistress in such a fashion. Of course the Marquise was alone! Yet the way the Duc was looking at her... She began to feel uneasy. Were his questions only so that he could provide protection for the Marquise, or did he have an ulterior motive? A personal motive? She was regretting being so frank and open with him, and even though he had convinced her it was necessary her uneasiness grew.

'You must surely realise the danger she could be exposed to—alone, out of sight of possible help should she be attacked again? You must not allow her to be alone, Francine. If she does not wish for your company, then somehow you must ensure that one of the men I have hired is always near at hand. Discreetly out of sight, of course, but on hand,' Alain continued, sensing the disquiet rising in her. 'Will you promise me you will do this—for your mistress's sake?'

How could she refuse? Francine nodded and watched him visibly relax. There the interview had ended, but not the suspicion in Alain's mind.

In the semi-darkness of the carriage, Alain stared across at the quiet woman opposite. She looked lovely tonight in a gown of deep rich purple satin which enhanced her fair colouring. Her hair was caught up in a mass of curls each side of her ears. Amethysts glowed against the whiteness of flawless skin. Each time he saw her he thought she grew more beautiful. Had a man come into her life who fulfilled her as her own husband did not, fulfilled her more than Alain himself swore he had that one wild night they had spent together? Had some stranger given her the air of fresh confidence with which she now conducted herself in public? The uncertain country girl had been replaced by a lady... whose poise and manner singled her out amid a crowd. Many times, as he mingled with his friends, he found himself searching the room for her, seeking her face amid so many others. And he knew he was not the only one. Many eyes followed her, devoured her, yet she seemed unaware of the interest. *He* could still cause her to blush by the bold way he stared at her. The conflicting images in his mind disturbed him, deepened his black mood.

When they arrived at Versailles, he spent an hour at the 'vingt-et-un' table and lost, for the first time in many months, causing a companion to comment on his lack of concentration. It was true, he could not think straight when he was so deeply troubled. When everyone began to make their way towards the boats which would carry them on the waters, it was not Alexandrine who leaned on his arm and gazed adoringly up into the aquiline features, but the daughter of the Comte de Morrière.

'Do they not make a delightful couple?' Mademoiselle de Charolais whispered to her companion as they lowered themselves carefully on to cushioned seats. 'The child is obviously infatuated with him.'

'Poor thing. He will break her heart within a week,' a woman in front of them returned with a flutter of her fan as she surveyed the occupants of the other gondola.

'Perhaps the Comte would not look so satisfied at the
sight of them together if he knew what had happened
to the first Duchesse de Belaincourt.'

'Be quiet,' Mademoiselle snapped. 'Nothing was ever
proved...'

'But everyone knows the Duc has a temper—and he
did kill two men when he discovered they had been her
lovers,' the woman replied, determined not to be silenced.
At the sight of Alexandrine's wide-eyes, she added.
'Don't you know about your host at Belaincourt,
Madame Boussières? I was so surprised when your
husband thought him a fit companion for you. The man
is notorious for his affairs...'

'If you wish to remain in this boat, *madame*, shut
your mouth!' Mademoiselle de Charolais ordered in an
angry tone. 'No good will come of disturbing old ghosts.'

Alexandrine barely contained her questions until they
had disembarked. As she laid a hand on the arm of the
elder woman, she heard her give a deep sigh.

'Not here, my dear. Let us find a quiet spot where we
shall not be overheard.'

It took them several minutes to thread their way
through the pressing crowds, but eventually they came
to some stone seats set beneath spreading chestnut trees
and sat down.

'You are bursting with curiosity, I can feel it,' the older
woman said, peering into Alexandrine's face. 'Are you
more interested in the man than you would have everyone
believe?'

'If I were, how could I hide it from you?' Alexandrine
replied lightly. 'Did—did Monsieur Ratan really kill two
men—deliberately?' How he had loved his wife! But she
had been bored with him and his lovely home and had
sought solace elsewhere. That love had turned to hate
and destroyed a once understanding and compassionate
human being.

'In duels—fair, I might add. There are few who can
best him with a sword and as, on both occasions, he was
the party challenged, he had choice of weapons. His op-
ponents stood no chance! There are those who say he

deliberately allowed himself to be manoeuvred into such a position so that he would have the advantage. I believe him capable of that—but of murder... I have not made up my mind. I like the man. I like his frankness. He's one of the few honest men at Versailles.'

'Murder!' Alexandrine breathed. 'What are you saying?'

'Nicolette was the most stunning creature,' Mademoiselle de Charolais said, with another sigh, as she wondered whether, were she herself more beautiful, she would have been at the side of the King tonight instead of that cold-hearted fish, the Duchesse de Châteauroux. Perhaps not. She was fifteen years older than Louis and he had never regarded her as anything more than a good friend, whose château was a short ride from his hunting lodge at La Muette, easily accessible to himself and the attendants known as marmousets. Mistresses came and went, she mused, but what they shared was something infinitely more lasting and worthwhile. 'I did not know her too well—personally, you understand—but she did little which did not reach my ears. I will not bore you with details, my dear, as to what led up to—how shall I put it? Let us say the unfortunate *accident* which deprived many men of her favours. I do remember, however, that there had been much talk because the Duc had voiced his intention of taking her back to the country. By force, I was told, if she refused to go with him willingly. It was a few days after the last duel and you can imagine how the whole Court was buzzing with different versions of what had happened.

'They quarrelled bitterly, publicly; they had a splendid house in Paris and Nicolette was always entertaining. At one of her soirées she went too far in her spiteful remarks—and the Duc de Belaincourt was heard by many people to say... something about hating her so much he wished he could see her dead.'

Alexandrine caught her breath, but dared not interrupt now that Mademoiselle de Charolais' memory was returning with such clarity. Murder! Was he capable of that?

'The next day in the afternoon Nicolette went hunting with a large group of friends. At some point during the afternoon they split into two parties, and it was only when both returned at dusk that they realised Nicolette was not with either group. A search of the forest was at once organised...and that was when her body was found, a mass of cuts, bruises and broken bones. It looked like a simple accident—the horse bolted, she fell and was dragged through the undergrowth, perhaps hit her head on something... But those who thought ill of the Duc pointed out that he had refused to accompany the hunt that afternoon as he usually did—and wondered aloud what could have made her separate from her companions like that so that no one heard the accident. And just what *had* caused her horse to bolt—if indeed it had. They suggested that her injuries were also consistent with having been severely beaten...it would not have been difficult for him to arrange... But no! As I have said, I do not believe him capable of that. There, now—have I satisfied your curiosity?'

'I—I am shocked by what you have told me!' said Alexandrine. 'I can hardly believe it.' She did not want to believe it!

As the sound of cheering reached them and the sky above exploded in coloured lights, accompanied by loud bangs, Mademoiselle de Charolais rose to her feet, indicating it was time they rejoined the others.

'Let us see if the lovers are still gazing at each other starry-eyed,' she laughed, wondering as she did so why Alexandrine's hand should tremble so she almost dropped her fan.

'Do you think he—the Duc—will ever marry again?'

'Who knows? Someone like the Morrière girl might be just what he needs—fresh and innocent. It is obvious he has no idea how history has repeated itself. Claudia de la Fontaine, my dear, and Paul Boussières! Really, do you never listen to what is going on about you?'

'I fail to make a connection,' Alexandrine said in bewilderment.

'Nicolette and Claudia shared the same taste in men. Alain Ratan and Paul Boussières.'

The remainder of the evening was a blur upon Alexandrine's memory. She remembered squeezing into a seat beside Mademoiselle de Charolais to one side of the raised dais where the King sat with the Queen and his mistress. Even though they had arrived late a place had still been saved for someone of Mademoiselle's importance, and the man beside her had been soundly slapped on the head with her fan when he would not move to allow Alexandrine a seat also.

Alain and Caroline de Morrière were together at the front of those who had been unable to find somewhere to sit and were forced to stand for the duration of the entertainment, which consisted tonight of music and then poetry. She felt herself grow cold at the thought of him coldly engineering his wife's 'accident'.

Alain's head was inclined slightly to one side as he listened to his talkative companion, who appeared to have little interest in what was being performed in front of her. But his eyes were locked on Alexandrine! Pretending not to notice their scrutiny, she turned away and allowed herself to be drawn into conversation by the man at her side. It was of no importance whom Alain escorted tonight, or any other night, she told herself fiercely, laughing at jokes which did not amuse her and firmly removing the hand which continually sought to hold hers.

But she did care...

CHAPTER FIVE

'I THINK we have lingered long enough at Belaincourt, Luc, do you not agree with me?' Alexandrine asked quietly, looking up from the chessboard. She knew her husband's mind was not on the game, for he was allowing her to win... 'Are you listening to me?'

Luc's eyes flickered to where she sat, and after a moment he nodded.

'As you wish, my dear. We shall spend a few weeks at the Paris house and then go to Noyen for the summer. You would like that, wouldn't you? I have heard from the steward I appointed to take care of the repairs that they will be completed very shortly.'

'Luc, why, that is wonderful! Do you think you will be strong enough to make the journey?' she asked, and a faint smile lit up the sallow features at the note of excitement in her voice.

'We need to be alone together, don't we? I have been an old bear these past weeks and spoiled what was intended to be an enjoyable time for you. I know how much you love Noyen. Perhaps, we can return Alain's hospitality and invite him to join us in a month or so, when we are settled. There will be much to do for a while...'

And every moment of the day would be occupied, Alexandrine thought, which was what she needed to keep her thoughts from the past—and the future. Selim had told her Luc was now responding to his treatment. It had taken longer than expected, but slowly he was responding, growing strong again, and that was all that she cared about. A few more months of precious life...

'Do you follow the hunt this afternoon?'

'Yes. Jeanne says it may be the last one for some while. There is talk of the King going to join the army in

Flanders. At Versailles, or sometimes listening to a play or poetry at one of the salons, I have tried to imagine what it must be like for those poor soldiers and I am ashamed to say I cannot! Frenchmen are being killed while the King idles away his days in pursuit of pleasure!'

She knew little of the war being fought over the succession to the throne of Austria, only what she had heard at Court. Many were uneasy that Louis had been drawn in to press the claims of the elector of Bavaria, especially when the Prussians made a separate peace. But she knew that the long influence of Cardinal Fleury was now over, and Louis was now subject to the iron rule of his mistress, La Châteauroux.

'Do not underestimate the King,' Luc replied. 'He is no weakling, as the Duchesse may find out to her cost if she pushes him too far. Mistresses do not last forever...'

And there was Jeanne waiting to step into the position when it fell vacant, Alexandrine mused.

'Luc...' She knelt beside his chair and took both his hands in hers. 'When we return to the house, will you——' she took a deep breath, knowing how this subject was taboo '—will you allow yourself to be examined by other doctors? It is not that I doubt Selim's skills in any way, but I feel sure there must be something else we can do. I don't want to lose you.'

The cry came from her heart and Luc's hand briefly touched the mass of blonde curls nestling at the base of her slender neck. Over her shoulder his eyes met those of the Moor, standing by the window.

'Very well.' She could not believe her ears! 'I do not doubt Selim, either, my dear, but if this would put your mind at ease...'

'It would.' Relief flooded across her face.

'You will accept that nothing can be done. I do.'

'No, I will not. There is always hope and my prayers,' Alexandrine replied fiercely.

'I bless you for those, but God has abandoned this sinner. It is no more than I deserve. Off you go now and get changed. Give my regards to Madame d'Etoiles when you see her and invite her to the house soon.'

Luc sat back in his chair with a deep sigh as the door closed behind his wife and the hands which lay on the lap of his robe began to shake. His lips twisted into a bitter smile as he fought to control the tremors—and failed. Each day they grew worse. It took every ounce of his strength to keep this new development from Alexandrine's eyes. They had spent little under an hour together and he was exhausted, drained by the effort to appear normal and on the road once again to recovery.

'Do you think she is convinced?' He took the glass being held out to him and drained it. These were increasing too, but without them...

'Yes. Because it is the way she wants it. She really cares for you,' Selim answered, long brown fingers momentarily resting against one of Luc's cheeks. 'You must rest.'

'I know. I have hurt her, Selim. To have struck her...'

'She is young, she will survive. You must clear your mind of such troubling thoughts. Come and lie down. These hands of mine will soothe away your tension and you will sleep.'

'She will only survive if I end this torment. I should have done so months ago...'

'But life has suddenly become dear to you. There is no need to explain to me,' the Moor said, as he helped him to rise.

'How much longer...?'

'Not long. Or as long as you wish.'

'For my sake, a little longer. For hers, not too long. She must not suffer as my father did. She must never know the terrible agony of mind that he endured for years—in silence.'

'You do not have years...'

'Is it true you have asked the King's permission to retire to the country for the summer?' Jeanne d'Etoiles asked, opening the hamper at her side and extracting a cold collation.

'I know news travels fast at Versailles, but it has not been three hours since I made my petition,' Alexandrine laughed, selecting one of the sliced titbits and savouring it. 'This is delicious—I shall have to send my cook to take lessons from yours!'

'My cook is the most secretive individual! Now, what is this all about? Where are you going? No one goes to the country unless they are in disfavour with the King, and he always speaks most highly of you and your husband. I think it amuses him to drop your name now and then and watch how the long ears wag.'

They were seated in Jeanne's phaeton in which she had been following the hunt at a discreet distance. Alexandrine had been riding Lady Blue, but was glad to rest the mare when Jeanne invited her into her carriage. Jeanne never drove in the midst of the other carriages and horsemen, preferring to remain somewhere in the rear. The King always knew if she was, Alexandrine thought, for there was no mistaking the bright pink coach and the perfectly groomed young woman who drove it with skill and panache, often to the chagrin of other women who accompanied the hunt, weary from hours of being cramped in one position, complaining incessantly of either cold or heat, or the fact that they had not been noticed by the monarch.

Jeanne was being noticed more and more and the presents of venison after a good kill always came her way. She accepted the gifts with an air that made many teeth grind in vexation, as times past were remembered when they had been less than polite to Madame Jeanne Poisson d'Etoiles, and now regretted it. Madame was on her way to the royal palace, it was suggested by some who considered they had the ear of those nearest to the King. The reign of the Duchesse de Châteauroux was coming to an end.

'Luc has suggested we spend the summer in Noyen, my old house. I love it there, Jeanne. It is only a small place, but now that the house has been renovated it will be a pleasure to live in. Even with all its draughts and leaky roofs I loved it as a child. There is so much I can do there now—for the villagers, too. They are mostly farmers and very poor.'

'And you intend to turn it into a thriving farming community?'

'Why not? Does it sound so ridiculous?'

'You would give up Paris, Versailles—for the country life? What is it you are not telling me, Alexandrine? Is Luc's health deteriorating? The Duc de Belaincourt was most concerned about him when we spoke the other day.'

'I did not know you had seen him recently...'

'He comes to my salon often—sometimes with a friend,' Jeanne answered with a smile.

The King, of course. How silly of her not to have guessed!

'I am pleased everything is going so well for you,' Alexandrine said, and Jeanne's head tilted to one side as she surveyed her, almost threatening to dislodge the saucy pink hat perched on top of the chestnut hair.

'For me, but not for you. I suspect you have a few secrets, Alexandrine. Are you not able to confide in me? I am your friend, am I not? In the company of the Marquise de Mezière I am accepted, and my life is at last shaping as it should—as it was predicted.'

'Nonsense, I did nothing,' Alexandrine protested. 'You have done it all yourself—with your belief in that prediction, your own accomplishments—and the salon. You should be very proud and pleased with yourself. And happy.'

'I am. Are you? When we first met and you confided in me about your marriage to the Marquis, I was so sorry that you would never know love. I have watched you emerge like a shy little butterfly into the world and, I admit, have waited breathlessly for the day you would come to me and say, "Jeanne, it has happened. I am in love!" Luc has made you the way he wishes you to be... What will happen to you when he is dead, Alexandrine? Will you know who you are? Or will you live the rest of your life in the shadow of the woman he created?'

'You sound like——' Alexandrine bit her tongue.

'Like whom? I can name a dozen men who would give every sou they possess to get you alone for ten minutes. I've no doubt many have tried,' she added with a laugh which made Alexandrine's cheeks flood with colour. 'Which one has succeeded in penetrating your defences? Marc Gyan? Now there's a handsome devil. Or perhaps it is the Duc de Tallart. Somewhat older than you, but horribly rich. You must think of the future, you know. A woman alone will need protection—friends— comfort...'

'Stop!' Alexandrine cried in horror. 'You are talking as if Luc were already dead. He isn't going to die. I won't let him! He's promised to see other doctors when we return to the house. Something can be done, I know it!' Yet even as she uttered the words, they sounded hollow and useless in her ears. Nothing could be done. Luc had told her that himself, and she buried her face in her hands, to hide the tears which sprang to her eyes. 'What am I to do, Jeanne? Every day he is different, I never know what to expect from him, or how to act when we are together. Several times, for no reason at all, that I can remember, he has flown into terrible rages, cursing me, accusing me of awful things... and then the next day I receive a present—jewellery or a dress—and when I go to him he is like an apologetic little boy. Selim says the illness is clouding his mind—the pain, and the knowledge that he is going to die. I accept that—and I try to understand and help him, but when he looks at me sometimes... so strangely...'

'Hush, my dear. If there is nothing you can do, you must accept it,' Jeanne murmured, pouring a little wine into an engraved goblet and pressing it into her friend's hand. 'Drink this. We will talk of him no more. I shall say only this. If you ever need a friend—at any time, day or night, now or in the future—I shall always be on hand. You will remember that, won't you? Whatever happens?'

'Now you sound like Solange, about to tell me there will be another man in my life! I have known but one——' She broke off, then realised she had said

nothing amiss, for Jeanne believed she meant that Luc
was that man. Yet that other man, that distant shadow
who hovered over her shoulder...why could she not erase
those words of prediction from her memory? If she were
free she would only want one man—Alain Ratan. A
stupid, foolish thing to desire, for already his attentions
were focused elsewhere now she had refused to continue
their brief, tempestuous relationship. Yet Solange had
been right—there were two men—and she had been right
to predict. 'Beware the hunter when coloured lights fill
the sky.'

For, on that fateful night at the Hôtel Boussières, as
people outside in the streets celebrated the coming of
Christmas with a colourful firework display, Alain Ratan
the hunter had stalked and captured his prey—her!

Alexandrine could not forget the night of passion
which had followed Alain's invasion of her room. No!
She would never experience that with any other man!
She wanted no other, and since she could not have him
she would live her life alone! She would not marry again
when Luc was dead, no matter what pressures she felt
upon her shoulders. She would be rich in her own right,
with property the length and breadth of France. If she
could not marry for love—spend the remainder of her
life with the only man who would ever mean anything
to her—then she would find solace in other things.
Noyen—the house—anything!

'Forgive me,' she apologised with a faint smile. 'I have
not been sleeping well these past few nights. My nerves
are a little ragged.'

'And no wonder, after all you have told me. And then
that attempt on your life!' Jeanne declared. 'I hope
someone has taken steps to ensure there will be no
repetition?'

'The—the Duc de Belaincourt has hired men to protect
us at the house...thank goodness they will not be
necessary at Noyen.'

'You think not? Noyen is some distance from here,
Alexandrine. Do not be foolish enough to leave them

behind when you go there. A lonely little country village!
Mon Dieu—a perfect place for murder and mayhem!'

'We are assuming Paul was behind the attempt on my
life.'

'Do you doubt it?'

'No. I have tried to think well of him, to understand
how bitter he has become because his father has taken
a young wife and deprived him of the inheritance he
believes should be his...'

'And will be his, if you are not well protected. If you
will not take this up with Alain Ratan, then I will,'
Jeanne declared, not understanding Alexandrine's reluctance to confide in Luc's closest friend. Odd,
that...considering the time they spent in each other's
company. Had she not known of the staunch friendship
between Luc and Alain she might have allowed herself
to consider another possibility—that Alain's interest was
closer at hand, in the beautiful, demure young woman
who danced with him, sat at his side as he gamed, walked
with him in the gardens discussing how she might en-
hance the gardens of her home. Always they were so
casual, so polite when they were together.

Jeanne's alert, probing little mind did not accept the
idea that this was the way of it when they were alone
together. How could it be! Alain Ratan was one of the
most sought-after men at Court. Women pursued him
with the same determination as many did the rakish Duc
de Richelieu, yet after the death of his wife Alain had
been immune to love. Affairs? He was said to have had
many of those—always with great discretion. Was he now
embarking on another, with the wife of the Marquis de
Mezière?

Jeanne hoped so. Alexandrine needed a young man
to bring her to life. Her marriage to an old, sick man
would be the death of her too, if something—or
someone—did not instil something worthwhile to live
for in her. She was so innocent! And yet, beneath that
innocence, Jeanne sensed a fire burning...though she
betrayed no desire to take a lover and had even looked
quite horrified when her friend had suggested it to her.

Poor Alexandrine, to deny herself the pleasures which could be hers—and in the arms of someone as handsome as the Duc de Belaincourt, too! Perhaps she was wrong—perhaps the two of them were enjoying a pleasant, if not amorous, relationship, with him carefully protecting her as he did all his other women. She would need to be protected, Jeanne thought, a frown furrowing her brow as she thought of Paul Boussières.

'What is it?' Alexandrine was looking at her curiously.

'Nothing...I was just thinking...look at those clouds! We shall have rain before the afternoon is out, and I do not intend to stay here and have this new dress ruined. I am going back to the château. Will you come with me?'

No, I shall follow the hunt a while longer, I think. Rain—are you sure? The sky does not look that dismal,' her companion remarked, staring up at the blue sky which was interlaced with white cloud, none of which looked very threatening.

'For a country girl, I am surprised at you. I smell rain in the air,' Jeanne said with a gay laugh as she gathered up the reins of the phaeton. 'Come and dine with me, or at least have some refreshment before you go back to the house. It's growing late, and the King will not hunt much longer. The light will soon begin to fade.'

'Very well.' Alexandrine allowed herself to be persuaded. She would never tire of Jeanne's pleasant company. 'But I must not stay long. Luc will be expecting me. Wait a moment while I tell my bodyguard.' Stoneface! It was the name she had given to the man Alain Ratan had made her bodyguard. He followed her wherever she went, at a discreet distance, his presence never interfering with her daily routine. He was a rough-looking individual, the new clothes which had been provided for him unable to hide the temperament of the man beneath them. She did not even know his real name, for they had never once spoken. He gave her the impression he did not want their relationship to go further than it did—a polite nod when she first appeared. His place was to the rear of her at all times, and

that was where he stayed. She had never seen a smile on
the pock-marked features, not even when he mixed with
other servants at Belaincourt. She had come to the conclusion he was one of Jules's acquaintances and therefore
it would be wiser if she kept her distance from him.

Motioning to the man, she told him to follow them
to Jeanne's forest château, and bring with him Lady
Blue, who was tethered not far away, quietly grazing and
enjoying the lull in the day's activity. A nod in response
to her orders. Not a word spoken. She saw Jeanne's
amused look as they moved off.

Would Luc be expecting her? she wondered as they
drove. There were days when he seemed unaware of her
existence. Selim had hinted that long before the end came
for him he might slip away from her in his mind and
not even know her. How terrible to become a mindless
being, incapable of controlling one's own life! And she
was so helpless! All she could do was sit with him and
talk with him when he was able. The rest of the time
she was a silent statue at his bedside, elegantly gowned
as always for when he awoke, hoping he would find
pleasure in her presence and her appearance. It was all
she could do for him—all she was allowed to do... So
little...

There was a carriage coming out of the tree-lined
driveway as Jeanne's phaeton turned into it, and she
brought the horses to a halt with a skill that made
Alexandrine envy her.

'My husband,' she said smilingly. 'You haven't met
yet, have you? Poor Charles-Guillaume is always being
sent away on business for his uncle. We hardly see each
other these days.' She extended her hand to the young,
good-looking man who jumped from the carriage and
hurried towards them, and he took it and touched it to
his lips.

How he loved her, Alexandrine thought, watching the
way he lingered with her ringed fingers in his grasp, the
gentle way they were pressed to his cheek.

'I was afraid I would miss you,' Charles-Guillaume
Le Normant d'Etoiles said, gazing up at the figure of

his wife. How he hated leaving her for even one hour, let alone weeks. There always seemed to be something separating them these days, yet they were still blissfully happy. She was socially a success, and his business dealings were becoming more profitable every day, thanks to his uncle's connections. 'I shall try to be back within a week, but...' He shrugged his shoulders. 'I have much to do. You will not be too bored, will you, my love?'

'Of course not, but I shall count the days until you are with me again,' Jeanne replied quietly, as she bent to place a kiss upon one cheek. 'Take care of yourself. Oh, forgive me—this is my very dear friend, Alexandrine, Marquise de Mezière. You know her husband well.'

'I am honoured that my wife has your friendship, *madame*.' Jeanne's husband bowed in Alexandrine's direction. 'I confess I have been neglecting her of late— my business, you understand. I am relieved she will not be lonely until I return.'

Lonely, Alexandrine mused as Charles-Guillaume backed away to his coach and climbed reluctantly inside. Jeanne waved to him until it had passed them and was out of sight. Lonely, with her salon which attracted so many intellectuals these days? Lonely, when she had caught the eye of the King of France?

'Does he...know?' she asked hesitantly, as Jeanne whipped up the horses and brought the phaeton to the front door of the château.

The pair of blue eyes which turned on her were dancing with mischievous lights.

'Know? That I shall become the King's mistress? Of course. I have been completely honest with him. I have told him I shall never leave him—except for the King— nor will I,' came the frank answer. As servants came hurrying forward to help them alight from the phaeton and a young groom took the reins of the horses, Jeanne paused to gaze for a long moment at the bright pink conveyance with which she had sought—and succeeded in catching—the eye of the King of France. 'I shall miss these days when I am forced to my bed,' she sighed, and Alexandrine's face grew alarmed.

'Are you ill?' If she was, there was no sign to betray the fact.

'No—*enceinte*. I had thought of going to the country to have my confinement, but the thought of the heat . . . and to be so far from my friends . . . No, I shall remain in the the Hôtel de Gesvres, and you must promise to come and see me often—if you can spare the time.'

'Of course I shall.' Pregnant! The question on the tip of Alexandrine's tongue was never uttered, for Jeanne looked at her as they seated themselves in the small, pleasant sitting-room which overlooked the gardens where refreshments were brought without a single order being given, and a soft laugh broke from her lips.

'No, it is not his. Charles-Guillaume *is* the father. I have not told him yet, he would fuss so and insist I stay in my bed until the child is born. I should go mad! I shall not be able to follow the hunt soon, but I refuse to live the life of a nun because I am not as strong as other women.' She had told Alexandrine how, as a child, she had been plagued with severe chest colds and other ailments which over the years had taken their toll of her strength. She tired so easily, although few people ever realised it from her bright countenance and apparently boundless energy, and whenever possible would lie abed until almost evening to recover. But, despite the frailty of her woman's body, she was strong in her resolve that one day she would be the first lady in France and sit at the side of the King. How could she be weak when such a destiny was before her?

She had heard talk that in certain quarters she had become known as *la bourgeoise*. Never was she allowed to be introduced publicly to the King or to be part of his intimate circle, and so she was forced to follow the hunt at a distance, to take such outrageous steps to have him notice her. Let them call her what they would! He *had* noticed her. She was on the road to Versailles and no one—nothing—would stop her now.

'Did I not tell you it would rain?' she remarked, glancing up as huge drops of rain splattered against the window-panes. 'You cannot leave yet, Alexandrine, you will catch your death out in such weather. If it continues I shall have the fires lit tonight. I hate the damp. No, perhaps I shall return to Paris tomorrow and we shall spend some time together. Would it help if I came to visit your husband? We have enjoyed such interesting conversations in the past.'

'No!' Alexandrine's answer was so swift that an eyebrow rose quizzically, and reluctantly Alexandrine confessed how far her husband's health was deteriorating. She did not want anyone else to see him as he was now. 'Selim is doing everything he can,' she said with a shrug of her shoulders, 'and Luc has promised to consult other doctors, but I fear it is hopeless. Sometimes, at night, when I sit by his bed, he does not even know me.'

'This Selim who attends him—does he sedate him that heavily?'

'It is necessary...not all the time, you understand, but several times...Luc has been so...unpredictable in his behaviour...turning on us all. And once...' A shadow crossed her pale face as she recalled a terrible rage which had come upon him, the force which Selim had used in order to restrain him until it had passed '...he has been violent...'

'*Mon Dieu!*' Jeanne crossed herself quickly. 'What is happening to him? If I did not know he is in the care of people who love him, I would think he is being poisoned! You must take care, my dear...already there have been mutterings in some circles about the strangeness of his illness. One moment he appears with you in near-perfect health, the next he is struck down again, and confined to his bed and allowed to see no one. Paul has made the most of that fact, you know. He is dropping subtle hints that perhaps you are ensuring his father does not change his mind about leaving all his wealth to you. He argues that if it were possible to see him they would be reconciled.'

'Nonsense! He tried to kill Luc! And me!'

'But can you prove either accusation? On both occasions, if I recall, the Duc de Belaincourt was involved. The first time in rescuing Luc, the second in sending his servant to your assistance.'

'What are you suggesting?' Alexandrine asked, her eyes widening slightly. She had been too concerned with Luc to even consider how people might gossip. 'Alain Ratan saved Luc's life...and Jules killed the man sent by Paul to murder me. He told me so himself, Jeanne. I shall never forget his voice—the words he spoke before he attacked me with a knife!'

'I believe you. And I am sure, if this became known, many others would, too, but Paul somehow has managed to retain a good many friends. He has the cunning of a fox, that one. Claudia, heaven knows why, is quite prepared to keep him, even though I swear she does not have one iota of affection for him. I suspect she has reasons of her own, and this liaison with him is of some importance to her. And the money Paul owes to his creditors! That has not yet been paid, and yet they are being patient. He should have been in the Bastille by now! Why, Alexandrine? Ask yourself that! What has he promised them, that they do not send him there? His father's wealth? But that will be yours—unless...' Jeanne paused significantly, allowing her words to penetrate Alexandrine's stunned brain.

'Unless I die...' she breathed.

'Or unless Luc's death, when it occurs—and we know how serious is this illness he suffers—can be made to look like something else. Do you not see how Paul is preparing the groundwork for his father's demise? Rumours now, accusations later...and who will come to your defence? The Duc de Belaincourt? Luc's friend— your constant companion since his confinement. And, some will say, your lover!'

He would not come to her aid, Alexandrine thought bitterly, for he had been among those turned away from the bedroom on Luc's orders. He had not believed they came from his old friend, and had ranted at her for keeping him from the sick man's bedside. When he had attempted to push past her, Selim had blocked the way, and Alain had left in a fury. *He* would believe the worst of her too! But it could not be avoided. Luc had made her promise no one would see him in his present sorry state. Soon, he had assured her, his strength would return sufficiently for him to receive guests. Was this the truth? Or was it mere words to bolster her flagging spirits? she wondered. The sooner they were back home again, the better. And now, when he was able to travel, there was the prospect of Noyen. Peace...seclusion. When the end came, she did not want him surrounded by vultures, waiting to tear him to pieces and then turn on the surviving and destroy them too.

She was conscious of her vulnerability in a man's world. Of the body she could use, as a weapon, if necessary, or as a favour given willingly to the man she suspected would only help her if she paid his price—and that price, she had decided, was too high, despite the love she still harboured deep in her heart for him. She was not of the same mould as La Châteauroux, or Claudia or countless other women who used their God-given gifts to further their ambitions, deceive their husbands, or satiate their own desires. No matter how difficult life became for her after her husband was gone, she would never lower herself to their level. She would fight tooth and nail to protect what had been left to her, but by other means. Just what those might prove to be, she did not know...

'*Madame*, you have unexpected guests.' Jeanne rose to her feet quickly as a servant appeared to announce the arrival of a group of rather wet and dishevelled ladies and gentlemen who wished to shelter at the château until the rain had passed over.

'Alexandrine!' A tiny gasp escaped her lips as she peered through the window. 'The King! And the Duchesse...and—and at least a dozen friends. *He* has come here!' Nervous hands smoothed down the skirts of her pale pink gown, then fluttered to the necklace of diamonds at her throat. Her eyes had begun to shine. Alexandrine thought her suddenly radiant. Then, it was as if a calm cloak of self-confidence settled about her shoulders. In a quiet, perfectly composed voice she instructed the visitors to be taken into the lower drawing-room and a fire lighted. Those who required it should have their clothes dried immediately, and mulled wine and brandy was to be served without delay. 'Come, Alexandrine, we must go to greet the King.'

'I—I shall remain here. No one will know and I shall leave as soon as the rain eases.' Alexandrine knew without asking who else was in the party. These days Alain was never far from the King's side and had swiftly become a constant companion at Mailly, Louis's favourite retreat, as well as at all the supper parties. More often than not he was accompanied by the delightful little Caroline de Morrière. It seemed that at last the Duc de Belaincourt was able to forget the scheming of his beautiful Nicolette, and look elsewhere for love and affection, and from the adoring way the girl followed him everywhere it was obvious to all that she was hopelessly in love with him. Would he use her as he had used Alexandrine? For one brief night of pleasure? The Comte, her father, was said to be a cautious man, who watched over his offspring like a hawk. A liaison other than marriage would be out of the question, but to have as his son-in-law one of the élite nobility, with the ear of the King, was too good an opportunity to miss. Did she feel pity for the girl? Alexandrine wondered. Or was she jealous?

'Of course you must come down,' Jeanne insisted. 'You are my friend...and the King likes you. Remember that. If you need protection one day, you could approach him and I do not think he would ignore you.'

All eyes turned to focus on the two women when they entered the drawing-room, where servants were busy attending to the needs of the new arrivals. The hot spiced wine was much appreciated by the women, who bemoaned their saturated gowns and the feathers drooping most tipsily from wide-brimmed hats. Few of the men were concerned with their appearance, but had launched wholeheartedly into the brandy, determined not to allow a little rain to spoil what had so far been a good day's sport, and still there was the prospect of the King's supper party in the evening. As usual, all would gather in front of the door to the royal chambers and await its opening, whereupon Louis would gaze at the crowd pressing forward, eager to be noticed, and then retire again to make out a list of those he wished to sup with him.

The ritual never changed. At Versailles it was always the same, and each day promised a chance of recognition and acceptance—a chance to be elevated from the minority who clamoured in the rooms every day of the year. Faces came and went, and it was quite probable the King never remembered all who had sat with him, Alexandrine thought as she sank into a deep curtsy before Louis, Jeanne at her side. Their entrance was like a breath of spring invading a stuffy room, for they were both perfectly groomed, their gowns immaculate, their demure smiles for the King alone.

'Madame Poisson...' She heard the hushed whisper from one side of her as Louis came forward and raised them both to their feet. 'Of all the nerve...' Abruptly conversation was curtailed as the Duchesse de Châteauroux sent a withering glance around her.

'Madame la Marquise, I am glad to see you at least managed to escape the ravages of the storm. And this is...? Forgive me, *madame*, I do not believe we have met.' Louis was playing his public role, Alexandrine realised.

'I am your hostess, sire. Jeanne Poisson d'Etoiles. I am honoured this old château should receive such an honoured guest. My door will be forever open to you should you ever be caught out in the rain again.' The name was delivered with pride. It had always been a source of embarrassment to the family, for it meant 'fish' and had been used in a most unpleasant fashion after Jeanne's mother was deserted by her husband. Jeanne was determined it never would be again. Soon the whole of France would utter it as they might a prayer upon their lips.

A soft chuckle escaped Louis's lips as he gazed into the porcelain features of the woman whose hand he still held. He touched ringed fingers to his lips. Did he hold them a little longer than was necessary? Alexandrine wondered, marvelling at the composure of them both. They were flirting with each other before everyone, Jeanne with her double-edged words and the King with his eyes. One day, they said, I shall acknowledge you before these gaping clowns. Until then what we have shared is for us alone.

'What more could I ask for? Comfortable surroundings, fine wine and——' suddenly conscious again, as an afterthought, of who stood behind him with her eyes boring into his back, he glanced around him '—and pleasant company. I thank you for your hospitality, *madame*, as do my friends. We shall not forget the haven you have offered us until the weather improves.'

'Will you take some wine to warm you, sire?' The Duchesse de Châteauroux had had enough of the cosy conversation between her lover and this upstart bourgeoise. She too had heard the silly rumours about this woman who some thought would usurp *her* place at the King's side. Louis had a healthy appetite, and often she, a robust, healthy woman, was exhausted by the demands he made on her. This Madame Poisson—her lips curled derisively as she considered the insulting name by which she decided she would refer to her from now on—looked as cold as her name, and so fragile! She would not last more than one night in Louis's bed!

As she managed to draw the King away to where a fire now blazed welcomingly in the huge stone fireplace, Jeanne said in a scornful whisper, 'She is jealous of me already—and it shows! Do you not think so?'

'I believe she fears you,' Alexandrine returned in the same low tone, aware of eyes still on them. Not least was she aware of those of Alain Ratan, a few feet away and beside, as usual these days, Mademoiselle Caroline de Morrière. The Comte, her father, was nowhere to be seen. Perhaps he had grown to accept the Duc as his future son-in-law and therefore to be trusted with her out of his sight, she thought. How foolish! He would seduce her at the first opportunity. And then she grew quite cold as a chilling thought struck her. Unless he was truly in love with the girl.

'Afraid,' Jeanne mused, oblivious to her friend's thoughts as she contemplated the tall figure of the King across the room. He was still as handsome as when she had first seen him as a little girl. She had loved him then. She loved him now. What they would share would be worth all the waiting and the uncertainty, the ridicule she had been forced to endure all these years. 'What a comforting thought. Forgive me, I think I should mingle, or they will be saying Madame d'Etoiles does not have the manners of a lady, let alone a bourgeoise.'

No sooner had she left Alexandrine's side than Alain murmured something to his companion, who smiled sweetly at him and nodded her head. Alexandrine turned to go, but, without seemingly hurrying to cut her off, he was ahead of her, blocking her path to the door.

'I have just heard.' There was controlled anger in his voice. 'That you are retiring from court,' he added as she looked at him enquiringly. 'Is this Luc's idea—or yours?'

'We have been your guests at Belaincourt too long, *monsieur*. You have borne us with great patience, especially Luc's illness these past weeks, but he agrees with me that we must take our leave of you. The King has given us his permission to go to the country.' Home to Noyen, where I belong, she wanted to add but knew it would not be wise to do so.

'Luc cannot be well enough to travel. Since I have not been allowed to see him for the past three days—and since he has not put in an appearance downstairs—I can only surmise he has not improved, despite the Moor's tender ministrations.'

She ignored the sarcasm which accompanied the words.

'It was my husband's wish that he receive no visitors while he is indisposed. He is a proud man; of that you should be only too aware. He does not like to be seen at a disadvantage. As for Selim's care, he is doing all he can—as he has always done. However, Luc has agreed to my request that he consult other doctors before we depart for the country. Their decision may determine whether or not we ever come back to Paris.'

Now you know, her eyes proclaimed silently. Once there I shall be free of you—perhaps—forever.

If the statement came as a shock to Alain, he did not allow it to show on his face. Except for a slight narrowing of the pale, glittering eyes which watched her, there was no reaction.

'So—once more he becomes a recluse. His decision or yours, I wonder?'

'When he is well enough, why not ask him?' Alexandrine challenged. He no longer intimidated her as in the past, and she knew it was because she had found a way to escape from the love that had made her weak-willed and vulnerable. Her love might last for many years to come, the memory of that one night when she had walked through paradise with him, but in time it would fade and so would the pain, and take second place in her life, no longer ruling her thoughts...her actions...her heart.

The memories she would retain of him would be mixed ones—of love and hate intermingling until it was impossible to separate the two completely.

'That I shall do, Alexa.' Alain cast a brief glance at the King and the Duchesse de Châteauroux, surrounded, as always, by those clamouring to be included in the royal conversation. 'Take care. The Duchesse is a dangerous enemy.'

'I don't know what you mean. I have given her no reason to dislike me. Why, we have hardly spoken more than twice,' Alexandrine protested.

'You are Madame d'Etoiles' friend. Nay, more than that—her confidante, I'll warrant. After all, you share the same fortune-teller! La Châteauroux is no fool. She knows her position is no more secure than that of her sisters. She had Louise, her own kin, banished from Court to keep Louis's eyes off her. If she will go to such lengths with her own family, what do you think she will do to the woman rumoured to want to take her place—and to those associating with her?'

'I think you exaggerate,' she returned with a shrug of slender shoulders, and Alain's features now darkened visibly at her casual dismissal of his warning. 'After all, did you not arrange for Jeanne to meet the King at Belaincourt on the night of your birthday? Has that little escapade not reached the Duchesse's ears? She still seems cordial enough with you.'

'But I have the friendship of the King, and she knows better than to push him too far. True friends for a King are rare. Louis values those he has.'

'His so-called friends are apt to desert him in times of need. Will you be different, *monsieur*?'

'I am different,' Alain said tersely. 'You see, I want nothing from the King. I am wealthy in my own right. I have a château and a town house in Paris and business connections throughout France. I seek no honours for myself. Friendship is as important to me as it is to him—which is why I care so much for your husband, Alexa. He is a true friend to me and I shall always be so to him. However, on the subject of the Duchesse—she and Claudia de la Fontaine are old friends—close friends. Need I remind you who now enjoys Claudia's favours? I will not say her bed, for I do not think him man enough to fill it.' He nodded as his words brought a sharp intake of breath from her. 'Yes—Paul, your stepson. He now has friends in high places, Alexa. Your future is not yet secure.'

'My—my future?' What was he implying?

'Your very bright future as the widow of the Marquis de Mezière. You do not think I believe that you will remain hidden away in the country if he should die? You will be very rich—and very available, will you not? Is this not what you have been waiting for since the day you married him?'

The cruel taunt brought fierce colour flooding into her cheeks. Instinctively her hand began to travel up-wards to slap the insolent smile from his face, but he caught it midway, his grip crushing her fingers as he carried them to his lips.

'Take care, Monsieur Ratan, lest you offend Mademoiselle de Morrière,' Alexandrine said coldly, and Alain's eyes mocked her attempt to shame him.

'Have I made you jealous? I hope so. That was my intention...'

'Why—you—you arrogant, conceited——' Words failed her as his grip continued to numb her fingers. 'You are hurting me—and people are beginning to stare at us.'

'Let them.' He did not release her, although his hold slackened slightly. For a long moment he allowed himself the pleasure of just looking at her and remembering more pleasant moments they had shared, even though he knew they had never meant anything to her at all. And, in the beginning, not to him...

She wore the rich blue riding-habit he had seen before and admired, and the necklace of lapis-lazuli was about her milk-white throat. Small sapphire studs were just visible beneath the mass of corn-coloured curls which fell in profusion about her ears. How her hair had grown! Who would have thought such a transformation possible in a few short months? Luc had. He had seen what no one else could, and had achieved what he set out to do with no misgivings whatsoever and never for one moment considering failure.

Alexandrine had resembled a country urchin when first Alain had seen her at the Hôtel Boussières. Now she was a desirable woman, sought after by many men at Court, and not merely for her company. And there were at least three in the room where they stood, he mused, who were enamoured of her. The Duc de Tallart was beginning to look extremely annoyed at the fact that Alain was monopolising her for so long. Poor Gervais, he stood no chance...or did he? She had married one old man, so why not another, equally rich? The thought irritated him, as did the sight of her dancing with other men. He did not own her, and he should not care, but it was growing increasingly hard to ignore the fact that she was willing to be pleasant with others and not with him. To bestow on them more than just a smile or a passing word, when she refused to continue what had begun between them.

There were two memories of her he knew would never leave him. One was the sight of her naked, trembling, that first night—slim-hipped, long-legged, her young breasts firm and rounded, crowned with pink rosebud nipples. The other was of the woman he had discovered in bed. Shy and at first protesting at his caresses, the kisses that were planted on her lips, her breasts, her throat—like a young bride on her wedding night. Yet at the same time unable to control the fires he ignited inside her. She could not have been a virgin, of course—for Luc had spoken of his love for her that first night back in Paris—and yet, for a moment, when she had cried out...he had thought...

But it had been for an instant only as her body surrendered to passion and came alive beneath his skilful caresses...

'It is not I who will be made jealous,' Alexandrine replied indifferently. 'I am immune to your ploys.'

'Are you? Why then is there such anger in those lovely eyes? You are annoyed because I have neglected you...as I intended you should be. You must learn not to play games with me, either, Alexa. I am a formidable opponent.'

'The game we once played is over.' Her voice shook with restrained temper seeing a woman's fan flutter as she bent her head to whisper to the man at her side and heard the latter chuckle. They were being talked about and he was deliberately making it happen. Had he gone mad!

'I want you, Alexa.' Alain said, and the pale eyes bored down into her very soul, stripping her bare of all pretence. This had happened before, she thought frantically, but then she had been susceptible to his charm—his lies. Not this time! Let him go to Claudia de la Fontaine for what he needed, if she would have him back. Or Caroline de Morrière.

'What you feel for me is lust...nothing more. You are incapable of anything else.' Her fiery eyes challenged his mocking gaze, and surprise registered for a fleeting moment in his face.

'What does a chit of a girl like you know of lust?'

She almost laughed aloud at the question.

'So now I am a girl! Can you not make up your mind about me, *monsieur*? Girl, whore, innocent or harlot. At one time or another you have intimated I am one or all of these... all without good reason, I might add.'

'As you say—perhaps all, perhaps only one. I know how a beautiful woman can blind a man—it has happened to me before!'

'So again I am a woman—to suit this occasion perhaps?' she flung back in a scornful whisper.

'Yes, you are... and it is the woman I want to hold in my arms again.'

'You will have to look elsewhere for consolation, *monsieur*. I love my husband, and what happened once between us will never occur again—with you or any man,' came the vehement vow.

'Then why are you still here with me?' Alain questioned, his mouth deepening into a cynical twist. 'Walk away, Alexa. That way I shall know I mean nothing to you.'

His hand fell away from hers, and as the blood returned to her cramped fingers she had to keep the pain from registering on her face.

'Mean something to me! You flatter yourself. I do not even like you.'

'Madame la Marquise, forgive the interruption, but there is a man waiting outside to speak with you.' A servant was at her elbow, and she eagerly grasped the opportunity to flee Alain's hated presence. Even so, she could not resist a parting shot in revenge for the way he had humiliated her with his suggestions.

'Oh, dear, I do hope it is not another of my admirers desperate for my company. I'm afraid, *monsieur*, even if I were foolish enough to consider you among them, you would be last in line!'

She did not hear the expletive which broke from Alain's lips as she picked up her skirts and followed the lackey to the front door of the château, where a boy stood, nervously clutching a piece of paper in his hands.

'Oh, *madame*, thank God I have found you! I've been searching the forest for an hour... I was ordered to bring you this—I'm from the stables at Belaincourt, and that huge black giant came running out of the house as if pursued by the devil himself and thrust it into my hand! I was to find you at once and bring you back to Belaincourt.'

Selim! Who else could he mean? 'Give it to me quickly.' Alexandrine knew a moment of great apprehension as she opened the folded paper, and the words leapt up at her like an omen of doom.

'Come at once. Grave news. The worst. Selim.'

Eight little words that sent her hurrying towards the stables.

'I had them saddle your mare, *madame*, I knew you would not want to be kept waiting.' The boy was ahead of her to assist her into the saddle. She gave no thought to leaving so abruptly, forgetful in her panic of the etiquette which demanded she ask leave of the King. She forgot the bodyguard who had taken Lady Blue to the château while she drove with Jeanne.

Grave news! It could only concern Luc. The worst! He was dead! Oh, no, not that, she prayed as she pulled the mount about and urged her into a gallop. Dead— and she had not been at his side during his last moments! She would never forgive herself!

All thought of safety, of the warnings she had been given never to ride alone, fled from her mind, nor was she aware that the boy had not followed her. As horse and rider vanished from sight amid the trees, he had turned quickly about and hurried behind the stables. Pausing only to satisfy himself that the man set to guard Alexandrine was dead, he stepped over the lifeless body, a smile stealing across his youthful features as he considered the money he was to be paid for such a simple errand. Slit a man's throat and send a woman to her death. He had killed before, and it was of no consequence to him to take another life or two, especially when one of them was from the hated nobility.

And his employer was a most generous man when a job was well done...

CHAPTER SIX

'MONSIEUR RATAN, have you seen Alexandrine? She seems to have disappeared,' Jeanne said, following Alain out on to the rain-sodden terrace, and grimacing as her dainty slippers became wet. A watery sun was forcing its way through the dark clouds and only a light drizzle now prevailed. The King had voiced his intention of starting back for Versailles within the hour. 'You were talking to her not ten minutes ago, were you not?'

'I was, but I am not her keeper.' There was still anger smouldering in Alain's eyes as he swung around to face her, causing her to wonder what had passed between them. A lovers' quarrel perhaps? 'Someone—a man— came to see her.'

'A man,' Jeanne echoed. 'But no one knows she is here. I shall go and find out what this is all about.'

'Take care, *madame*. you might interrupt a lover's tryst,' he remarked sardonically, making no move to follow her.

'It is you who should take care, Monsieur Ratan— your jealousy is showing. Someone might see,' came the provocative retort which made his lips tighten still more.

Jealous! Damnation, he knew he was, and it was growing hard to control. The only way to rid himself of this obsession was to have Alexandrine again...to exorcise the ghost of her which haunted his nights. She was only a woman—and another night with her would prove to him once and for all that she was nothing special. No one to lose sleep over. No one with whom it was worth contemplating anything other than a few stolen moments of passion.

Passion! She had that well enough! Who did she share it with these days? Luc? Impossible. There were so many others... Her parting taunt had touched him more than

134

he wanted to admit. He had returned to Caroline in a spiteful, mean mood and had left her almost immediately to drink with some friends, aware that had he remained with her he would have been rude and unpleasant, and she did not deserve that from him. She was a sweet, innocent little child and he enjoyed her company... but that was all. He had said nothing to the Comte, even when it became obvious the man was considering him prospective son-in-law material, for it suited Alain to have his name linked with Caroline's and served a dual purpose. It not only set the gossips talking about something else so that they forgot his continual escorting of Alexandrine, but it also provoked her.

'*Monsieur*, something is wrong.' Jeanne came hurrying across the terrace to him, her face quite pale and agitated. It was one of the very few times he had seen her lose some of her magnificent composure. Nothing seemed to upset her, yet here she was almost on the point of tears. 'My servant tells me someone came from Belaincourt with a note for Alexandrine. He was standing quite close to her when she read it, although he could not see it all. Something about grave news, with a strange signature—Selim.'

'The Moor! Luc!' Alain's first thoughts were the same as Alexandrine's had been. 'I must go too. He must have had a relapse.'

'Wait!' Jeanne caught at his arm with trembling fingers. 'The boy who brought the news did not return with her. She rode off alone and he went in another direction, so Daniel tells me.'

'Alone! Where was the man I ordered to be with her? Was he at the hunt?' Alain's voice was suddenly harsh.

'Why, yes...I remember seeing him, and Alexandrine remarked about her extra shadow. And when we came here...yes, he went off towards the stables when we came inside... *Monsieur*, wait! What is happening?'

Alain did not hear the words she called after him as he broke into a run towards the stables. Riding alone in the forest? Drawn away by a note delivered by a boy who did not return with her? What devilry was afoot

now? And who was behind it? Paul! He shut his mind
against that reasoning. The note was probably genuine—
it had to be—and she had gone in all haste to be at Luc's
side, retaining that appearance of the dutiful wife rushing
to the bedside of a sick husband. The Court would love
it!

When he arrived at Belaincourt he would find her
there—safe!

'Jules, where the devil are you, man?' He stared
angrily inside the stables, furious not to find him there.

He was already mounted and about to urge the huge
black stallion out into the open when Jules appeared in
the doorway.

'Monsieur le Duc...murder has been done. Fuete is
dead...round the back, his throat cut. From behind,
I'd say. He probably never knew who did it.' Jules's eyes
were narrowed to tiny slits. Fuete had been one of the
men he had hired on Alain's behalf from across the Pont-
Neuf. They had grown up as children in the back alleys,
and learned the art of survival from an early age. Despite the fact he had been older, Fuete had always looked
up to his companion, admired the skill with which Jules
picked pockets and locks, and relieved so many rich
people of their valuables. Now he was dead, and attacked from behind—the coward's way! Every man
should see the face of the one who would kill him, Jules
believed, and his gutter upbringing demanded he revenge the friend who had been taken from him.
'Whoever did it went off towards the village. I tried to
follow, but then I thought I'd better warn you to keep
the Marquise in sight. It can only mean one thing.'

''You are too late...Fuete's murderer brought the
Marquise word that she must return to Belaincourt immediately. She rode off alone...the little fool! I'll take
the short cut and try to get ahead of her. You track our
man, if you can. Find him, Jules! It might make up for
the fact that you were not where you should have been
when it happened. You will explain that to me when I
get back.'

Alain spurred the stallion out of the stables, forcing Jules to jump back to avoid being knocked over. The man swore as he ran for his horse. One mug of ale, and it was going to cost him dear. He had lost a friend, and would have to face the Duc's anger for not being at his post. Which was worse? he wondered.

Alexandrine rode her horse at a reckless pace through the forest, uppermost in her mind the one thought that she had again betrayed Luc. Not with a man this time, but with her absence from his side when he must have sorely needed her.

She urged Lady Blue on faster. A fallen tree-trunk loomed up in the path ahead, but the mare cleared it without faltering in her long stride, although the jolt Alexandrine received as the animal came down to earth again almost unseated her. The wind tore at her gown, billowing it out behind her like the sail of a ship. Her hair had come loose from the confines of the combs she had placed there earlier that day, and tossed about her shoulders in wild disarray. She had lost the combs during the first few moments of her hectic ride when a low branch had slapped painfully across her face and caught in her hair. It had scratched one cheek and drawn blood, but she had not noticed, never for one moment taking her eyes off the narrow, twisting path ahead which would take her back to Belaincourt.

She should have told Alain, she thought at last, and realised she had forgotten about her bodyguard. A swift glance over her shoulder told her he had not seen her leave, or he would have been close behind her as always…and where was the young lad who had brought her the terrible news? She had believed him to be accompanying her back to the house. Perhaps *he* had gone to convey the news to Alain. What did it matter? Nothing was important except that she get home as soon as possible to be with her husband.

This morning, when she had looked in on him, he had been sleeping soundly. His first peaceful sleep for days, Selim had told her. The medicine was again having the desired effect. The Moor sounded quite confident when he spoke of their being able to leave for Noyen within a month. Had he lied to her? Deliberately deceived her because he knew Luc was not improving? Could he, as many suspected, be a charlatan—a quack whose potions did no good whatsoever for his patient?

No! She must keep her faith in the man. He alone knew Luc's many varied moods and was able to humour him when he was in a bad temper. He had proved his skill at healing, his vast knowledge of herbs and various potentially dangerous wonders which, when mixed correctly, became beneficial, not detrimental.

Two riders were upon her before she was aware of their presence. They came out of the trees to one side of her at a fast gallop and were alongside her immediately. Startled, Alexandrine wrenched at Lady Blue's reins as one of them tried to reach out and grab them. They were not from Belaincourt! The hard, unshaven features were those of peasants—farm labourers or the like. She had seen many faces like theirs staring at the richly ornamented carriages which passed through dismal, poverty-stricken villages *en route* to Versailles, and she had been alarmed by the hatred registered thereon. While the idle nobility amused themselves at the King's favourite abode, gorged themselves on the best food in the land, the poor lived in a perpetual state of hunger, decimated by disease, their stomachs crying out for food, their hearts for justice. The bread riots of 1725 were still vivid in the minds of common folk, if barely remembered in those of the upper classes whom it had not touched.

She was about to be robbed, Alexandrine thought, spurring her mount on faster. And she was sure she would not afterwards be spared. She never wore much jewellery when she went riding or followed the King's hunt, unlike many women who reclined in their carriages dressed as if for a grand ball and laden down with a fortune in jewels. Even so, the lapis-lazuli necklace around her throat was extremely valuable and one of her favourite pieces. And the sapphires in her ears would keep a less fortunate family for well over a year.

Lady Blue slipped on an uneven piece of ground and slithered unsteadily down a slope, scattering mud and water in all directions. Alexandrine was thrown violently forward, but somehow managed to keep her seat, clinging to the saddle with all her strength so that she would not be tossed down on to the rain-soaked ground as Lady Blue continued her perilous descent to the bottom of the slope.

She heard shouting behind her, and cursing, growing louder in her ears. On open ground once again, she wheeled the horse about to bring her back towards the correct direction to take her back to Belaincourt and safety, only to find one of the men had managed to get ahead of her—and she could not turn, for the second was behind her, closing with her as she raised her riding crop in one hand and slashed viciously across the face of the man who barred her path. Then, kneeing Lady Blue, she galloped past him. His howl of pain was lost in the wind which whipped it away immediately.

She was alone! No one knew where she was! Why had she not told Jeanne she was leaving? If only the messenger had remained with her—if only...

Fear gripped her, and for a moment her mind was numb with shock. This was no coincidence...she had been lured away from the château with this in mind. Not to rob her, but to kill her! So distraught had she been by the news brought to her that she had not questioned its authenticity. Or was she letting her imagination run away with her? She prayed it was so.

Lady Blue was tiring fast, and Alexandrine knew she would be unable to maintain the fast pace for much longer. And the way ahead was strewn with fallen branches blown down in the fierce winds of the past few days, causing the mare to slow her stride and avoid them. Alexandrine had strayed totally from the right path and, although she had ridden many times in the forest, all around her now seemed strange. She could recognise no visible landmarks.

Her eyes streamed from the wind, blinding her. Again one of her pursuers managed to get ahead of her, forcing her to rein in abruptly to avoid a head-on collision with him. Startled, Lady Blue whinnied and swerved—then stumbled and threw Alexandrine from the saddle. She landed on the ground with a sickening thud that knocked every breath from her body. Mud plastered her face and arms, clung to the beautiful blue gown as she rolled over and over, unable to control the downward momentum, until she came to a halt against a large oak, barely conscious.

Voices—far off, growing closer. Shadows looming over her...through the mist which obscured her vision came the faces of the two men who had chased her. She felt the necklace ripped from her throat, so cruelly that the stones cut into her soft skin, but she was too weak, too wretched—too frightened—to move or utter a sound. She closed her eyes again...if they thought she was dead perhaps they would leave her.

'No, leave the rest of the stuff,' she heard one voice order. 'The necklace will be enough to convince him that we have done what he wanted.'

A hand was laid against her heart and lingered there for a long moment, then moved slowly up to where the bodice of her gown had been ripped in the fall, exposing one creamy shoulder and the rise of a rounded breast. She barely suppressed a shudder as calloused fingers cupped the softness and squeezed it roughly.

'Pretty little filly, isn't she? What a waste....'

'None of that! This has to look like an accident. She looks half done for now, she'll not give you any trouble. Cave her head in with a rock—that should do it. We'll meet later at Yvette's and divide our pay. And don't linger here...'

Silence. A silence so terrible that Alexandrine wanted to scream. Dared she look and see what was happening? She heard the sound of a horse being mounted and ridden away. One man had left, but in her condition what could she do? Slowly, fearfully, she lifted her lids a fraction. There was a man a few feet away, wandering over the ground, looking for something... For a rock to kill her with? Everyone would think she had been killed when

Lady Blue threw her? Dear God, was there nothing she could do?

An agonising pain shot through her head as she gingerly lifted it from the muddy earth, but she bit her lips and kept going. If she did not she was dead. She had gained her feet and was tottering towards her mount when the man turned and saw her. In two strides he had covered the space between them, and had flung her to the ground again. This time she did not rise. The last of her strength was gone.

'So there's more life in you than we thought, is there, my beauty?' Garlic breath was hot upon her face as he bent to press his mouth against hers. 'Don't you taste sweet now? And smelling like a spring flower. Not like my woman. Who's to know, eh, if we have a little fun...? You won't be telling anyone, will you?'

Alexandrine screamed—just once—as his weight held her pinned to the ground and he began to pull open her bodice...

Alain had ridden within sight of Belaincourt without catching a glimpse of Alexandrine, and he knew he had come too far. She was somewhere behind him... and he had wasted precious time. He cursed himself as he wheeled his stallion about and headed into the forest again.

A single piercing scream so short in duration that for a moment he thought he had imagined it, reached him. He reined in and sat listening intently, but the only sounds about him were of the wind in the trees, the call of birds above his head and the heavy breathing of Midnight Blue, lathered and sweating profusely from the ride.

It had to be her—and she was in danger! His instincts had been right. Lifting his head, he pursed his lips and emitted a sharp, high-pitched whistle. Nothing. He repeated it and from ahead came a familiar whinny in return. Lady Blue had responded to his call. Alexandrine was somewhere near, and Alain gave his horse its head, knowing the animal would lead him to the mare.

He rode like a man possessed, engulfed with a murderous rage. *She* had not listened to his warnings of the danger of riding alone! *She* was to blame for her predicament, and no one else! How easy it would be to burden her shoulders with blame! Had he not been so incensed by her attitude at the château he would have noticed her departure. *He*, who had sworn an oath that neither she nor Luc would again suffer from the warped inspirations of Paul Boussières' mind!

Yet he had been ignorant of her departure! Jules had been elsewhere, damn the man! Her bodyguard—had he seen something, he wondered, or had he indeed been struck from behind, as the other man believed? He too had failed in his duty to protect her. Excuses were so easy to find for someone seeking them out of desperation—as he was.

His anger had caused him to ignore her—and fate, or Paul Boussières, had done the rest. Until he found her he would not know who—or what—had intervened on this pleasant day to turn his existence once more upside-down, and to place her in peril of her life!

There was danger! The desperation in the scream had seared him like a sword thrust. He prayed he would not be too late. At that moment he did not care that if he saved her she would return to her husband—his best friend! That she might take lovers from among his circle of acquaintances! Nothing was important save that when he did find her she was alive...

Without warning, as the trees thinned out and gorse and evergreen bushes took the place of towering oak and Spanish chestnut, he came upon them. An ill-dressed oaf was fondling the inert form which lay trapped beneath his bulk. As he threw himself from his horse, Alain was aware only of the grimy hands, with their bitten nails, which were touching Alexandrine's flesh, and a red mist swam before his eyes. Was she dead? She made no sound! Did not move!

The man was so intent on discovering the delights of the soft, milk-white skin, the full, rounded breasts—not sagging with age and child-bearing like those of the woman with whom he lived—that he did not hear Alain's approach . . .

Awareness of danger came too late! His hand fell to the knife at his belt and he came up on to his knees, his lips drawn back over his teeth in a snarl. He saw no mercy on the dark features of the advancing man, and as he sank his blade into Alain's shoulder he saw his own death in the pale eyes. At the same moment blood welled into his throat, choking him, as Alain's sword took him full in the chest. He was dead even before he was heaved unceremoniously to one side.

So still, so pale, Alain thought, as he dropped to the ground beside Alexandrine. Her gown was torn open to the waist and dark smudges were already beginning to show on her shoulders and breasts. But the brute had been too intent on enjoying the beauty helpless before his lust to hasten in his actions, Alain realised, pushing her skirts down to cover the long, slender legs.

Relief that he had arrived in time made him momentarily weak, and only then, as he sat back on his heels, dragging in deep lungfuls of air, did he realise the pain in his right shoulder. His coat was soaked with blood, and he stripped it off, tore a sleeve from his shirt and folded it into a tight wad to pad the injured shoulder and stem the flow of blood. He was beginning to feel a little light-headed. Mere relief, or loss of blood?

Alexandrine moaned, and immediately he was beside her again, cradling her in his arms. But the moment she became aware of his touch, tight fists pounded at his chest and, weak though they were, they brought a gasp of pain from between his clenched lips.

'Gently, *m'amie*, do you want me to pass out before I can get you safely back to Belaincourt? Hush now— be still! You are safe now.'

Safe! Alexandrine fought against the arms which enfolded her and held her fast against a broad, firm chest. She was about to be raped—and then murdered! Safe?

That voice! She knew it—yet where? Her eyes fluttered open on to a face she knew well. No putrid breath upon her cheek, or leering grin, or callused hands invading her body.

'Alain!' Only once could he ever remember her calling him that—at the Hôtel Boussières that fateful night.

'You are safe,' he repeated gently, afraid that the terrible panic still visible in her eyes indicated she had not yet accepted that her ordeal was over. 'As soon as you are able, we will ride back to the house.'

'Safe!' Trembling fingers touched the bronzed cheek above hers. 'With you!' Her laugh bordered on hysteria, but the anger he knew he would have felt had she uttered the words at any other time did not now materialise. It was his wound, he thought, drawing her closer still against him. He could not think of anything else but how good she felt, how soft her body was, how her bare breasts were warm against his chest.

'Do you realise I almost lost you?'

Did those words come from him? Her glazed eyes widened. Her lips parted as if to protest as he bent his head to hers and took her mouth—silencing her, silencing himself. Silencing the whole world until that long kiss ended.

'Alain.' She said his name again, a touch of awe in the whisper. Her fingers touched his cheek—his mouth—locked behind his head as she turned her face against his uninjured shoulder and wept.

Her whole body was racked with uncontrollable sobs. There was nothing he could do but hold her until they had passed, rocking her against him like a child—and all the while knowing the life-blood was ebbing from him. But it did not matter. Nothing mattered in that moment when time ceased to exist and a man and a woman silently acknowledged what they could never put into words—their need, desire...love?

Alain gently tilted back her head as the tears began to subside, and swore as he saw the scratches on her cheek, the bruised mouth, the condition of her clothing.

'I—I am not hurt...Luc! There was a message from Belaincourt...'

'A ruse to get you alone.' It would serve no purpose to tell her, yet the man who should have watched over her was dead, and he swallowed the recriminations which rose to his lips.

'How—who? Oh, no—not Paul! Do rot tell me it was he who planned this? Do you know what that—that *thing* intended to do to me?'

'I know very well; that is why he is dead,' Alain returned, tight-lipped, and her eyes flew from his face to the body lying nearby. Instantly she began to tremble again, and he laid his lips across her scratched cheek and then her mouth. His fingers, light as a breath of wind, brushed across her exposed breasts. It should have been unthinkable, with a man lying dead beside them, and her body crying out to be assuaged by a perfumed bath and blessed sleep to restore her shattered nerves, that he could arouse her—but he did.

She caught her breath as she stared up into the narrowed green eyes and felt as if she was tottering on the edge of a steep cliff...one step further and...

'Alexa——' Her name was lost on his lips as they took hers, and the fire which leapt unbidden between them devoured her!

For Alain the explosion of passion was as devastating—as complete. If he had been a moment later...*Mon Dieu*! He could not bear to think of it. Rage rose again in him as he thought of her being straddled by that ape of a peasant, then died as he opened his eyes on to the dark marks on her shoulders and laid his mouth gently against each one in turn.

She was his for the taking—how ironic that he was in no condition to take advantage of the situation, to settle the score which had plagued him for months.

Yet, had he not been wounded, would he have been so cruel? He was capable of inflicting pain...but to her? His head began to swim...thank heaven Belaincourt was within easy reach for them both.

What was it she had said to him once? He heard again those words that had incensed him so: 'The debt is now paid in full. That is the way it is done in Paris...'

Alexandrine opened her eyes on to the dark face, totally devoid of expression. A moment ago she had thought . . . he wanted her—she could feel it in his kisses, his touch, and she knew that this time she would not have fought him . . . or her own feelings.

'I shall claim my reward at a time when we are both able to provide mutual satisfaction. Is not that the way it is done?' The taunt died on his lips and pain contorted his features. Only then, as she lay stunned by the callousness of the words which succeeded in their intention of reminding her how completely she had deceived him, did she become aware of the bright red stain spreading across the shirt before her eyes. Instantly his words were forgotten.

'You are hurt! Let me help you . . .' She bit her lips as everything swam giddily out of focus, and Alain gave a mirthless chuckle.

'Perhaps we should help each other, Alexa. Give me your arm.' Another thoughtless moment and he would have taken her. His tongue had saved him yet again. Would he ever be able to say the words which were in his heart, or would they forever taunt and hurt each other? Was that their destiny?

The ride back to Belaincourt, although a short distance only, was an agonising one for Alexandrine. Not until she tried to help Alain to mount Midnight Blue did she realise she had injured her back when she fell. Failing in the first attempt to drag himself into the saddle, he leaned weakly against her, fighting back the pain which threatened to drag him down into the realms of unconsciousness, and she had to bite her own lips to stop crying out as she took his full weight and became aware of the fragility of her own condition.

Somehow she managed to heave him upwards, and he did the rest, gathering up the reins with a grimace.

'Get me home,' he said in a harsh whisper. 'I am in your hands. God help me!'

In her hands and helpless as a new-born babe. The situation was becoming more ironic every moment. The fingers of his injured arm were becoming numb. The pain washed over him in great waves, and he slumped across the horse's back, not seeing the pain also in Alexandrine's face, as she mounted and a hundred red-hot needles stabbed viciously along her spine.

I shall get you home, she thought, as she gathered the reins from his lax hands. You are safer with me than you will ever know. Her own discomfort became bearable because she knew his was greater, despite the fact that he refused to utter one groan which would betray his pain to her. Did he think she enjoyed seeing him so helpless? He was hurt because he had come to her aid—as once before when Paul had attacked her—and the love she had tried desperately to suppress welled up inside her as she looked into Alain's ashen features.

'Not far now.' Her lips trembled as she uttered the reassuring words and a tight smile deepened the compressed lips.

She could have broken down and wept when Belaincourt came into sight. Alain tried to straighten in the saddle as if loath to allow himself to be seen in such a state, but the effort proved too much for him and Alexandrine had to grab his arm and hold it fast to prevent him from losing his balance. At her urgent cries, servants came running from all directions, to ease him gently from his horse and carry him inside. Alexandrine limped in their wake, up the wide marble staircase to the corridor where her rooms were, and watched with widening eyes as they stopped at a door a few yards from her own and carried Alain inside. His rooms were adjacent to hers! The realisation froze her momentarily to the spot. How could she not have known? But no one had told her. So close—yet he had never once attempted to invade her privacy. What satisfaction did he gain from having her so near?

Was it his way of telling her he knew she and Luc were not man and wife—and never would be? She searched her mind to remember a thoughtless moment when she might have inadvertently revealed the truth, but was certain there had been none. She even pretended with Jeanne that they now shared an amicable relationship,

although she was not sure that her friend accepted the
new story.

'*Madame*...what has happened to you?' Francine came
out of the apartment, and gasped in horror at the sight
of her mistress standing in the corridor, her beautiful gown
covered in mud, her hair awry and mud clinging to the
fine strands about her ears, as did a multitude of other
debris as if she had been dragged through some bushes.
Her face was dirty and scratched, and blood had dried
on one cheek. Francine's eyes were drawn to the bodice
Alexandrine had somehow managed to tie together so that
it did not gape as before. Even so, there was more of her
to be seen than modesty usually allowed. 'Was it—*him*?'
She glared after Alain.

'Monsieur Ratan has just saved my life—again!'
Alexandrine snapped, and then was instantly contrite for
her sharpness. 'Find Selim, quickly. He is hurt and needs
him.'

When the Moor entered Alain's bedroom, he found
Alexandrine bending over him on the bed. She had re-
padded the still bleeding wound, but he had fainted dead
away before he had reached the bed and knew nothing
of her ministrations. She had sent servants for clean
towels and hot water and bandages, taking charge of the
situation as if by right. No one had challenged her orders,
too alarmed by the sight of their unconscious master to
do anything but obey the dishevelled woman who held
his hand and wiped his wet brow with her own perfumed
lace handkerchief.

As she became aware of being watched, Alexandrine
sprang to her feet, feeling as if she had been caught in
some misdemeanour as she raised her gaze to that of
Selim.

'You have need of me, *madame*. Yes, I can see you
do,' he added, inspecting her appearance.

'The Duc has been hurt...stabbed when he came to
help me. I was waylaid in the forest...two men chased
me...they were going to kill me...' The words tumbled
out in a rush.

As dull comprehension of what had happened at last forced its way to the surface, and she found herself too weak to resist it further, huge tears sprang to her eyes. She realised her back was on fire and lifted trembling fingers to touch the scratch on her cheek. She was remembering it all now...the fall when she thought she had broken every bone in her body...the voices discussing her death so calmly...the weight of the man intent on raping her, the brutal lips clamped over hers...

Selim took her by the shoulders and shook her. Her head snapped back and the wildness faded from her eyes. Slowly she became calm again, and in doing so was swept with shame. Not once had her thoughts been for Luc!

'My husband...' she whispered, as servants filed silently past them with the requirements she had ordered. 'There was a note which brought me back here...from you...' Her voice was barely audible.

'I sent you no note,' Selim replied, releasing her. He stepped to the bed and bent to examine the unconscious man there. 'You have never seen my signature, *madame*, so how would you recognise it?'

'I wouldn't—I didn't...but it was your name and I thought——' Alexandrine broke off, aware how silly she had been. In such haste she had not questioned the authenticity of the message. 'I thought Luc was—dead. I didn't think,' she murmured, a hand against temples which had begun to throb maddeningly.

'The Marquis has been sleeping ever since you left this morning. He took a little nourishment a few hours ago and then went back to sleep immediately.' Selim's eyes held hers, and in them she read the question for which she had no answer. At least, not one she could openly confess to him—or to her husband. Concerned for Luc, she had come riding back to Belaincourt in all haste and been attacked *en route*...yet instead of going to her husband's room to satisfy herself he was alive, she had been by the bedside of the Duc de Belaincourt, holding his hand...

Motioning to the steward Gaston to help him, Selim removed Alain's blood-soaked shirt and began to cleanse the wound. Alexandrine felt nausea rise in her stomach at the sight of the ugly gash.

'I suggest you go back to your room, *madame*. I shall be a while here, and there is nothing you can do,' the Moor said, without looking around at her. He heard her move away with something that sounded to him suspiciously like a sob, and shot a quick glance over his shoulder. A frown masked the black features as he saw she was limping heavily.

As she reeled through the doorway, Francine was at her side, possessively pushing away the servant who rushed forward to help her. She supported her mistress into the sitting-room. She could see at a glance that Alexandrine was near to collapse, and so did not vex her with unnecessary chatter as she guided her into the bedroom, undressed her and helped her into the bath which had been prepared as Alain was settled.

The water had been heavily scented with different oils and, on the instructions of Francine herself, not poured into the porcelain bath until it was cool enough not to scald her mistress's sensitive skin. Even so, she saw Alexandrine wince as she lowered herself into it and immersed aching back and shoulders beneath the pungent water. Gently Francine washed the bruised face, taking great care with the scratched cheek, before lathering her mistress's hair with scented soap, rinsing it several times with fresh water to which had been added lemon oil to restore its lustre.

As Alexandrine emerged to be dried, the maid silently cursed whoever had inflicted the bruises on her mistress's body. She dared not ask what had taken place to bring them about, or why Alexandrine was limping heavily. She remembered the times Paul had summoned herself to his room—and ultimately his bed—and how she had crawled from it hours later, vowing revenge upon the perverted mind which had delighted in causing her pain. She had never told Jules, afraid he would not allow her to remain in the Boussières household under the same roof as a monster. Afraid, too, that he would kill Paul and become a hunted man for the rest of his life. The problem had resolved itself when Paul had been barred from his father's house, and she had been able to sleep in peace at night. Now it reared its ugly head again. If she did not tell Jules the truth, the next time Paul Boussières sent men after her mistress they might succeed in their task, and she would be to blame for not warning Jules of the man's warped mind.

'I am not hurt,' Alexandrine said, sensing her disquiet. 'I think I am more afraid...Monsieur Ratan is so sure Paul sent men to kill me a second time...'

Believe it, Francine thought silently. He is capable of anything. Aloud she pleaded, '*Madame*, do not speak of it now, you are too distraught. Please rest.'

Alexandrine limped slowly into the sitting-room, halting before the pair of pastel-grey doors she now knew would open on to Alain's bedroom.

'How can I, when I do not know how badly he is hurt? There was so much blood. If anything should happen to him because of me...'

She eased herself into a comfortable chair and the maid placed several cushions behind her back until she could lean back and relax, knowing, as she stared down into the pale face, the eyes brimming with unshed tears, that her mistress was in love with the injured man who lay in the adjoining room.

She had suspected since last Christmas, when they had been alone together at the Hôtel Boussières, that they were lovers, a suspicion confirmed by Alexandrine's proximity to their host at Belaincourt, although, to Francine's knowledge, neither had taken advantage of it. Not that it would have been necessary, considering the time they had spent together riding, or at Versailles. Those carriage rides home! Yet her mistress had never, by one word or a look, given any indication that she was being unfaithful to her aged husband.

Francine, with the fatalistic ideas of a romantic and in love herself, did not blame Alexandrine for seeking happiness elsewhere. It was a strange marriage, not yet consummated, even though all was done to pretend otherwise to the house servants and all outsiders, especially at Court. Such a deception must have played greatly on the nerves of the young wife and made her more susceptible to the overwhelming charm of Monsieur le Duc de Belaincourt. And they made such a handsome couple together...

And it was thought by everyone in the house that the Marquis de Mezière was so gravely ill that he could not live more than a few more months. At least her mistress would have someone to comfort her...

'I cannot sit here like this!' Alexandrine ejaculated. 'Go and see what is happening, Francine.'

She sat in an agonised silence until the maid returned.

'Well?' She was gripping the arms of the chair so tightly that her knuckles grew white. 'How is he?'

'Conscious, *madame*—and raising the devil, as no doubt you can hear.' Francine broke off, and loud voices came to them from the other room. 'He told Selim to go to the devil and take his potions with him.'

'What? Why? The man is trying to help him,' Alexandrine gasped. 'Is he feverish?'

'Not he. In full command of his senses is Monsieur le Duc, and raging at Jules because he did not catch the fellow who brought the note to you. I wasn't allowed into the room. Selim told me he would come to you in a moment and then the door was shut in my face, but——' a faint smile touched her sallow features '—I knew you would want to know what was going on, and so I listened outside. The Duc had sent my Jules to follow whoever it was and bring him back. He was furious that he returned alone. His language——'

'And well deserved,' Alexandrine interrupted. She had no sympathy for the man Jules. Had he been vigilant he might have seen her ride away and followed her.

'Not just because Jules did not catch him, *madame*. Fuete, your bodyguard, was murdered to prevent his riding with you. Jules found his body behind the stables. He was a friend. He is as angry as the Duc that the murderer escaped.' She shuddered when she thought how Jules would act when he caught up with the killer. No matter how long it took, she knew he would. Jules would kill again, as he had done in the past. Would that way of life never end for him? What evil star followed them and brought them ill fortune wherever they went? Soon she would visit Solange again. She had to know what the future held for them. And it would do no harm to ask for the Marquise also.

Alexandrine, who had known nothing of the events which had taken place before she left Jeanne's château, sat in a stunned silence. Alain had to be right. Paul was behind the whole thing. She was not safe even at Belaincourt! How easy it would be for him to strike at her at Versailles...but, despite what Jeanne thought, she felt she would be safe at Noyen. The house was not isolated and she was known there. A stranger could not enter the village without her knowing it. There Luc could live in peace and tranquillity until...

She shook her head to remove thoughts of death from her mind and the action caused her to wince visibly. Selim did not miss it as he entered and closed the door after him.

'I did not hear you knock, Selim.' Alexandrine's tone was sharp. She had not forgotten the look in his eyes, nor the question which lay between them. The familiarity which had existed between them vanished with the thought that he might have guessed of her relationship with Alain Ratan.

'I expected you to be resting—if not asleep after your harrowing ordeal. I have brought salve for the mark on your cheek and it will ease the pain of your bruises.' The Moor's eyes narrowed as her fingers gathered the neck of the robe more closely about her. 'You were limping, *madame*.'

'It is nothing. I am just stiff. I fell from my horse...'

'Nevertheless, I think it advisable that I examine you.'

'That will not be necessary,' she answered stiffly. 'How is Monsieur Ratan? The wound looked terrible.'

'He has suffered worse, so he tells me,' came the reply, accompanied by a half-smile. Despite what he suspected about the Duc, and what he had heard of his reputation, Selim respected him as a man. He was no coward. That

had been borne out by the way he had endured attention
to his wound. Although deep, it was clean and would
heal well. He had lost a considerable amount of blood,
but that would be rectified by sleep and the powders
Selim had left with him, which he had refused to take
until he had finished his conversation with Jules. Weak
though he was, Alain would not give way to his pain or
the necessity to rest until he had explored every avenue
of escape for the men remaining at large and found a
way to block it. 'In a day or two, he will be able to get
up. He is not a man to linger in his bed.'

'I shall look in on my husband before I retire,'
Alexandrine declared.

'Why wake him, *madame*? He was not expecting to
see you this evening.' As she opened her mouth to
protest, Selim added gravely, 'He must not be told of
this—at least not now. He must not grow excited. I will
not answer for the consequences if you insist on it. Tell
him at Noyen, *madame*, when it is a shadow in your
memory and you can speak of it calmly.'

'Do you think I shall ever reach Noyen?' Alexandrine's
voice rose sharply. 'Twice Paul has sent men to kill me.
It would be so easy with me dead, would it not? Luc is
so ill. He could return as the dutiful son...' If only they
had some proof of his guilt. But all those who could
have spoken were dead!

'Not while I live, *madame*. Nor will you ever again
be exposed to the diabolical plans of Monsieur Paul,'
Selim said solemnly, and she looked at him long and
hard. Was this a promise of his protection? Why? Despite the easing of the tension between them, especially
since they had come to Belaincourt, she was sure the
Moor did not truly like her—or trust her. No more than
when they had first met.

'Two men have died because of me. Men died who
were guarding Luc the night Monsieur Ratan rescued
him. How many more must die? Is there nothing we can
do against this madman?'

'I could arrange to have him found floating in the Seine,' Selim mused. 'While we are conveniently away at Noyen, of course.'

The suggestion was so outrageous that it took her breath away. But she saw he was serious.

'You will do no such thing!' she gasped, and a low chuckle rose in the man's throat.

'A pity. I would have enjoyed arranging it. If there is nothing else I can do for you, *madame*, I shall return to Luc now. He is progressing well and should be able to travel by the end of the week. Perhaps you would care to see him in the morning.'

'Yes. Please tell him that.'

As the door closed behind the Moor, Francine sucked in her breath.

'That man! He makes me shiver. The way he watches everyone. It is as if he——'

'Can see into your heart—and soul,' Alexandrine supplied. 'I know.'

'He's part devil, of that I'm sure.' The girl said, crossing herself.

'Yes.' Slowly Alexandrine eased herself out of the chair. 'I believe he is.'

Early the following morning Francine flew along the corridors past startled servants, scarcely awake, to fetch Selim. Her mistress was in great pain, she told him and had not been able to sleep a wink all night . . . and she could not move.

Alexandrine lay on her back, her face twisted with agony. Even the slightest movement caused her to cry out.

'Help me to turn her over—and remove her nightgown,' the maid was ordered.

'No!' Alexandrine gasped as hands reached out for her.

'If you do not, you will remain this way, *madame*,' came the quiet answer and, her protest ignored, she was carefully turned on to her stomach and her gown removed.

Cool, confident hands were laid against her burning back. She gasped again and her hands bunched into tight fists.

'Do not be alarmed, Madame la Marquise.' Selim's sardonic tones mocked her indignation at being forced to accept *his* help. 'You have nothing to fear from me. I have owned so many beautiful women in my lifetime that I am not easily aroused by the sight of an unclothed body. Do not fight me—you do not have the strength!' he commanded in an authorative tone, as she lashed backwards at him with a clenched fist and cried out. 'Accept the inevitable. You need my skill. It will not be the last time.'

What was he insinuating? His words both confused and alarmed her. The pain was dulling her senses. She pressed a hand against her mouth, suppressing her groans. He was killing her, not helping her! His hands seemed to know exactly where the pain was. He was enjoying this! Deliberately causing her more discomfort...she could not stand it...

And then, without warning, there was blessed peace. The hands continued to move over her back, along to the base of her spine, upwards to the hollow between her shoulders. Never still. She did not know how long he bent over her, the steady movements never lessening, the pressure easing slightly only now and then.

At last he drew back, and Francine was bending over her, lifting her head to make her drink the contents of the glass against her lips. She did so drowsily, wanting now only to sleep before the pain began again.

'Tomorrow you should remain in bed, *madame*,' Selim advised. 'If you need me again, I shall come at once, but I do not think the problem will occur again. May Allah grant you sleep.'

'Thank you...' The words were scarcely audible and Alexandrine thought he had not heard them, for there was no reply, but as he turned towards the door Francine noticed a satisfied smile spread across the ebony features, and hated him for his smugness.

However, as she turned back to the bedside, all feelings of antagonism disappeared for she found Alexandrine was sound asleep. Her lovely face was relaxed—serene. Perhaps she was dreaming of her lover, the girl thought, as she settled herself in a nearby chair, for what else could bring such a smile to those soft lips?

CHAPTER SEVEN

'You fool!' Claudia de la Fontaine raged as she scowled at the man before her. 'Her—yes! But not Alain.'

She wanted to strike out at the cynical smile masking the pale features, but she restrained herself. Paul had been drinking all day, celebrating his failure, although he did not consider it such. Both Alexandrine and Alain Ratan were, according to a talkative servant at Belaincourt, confined to their beds after a savage attack had been made on them both in the Forest of Sénart. The Duc had been carried unconscious to his bed and Madame la Marquise de Mezière had a back injury which was causing her great pain. And Paul considered that a victory. The man was an idiot, and Claudia was fast losing her belief that he might be able to get Alain back for her.

Her full mouth curled contemptuously as she paced the room, occasionally looking across to where Paul sat, sampling her best brandy. From the very beginning of their relationship, if it could be called that, she thought, even with all she had to offer him, he was still a brute in bed, oblivious to her needs or her feelings. He took her when it pleased him, and she had discovered how unwise it was to refuse him, especially when drink inflamed his vicious temper. Soon—very soon—she would have to find a way to be rid of him. He was becoming an embarrassment to her.

'Calm yourself, my dear Claudia. These rages do not become you. *I* want them both dead!'

'So far you have made two attempts on her life and failed miserably both times. You abducted your father, but could not keep him long enough for him to alter his will in your favour. Is that why you tried to have Alain

158

killed too? Because he interfered in your plans? Rescued the Marquis?'

'You know why I want him dead! She refused me, because they are lovers! Cuckolding my father under his very nose!' Paul cried, slamming his glass down so quickly on the table that the stem broke and wine spilled over the polished surface.

'Look at you! The moment you begin to talk of her you are a fool! A besotted fool!'

'Take care, *madame*.' He was on his feet in an instant, long thin fingers closing over her wrist in a painful grip. 'I am no one's fool. Hers—or yours. You are useful to me, otherwise I would not waste my time with you. What Alain ever saw in you is beyond me. In bed or out, you have nothing to offer a real man.'

'And what would you know about being a man? You, with your penchant for little boys and frightened kitchen maids. I warn you, Paul, if you harm one hair of Alain's head again, you will answer to me. I am not afraid of you, and I have enough money to hire a dozen assassins to deal with you.'

'I am sure you have. What a pity you would not be alive to enjoy the news of my death! You would precede me, my dear, be certain of that. However, I agree with you that, having failed to remove my dear stepmother from this earth, it would be madness to try again—at least so soon. For the moment they shall both live. Now, my father is a different matter. His continuing bad health is most fortunate.'

'If he dies you will never be able to prove he was poisoned,' Claudia returned, pulling herself free from his grasp and retiring well out of reach. 'The Moor who tends him has earned quite a reputation as a learned man. Several of my friends have consulted him about their ailments with the most surprising—and gratifying—results. He will not be easy to accuse.'

'I shall have my witnesses—when the time comes,' Paul assured her, contemplating the fresh glass of brandy he had just poured himself. 'You see, Alexandrine is in the habit of consulting a fortune-teller across the Pont-Neuf.

Well, actually, she has seen the woman only once, when she was with Madame d'Etoiles, but no matter; who will believe one visit only, when I prove she has been given poison to rid herself of her husband?'

'The fortune-teller told you this?'

'No, but she will, when the time is right. She will say anything I want her to say.' The confident smile which spread across his face made Claudia inwardly grimace. She knew how he loved to inflict pain—and, worse, to watch the agony of those at his mercy. An hour alone with Paul Boussières would loosen the most stubborn of tongues. Yet what did it matter to her? It might remove Alexandrine from Alain's life! She was sure they were lovers. Even the Duchesse de Châteauroux, her friend and confidante, had commented on how intimate they were at the château of that little upstart bourgeoise Jeanne d'Etoiles.

The name of the latter was now commented on freely at Court, and Claudia was well aware of the speculation that the Duchesse would soon be toppled from her position of power. If that happened it would not affect her unduly. What was the loss of one powerful friend when there were so many men about who could offer her the same protection? But if Alexandrine remained close to Madame d'Etoiles after she became the King's mistress, and there was every chance of that happening, then Claudia suspected her days at the glittering palace of Versailles would be numbered. Anyone who had snubbed the little bourgeoise and made fun of her, as she did, who had allied herself with Paul Boussières and his cronies, would doubtless be made to feel most unwelcome.

Alain Ratan was all she wanted. She would go to any lengths to have him, save putting her own pretty neck in jeopardy—and that was what Paul Boussières was making her do. She was mad to involve herself with him further. For two days she had not known whether Alain was alive or dead, until her enquiries, made through a trusted servant to one from Belaincourt, at last brought her the news she desired. Two days this excuse for a man who reclined in *her* chairs, drinking *her* brandy and strutting about the house as if he owned it, had made her wait. He had known from the beginning what had happened, but, as usual, he loved to prolong the inevitable. He was a loathsome, degenerate creature and she hated him. She also feared him and what he had threatened to do to her if she crossed him, and knew she must tread carefully in her dealings with him.

'Are you not going to dress?' Paul queried as she rang for a servant and ordered hot water to be brought for washing. 'We shall be late in attendance at Versailles.'

'You will have to make my excuses tonight. I have a headache.'

'A fit of cowardice, don't you mean?' he challenged, rising to his feet. 'You are so transparent, my dear. Go and get ready, and don't keep me waiting too long. We must keep up appearances, must we not?'

'And what have you done to show your abhorrence of the attack on your father's wife? What of Alain?' Claudia retorted. 'He was once your friend. You drank and played cards together, I can even remember your telling me of the visits you used to make together across the river to a certain Madame Lafarge who ran a house of—shall we say?—entertainment. And who used to carry you home when you were drunk? Alain! Who kept you out of trouble when you insulted better men than yourself and found yourself in a fight? Alain!'

'You remember too much!' Paul snapped. 'Never retain memories of the past, Claudia, they can only bring you pain.' The warning was only too clear. 'As to what I have done... Why, I have sent a note of sympathy to them both. And offered my help, if required, to catch the villains who perpetrated the cowardly act.'

'A futile gesture,' she said scathingly, and Paul looked at her almost contemptuously.

'Is there nothing in that head but thoughts of money—and Alain Ratan? Of course it was only a gesture, but one which may prove of some use in the future, if I am ever linked with this incident... or any other. Think of it! Since my foolhardy attempt to kidnap my father—

for which I am wholeheartedly ashamed—I have tried in so many ways to make amends, to do penance and have him accept me back as his son. I have pleaded with him in a dozen letters, most eloquently versed, I can tell you, to see him for a moment only if that is all he will allow me. I have discussed my situation with his friends, asked them on my behalf to aid me in my quest to return to the fold.' If she had not been looking at the smile which masked his features, proclaiming every word he uttered to be a lie, the conviction in his voice would have made Claudia believe. Others would be convinced, she had no doubt of that. They would see a miserable wretch of a man, torn with recrimination for the thing he had tried to do, racked with remorse, desperate to regain his father's favour...

'I am rejected by my own flesh and blood...I am not allowed to see my father even when he is ill. Is it any wonder I begin to believe I am being deliberately kept from him? To believe that someone close to him has some vile purpose in mind by alienating us? And yet, when my stepmother is attacked, do I not send her sympathy? Offer help if she needs it? Do I not plead with her—yet again—to intervene with my father so that I am allowed to visit him?' Paul paused for a long moment to allow his words to sink into her. 'If you could see the look on your face! I'm good, am I not?'

'Yes, very—and frightening.'

'You would do well to remember it when your confused little mind again thinks of me as a fool.' Paul flicked down the lace ruffles about his wrists and perused his appearance in the large gilt-framed mirror over the fireplace. 'I cannot wait for you. I shall go on ahead. By the way—when you are at Belaincourt, use your eyes and find out how many men Alain has brought in to guard his guests.'

Claudia opened her mouth to refute the implication, and then decided otherwise. To see Alain was exactly what had been uppermost in her mind. To reassure herself he was not seriously injured and to try in some way, no matter how small, to regain his favour.

'You *are* going to Belaincourt, are you not?'

'Perhaps,' she murmured.

'Go, but he won't take you back, you know,' Paul taunted from the doorway. 'Not while *she* shares his bed. So you see the necessity for getting rid of her as soon as possible. Make yourself useful while you are there and I might be able to devise something which will be more successful the next time.'

His face impassive, Selim handed the letter back to Alexandrine. She read it again, for the third time, before slowly tearing it into tiny pieces.

'I think that is the wisest thing to do with such—such impertinence, do you not agree? Help me, indeed! Anyone would think that he . . .'

'Was concerned for your well-being. Perhaps that is how he wishes it to appear,' the Moor replied. 'I have sadly underestimated that young man's cunning. The fault is mine. It will not happen again. I should have been prepared for the way his mind would work . . .' He broke off as she looked up at him curiously. 'How is your back this morning, *madame*?'

'You have miracle hands, Selim. I slept like a baby all that night and most of yesterday. Today I shall get out of this bed.'

'May I respectfully suggest you do not over-exert yourself for a day or two? The bruising was considerable.'

Respectfully suggest. Alexandrine's lips deepened into a smile at his words. He had not been so respectful in Alain's rooms that day—or when he had come to her in the early hours of the morning and treated her as if she was one of his harem women!

'Has anything happened? I mean, about the men who attacked me?'

'The Duc still has his men out searching for them, but after the rain last night it will be difficult to find any tracks. Those they did find lead towards Versailles—the village, not the palace. Some tavern, I believe, a local meeting place . . . and the inhabitants were too closemouthed to talk. The offer of a reward for information might loosen a tongue or two.'

'And you have said nothing to my husband?'

'No, nor do I intend to. I think it advisable that you come and see him this afternoon, *madame*. I have told him you were thrown from your horse, which slipped on muddy ground, and have been resting. He knows nothing of the Duc's injury... or of the letters you have both received.'

'Both of us!' Alexandrine was startled by the news. What was Paul up to now?

'The wording of both was similar. Asking if you were both recovering and if you needed his help, which would always be available. Asking for your understanding and compassion, a chance to speak with his father.'

'I would not trust Paul within a mile of Luc,' she retorted. 'Have you made a list, as I asked, of other physicians you consider capable of seeing my husband when we return to the house? The sooner we are safely at Noyen, the happier I shall be.'

'There is none I consider more able than myself, and not one is capable of alleviating his suffering more than I can, but to ease your mind I have done as you asked. I have sent word to certain physicians that upon our arrival back in Paris they will be required to call upon the Marquis.'

'Thank you, Selim. Yes, that does make me feel better.'

'Because now the whole world—or at least the Court—will see that you are doing all you can?' the Moor replied, a mocking edge to his tone.

'If that is the way you wish to look at it, then do so. My only concern is for my husband's welfare.'

'I am pleased to hear it, *madame*. The Duc is also recovering quickly, and wishes me to assure you that he is not in pain,' came the parting shot before the door closed behind him.

'That man grows too sure of himself,' she muttered, frowning at Francine. 'Why is it I suspect all our destinies are in his hands?'

'If they are, God help us,' the girl replied.

Alexandrine marvelled at the lack of pain in her back as she walked in the gardens later that morning. She felt stiff and there were several unpleasantly coloured bruises on her arms and shoulders, which were luckily hidden from view by her gown. The salve Selim had given her for her cheek had greatly reduced the swelling, and she had heeded his advice not to cover the scratch with powder, which he warned would only aggravate the injury and might delay healing. She had grimaced at her reflection, for there was a huge purple bruise just beneath her eye. Thank goodness she would not be returning to Versailles to be stared at like this.

Jeanne's phaeton appeared in the driveway as Alexandrine was returning to the house, and the greeting she received from Jeanne was so affectionate that it brought tears to her eyes.

'*I* should have realised something was wrong sooner! But I had seen you talking with Alain, and when you disappeared...well, I thought perhaps the two of you were going to slip away somewhere! I shall never forgive myself for waiting too long to approach him—a few moments earlier and you might have been spared that hideous brute's trying to rape you.'

'Does everyone have spies at Belaincourt?' Alexandrine asked incredulously.

'Alain told me what had happened. I came to see you yesterday, but your maid told me you were resting and so I did not want to disturb you. But I could not go away without knowing you were all right.'

'Monsieur Ratan was unconscious when we took him upstairs. I am surprised at his swift recovery,' returned Alexandrine, as she ushered her guest into the downstairs drawing-room and rang for hot chocolate to be brought.

'He reminded me rather of a hunting dog on a short leash.' Her companion laughed softly, remembering the scowl on Alain's face when he had received her. 'Ready to snap at the slightest excuse. And he did, when I said I thought he should not have left his bed to greet me. Beds are for people to die in, he said, in that fierce way he has when he is not really angry, but thinks he ought to be. I told him he would probably draw his last breath in the bed of some fascinating woman, and he laughed then and said he hoped the fascinating lady was there with him.'

'He—he told you all that happened, then? That the boy who brought me the message did not come from here, but had been hired to lure me into a trap?' How many times during yesterday had Alexandrine's eyes been drawn to those communicating doors? Once she had even risen from her bed and gathered up her robe, intending to quietly open them and peer through. She had not wanted to be seen, only to be sure he was not more seriously hurt than Selim had told her. But at the last moment her courage had failed her, and she had slipped miserably back between the sheets again. The distance between them, short as it was, had seemed like a thousand miles. But, if the space had once been traversed, there would have been no turning back. She had fallen asleep with his kisses burning her mouth, words whispered in her ear which still puzzled her: 'Do you realise I almost lost you?' *'M'amie'*—my love—even if he had not meant them she did not care!

'Yes, everything. Thank God he rode like the wind. He has not found the men, I know, but he will,' Jeanne said confidently. 'I know it. You say you have not seen him yet?' She cast a speculative look at Alexandrine, and one eyebrow rose when the latter shook her head. 'Are you going to allow me to die of curiosity? I saw the way he looked when he left me to come after you! He killed a man to defend your honour—and your life! I do not believe you are merely friends, even though you insist on calling him *monsieur*—so formal, so polite.'

Not always so formal, Alexandrine thought, as she bent her head over her cup of chocolate, unable to bear Jeanne's searching stare. She had called his name in relief in the forest—Alain! Whispered it in disbelief—Alain! Whispered it against his lips as he kissed her!

'Believe me, there are times when I do not feel polite towards that man,' she declared, and Jeanne gave a tut of disbelief. 'It is true. We—the relationship we share is fraught with antagonism—we argue——'

'And make up?' Jeanne suggested hopefully, and her words brought a smile to Alexandrine's lips.

'Yes, we do that, but there is always another time when we cannot bear to be in each other's company. It will always be that way. It has to be.'

'Because of Luc?'

'Yes.'

'I should not be so tactless as to suggest that your husband's ill health may soon deprive you of his protection. What then? This is exactly what we were discussing the other day, not an hour before you rushed out of the château without a word to anyone and were almost killed. You need a full-time bodyguard, Alexandrine. I believe Alain when he says Paul Boussières was behind it.'

'So do I. You must not blame yourself in any way, Jeanne. I simply did not think. After all Alain's——' she coloured slightly as Jeanne's expression warmed with the familiarity '—warnings, I still acted like an idiot. I cannot stop thinking of the men who have died since Luc married me and brought me to Paris. Where is the happiness Solange promised me?'

'So—you begin to believe, after all this time?'

'I have to believe in something!' Alexandrine cried. 'I am the cause of so much distress and unhappiness.'

'Nonsense. You are being used by an unscrupulous young man who resents the fact that you have taken the place in his father's life he considers rightfully his. You have brought Luc more happiness this past year than his son ever did. All that one gave him was debts and nights of worrying whether he would come home in one piece. Paul has always associated with very strange people.'

'Have I? Just lately I despair of things ever being the same for Luc and me again. I pray Noyen is the answer, but if it is not?' She lifted her shoulders in a shrug of despair, which brought a frown to Jeanne's face. So all was not as well as Alexandrine pretended. How she wished she could bring her friend to open her heart to her, but she could see this was not the time.

She shifted uncomfortably in her chair and Alexandrine quickly rose and brought a cushion to tuck behind her. It was still difficult to believe she was four months pregnant. Her features were, if anything, slightly thinner than a few months ago, and with the enormous panniers she wore beneath her gown there was nothing to give away her secret.

'You really should not be driving alone,' Alexandrine chided.

'I came to give you advice, not receive it,' Jeanne said, helping herself to a piece of vanilla truffle from the plate at her elbow. 'I see you have discovered one of my weaknesses too.'

There was a startled exclamation from the doorway and, looking up, both women found themselves being stared at by Claudia de la Fontaine. To Alexandrine's mind, the woman looked confident in brilliant red satin, a cloak of the same colour thrown about her shoulders. The contrast against her pale skin and the jet-black hair was stunning.

For a moment no one spoke and then Claudia said stiffly, 'I was asked to wait in here...I did not realise the room was occupied.'

'Come in, *madame*, and make yourself comfortable.' Alexandrine hid her dislike of the arrival, remembering she was only a guest at Belaincourt, despite the freedom with which she roamed about the house and the way that the servants granted her every wish without a murmur. 'We are just having some chocolate; would you care for some?'

'No, thank you. I shall not be here long.' Claudia's violet eyes rested on the bruise marking Alexandrine's cheek. She barely managed to conceal the surge of delight which went through her to see her rival so disfigured.

'I avoid such fattening things—tempting though they are to some.' Her gaze flickered to Jeanne, helping herself to another piece of truffle. Neither woman had ac-

knowledged the other, nor would do so. 'I have heard
of your unfortunate accident the other day, *madame*. I
can see you did not escape unscathed, despite Monsieur
Ratan's brave attempt to save you from...whatever it
was that made you take fright so violently that your horse
threw you!'

'Your facts are a little wrong, *madame*, but one comes
to expect that when they are received second-hand from
servants,' Alexandrine replied, with iced politeness. 'I
was set upon by two men who intended to kill me. I am
sure you can draw your own conclusions as to why—
and who might have paid them to undertake such a
venture.' She drove the point home with a smile as she
set her chocolate cup aside. 'But, as you can see, I have
suffered no great injury; no more did Alain. Shall I tell
him you called to enquire after him?'

Claudia's lips tightened visibly at the casual use of the
name, conscious of the smile on Jeanne's face as she
sipped her chocolate...and listened.

'I shall be able to do that for myself, *madame*, in a
moment, as soon as he receives me,' she retorted, and
spun about expectantly as Gaston came down the stairs
and across the hall towards her.

'Monsieur le Duc asks me to convey his regrets,
madame, but he does not feel able to receive visitors at
this moment. He is sure you will understand...after what
happened.'

Understand! Claudia's mouth gaped, and then, realising the two women were still watching her, she forced
a smile to stiff features and slowly turned again in their
direction.

'I shall call again,' she said to Alexandrine. 'Good
day, *madame*.' Jeanne was totally ignored as Claudia
swept to the door. As the sound of her carriage disappeared, being driven at a fast pace which seemed to indicate she was taking out her temper on the unfortunate
driver, Jeanne threw back her head and the room was
filled with the sound of laughter.

'Her face, Alexandrine! Did you see her face? Good
for Alain! He's finished with her once and for all.

Perhaps he has found someone else...' She looked significantly at her companion, but Alexandrine refused to be drawn further on the relationship they shared. She had said more than enough as it was.

He had been well enough to see Jeanne, but not Claudia. The snub had been deliberate. Did he believe she knew about the attack on them, perhaps had even helped Paul when he planned it? No, Alexandrine dismissed that as unacceptable. Claudia would do nothing to harm Alain Ratan—he was too important to her.

'It is time I should leave.' Jeanne began to ease herself from the chair, and then gave a gasp which brought Alexandrine to her side immediately. 'I think perhaps I shall take your very good advice and rest. Do you think you could find me someone to drive me home?'

'Are you in pain? Shall I fetch Selim?'

'No, it is only a warning twinge.' And the fact, Jeanne knew, that she did not eat enough for one at times, let alone two. Why was it that a woman must lose her figure just because she carried new life inside her? She hated the months of confinement, and fought against them. It would have made no difference if the child she carried with her had belonged to the King himself; she still knew she would not want to go through all this again. The endless, tedious waiting, the forcing down of food she did not want, the weeks she could expect afterwards of fighting to regain her figure. 'I promise I shall return to Paris and rest until the time comes. Don't forget to come and see me before you leave for Noyen...and you must write to me every week, and let me know how Luc is.'

'How was Monsieur le Marquis?' Francine asked, as she brushed Alexandrine's hair that evening before she retired. Her mistress had been unusually quiet when she returned from the afternoon visit. She had given instructions that her things were to be packed in readiness for the return to Paris, but had not mentioned her sick husband or when they were to leave.

'Better.' Alexandrine said, with a slight lifting of her shoulders. But was he? He had known her, but he was changing so rapidly before her eyes. So thin now, and how his hands had shaken when they had clutched hers...tightly, almost desperately, as if clinging to her was like clinging to the last threads of life! Yet he had been fully lucid and able to converse with her for over an hour, and some of her fears had dissolved as he had talked to her of Noyen, of all they would do there. She knew he would never live to see his ambitious plans finished, but his interest in the house and the small village brought him pleasure and a new interest with which to fill the hours—the days—the weeks ahead.

She had allowed him to dwell only briefly on her bruised face which he had taken between trembling hands and gently kissed. The gesture had brought a rush of tears to her eyes, and she had made sure to confirm only what Selim had told him and not elaborate further.

'Shall we be returning to Paris soon, *madame*?' Francine could not hold back her questions. Jules was becoming insistent that she leave Alexandrine and married him. There was nothing to stop them now, she accepted. He had a well-paid job and a house waiting for her. How her imagination had run wild when he had first shown her the run-down little cottage! So much to do to make it a real home, but it was more than big enough for the two of them, and when she had the first of their ten children, Jules had told her as they had examined the rooms, he would build more.

Alexandrine looked at her maid's reflection in the mirror as she heard her sigh.

'You are thinking about that young man of yours. Has he asked you to marry him yet?'

'Oh, yes, *madame*. He wants to do things properly,' Francine replied quickly, colour stealing into her cheeks at Alexandrine's probing stare. They still stole the odd moments together in the stables, or wherever a little privacy could be found. Once they had spent a whole afternoon in the cottage, lying in each other's arms, dreaming of the future. Jules had so many ideas, while Francine was content just to be with him. She wanted nothing more than to cook his food, mend his clothes and lie beside him all night long. She knew he wanted more for her... fine clothes and jewels and a carriage of her own. Imagine—her! A nobody from the back alleys of the Left Bank, being so grand.

'And of course you want to marry as soon as possible and set up your own home. I understand. When do you want to leave me?'

'Oh, *madame*—I don't! I wish I could marry Jules and stay with you!' Francine cried. 'You have been so good to me. Perhaps, as Monsieur le Marquis's health is improving, you will not need me when you are at Noyen. There will be other servants... And when you return to Paris——'

'I may never return,' said Alexandrine quietly. 'I think my husband will die at Noyen. Selim is sure he has little life left in him. I pray he will live long enough to enjoy the summer there, but...' She lifted her shoulders in recognition of the inevitable. 'By Christmas I think I shall be alone.'

'No, *madame*, you will not. I shall stay with you. You will need me,' Francine declared, and Alexandrine caught the girl impulsively by the hand and squeezed it gratefully.

'I have accepted what must happen. It must not spoil your happiness. I shall understand if you come to me and say you wish to leave. Remember that.'

'Stay here,' Alain ordered Jules, and the man frowned at the order, wondering what had brought the Duc out at this late hour.

'You may need me, *monsieur*,' he said meaningfully. The look Alain directed at him told him otherwise, and he stepped back to the carriage with a nod. 'As you wish.'

As soon as Alain entered the crowded entrance-rooms at Versailles, his swift pace slackened and became a casual saunter. The grimness vanished from his features as a smiling mask settled into place. Only the pale, glittering green eyes remained the same as they swept the sea of faces around him, and several men who knew him, and had seen that same look in their depths before, did not linger to make more than the usual polite conversation before hurrying away.

'My dear Alain, how good to see you up and about. I heard you were at death's door.' His close neighbour Claude Latour came up to him and clapped him heartily on the shoulder. As pain jolted through his body like wildfire, Alain somehow restrained the urge to knock the man down. 'Isn't the Marquise with you tonight? Too exhausted after her ministrations, eh? Lucky fellow...I wouldn't mind that one taking care of me.'

'I *shall* take care of you, and in a way which will be most unpleasant, if you do not seal that very loud mouth,' Alain snapped, pinpoints of emerald fire freezing more comments on the other man's lips. Without another word, Alain brushed past him and went upstairs to the gaming-rooms.

The Mercury Salon was full, as usual, and he paused only momentarily to acknowledge people who wanted to detain him. He was in no mood for conversation. That was not why he had come. His searching gaze found what he wanted. Claudia de la Fontaine was watching a game of picquet, surrounded by fawning admirers. She had come straight to Versailles from Belaincourt, he saw, for she still wore the same brilliantly red dress which attracted many eyes—as did the magnificent necklace of lapis-lazuli she now wore at her throat.

Alain felt the anger mounting inside him as he saw it. Here was the proof he had come seeking. He had been prepared to throttle it out of her if she would not willingly tell him what he wanted to know, but now force would not be necessary. The necklace linked her to Paul—who else would have given it to her? Linked Paul to the men who had attacked Alexandrine and tried to kill her. Linked them both to murder and robbery.

He had stood in the upstairs window to watch her leave after Gaston had delivered his message, and had seen the anger on the lovely face as she looked back at the house before climbing into the carriage. She had not been wearing the necklace then, and Alain concluded it could only have been because she knew Alexandrine would instantly recognise it as hers. Then had she known in the beginning where it came from?

He remembered the bruise on Alexandrine's cheek, the pain she had endured because of the attack made on her, and he recalled the sight of her half-naked and helpless beneath the man he had killed—and his hands clenched into tight fists. So great was the emotion that surged through him that he was forced to turn away and compose himself.

Henri, Duc de Blas, left one of the tables and came across the room, a hand outstretched to where he stood. Alain took it and shook it warmly. A firm grip. He liked that. He liked young Henri too, and did not move away as he might have done had it been anyone else.

'I heard you were hurt! Set upon in the forest by a dozen men.'

'There were two only,' Alain returned, with a tight smile. 'And, as you can see, I am in perfect health. Well, a little sore...but not dying, I assure you.'

'I'm glad to hear it.' His companion's relief was genuine. He began to reach into his pocket. 'I've been lucky tonight. I can repay some of the money I owe you.'

'Another time,' Alain interrupted. 'Take your good luck and go home before it turns sour on you. We can settle what is between us over supper some time.'

'It's something I must settle with you, Alain. If you were to go with the King and be killed, with me owing you so much, I would feel terrible,' de Blas insisted, and Alain frowned in puzzlement. 'Have you not heard? Well, it isn't confirmed yet, but the whole Court thinks the King is going to take himself off to join the army at Lille. Things have been going so badly he has been talking of new campaigns, before the winter sets in.'

'No, I had not heard.' It was like Louis, he thought, wanting to be where the action was. How life at Versailles must bore him. Perhaps that was why he needed to surround himself with beautiful, distracting women. But there would be times, he knew, when even they could not fill the gap in his life, the need to be a man, not just a King.

'Will you go—if it is true? You have a cavalry company at Lille, haven't you?'

Alain nodded. It would solve the problem looming up before him, he acknowledged, prevent him from walking headlong into the spider's web which would entrap him. But did he want to be saved? Could he abandon Alexandrine to whatever fate Paul Boussières had in store for her without a qualm? Leave Luc in the hands of the woman he was afraid to trust, yet could not keep away from? He should leave them to lead their own lives, but he would not. If it was in his power to prevent such incidents as had occurred twice before then he knew he must stay and do so.

'Perhaps.' He was non-committal, but his mind was already made up and his reasons, no matter how hard he tried to disguise them, were totally selfish!

'Lucky devil, at least you are free to do as you please,' Henri said, with a rueful smile, thinking how his wife would react if he suddenly announced he was going off to the war.

'I shall be the one sleeping alone tonight,' Alain replied, thinking of the unobtainable in the next room at Belaincourt, so close there were times when he could have sworn he could hear her breathing. How many times had he been tempted to open that door and go to her, make love to her and erase the dream from his heart? That was all she was—a dream, a myth which was distorted in his mind. She was not perfection; she was as full of flaws as the next woman, and as deceitful and scheming. If he destroyed the illusion which haunted him, then his mind could rest and he could look elsewhere for the company he had denied himself since knowing her. He moved towards the picquet table.

Claudia knew his touch instantly, but she did not turn at once to look up at him. She still smarted from the humiliation of knowing Alexandrine and Jeanne had been witnesses to his refusal to see her. Yet she hesitated for a moment only, lest he take offence and move away.

'Alain.' He took the hand she raised and touched her fingers to his lips in a slow, lingering caress that brought a smile of satisfaction to her lips. Perhaps he had been indisposed after all, although to look at him no one

would know, she thought as she turned and allowed him
to lead her away from the table. Curious eyes followed
their progress across the room, and her moment of
triumph intensified. Paul thought Alain did not want
her back, yet here he was seeking her out again, leading
her away from those watchful eyes and the whispers. He
was hers again! And everyone could see it. 'I thought
you were still angry with me—sending me away when I
had made the journey to see you.'

'Your solicitude touches me, Claudia.' They slipped
away and out through a side door to where the night air
was sweet with the perfume of orange blossom. She
pressed as close to him as the panniers of her gown would
allow, needing to have the long weeks of separation wiped
from her mind by the feel of his arms about her, the
firm mouth on hers, claiming what she would never be
able to deny him again.

'Alain, how strange you sound…almost angry…' She
laughed softly, tucking her arm through his, drawing him
towards the Parterres du Nord, so that the darkness hid
them from anyone coming out through the doors after
them. 'You have not yet forgiven me my terrible behaviour that day before Christmas. I was rude, I admit
it. I should never have come down and interrupted you
with the Marquise—but I was jealous. There, now you
know my dark secret. I shall always be jealous where
you are concerned. Tell me everything is the same as it
was between us. I shall ask no more of you than you
gave me before. I will take less…I cannot bear not to
be with you…'

The longing in her swept away all pride, all reserves
of dignity, and she flung her arms around him, lifting
her face pleadingly to his. 'I want you…only you.'

'And Paul Boussières?' Alain asked. He turned her
so that her back was against one of the statues, her body
imprisoned tightly against his. He heard her sigh as his
fingers cupped her breast, his mouth took hers and she
surrendered unrestrainedly to the wanton desire in her.

'He means nothing to me...I wanted to hurt you,' Claudia whispered, trembling as he laid his lips against her bare flesh. 'Oh, how I've missed you.'

When their relationship had first begun, Alain had found it satisfactory without placing any great demands on him, which was the way he had wanted it to be. Never again would he be bound by any chains! But after a while her possessiveness had begun to annoy him, and there were angry scenes, bitter and recriminating. He had always walked away from them. She had always come after him, and they had resumed as before, sometimes for several months before her jealousy rose up to repeat the incident. There was never more than one woman at a time in his life and Claudia knew it, but she wanted more than they had agreed upon in the beginning... She wanted to be mistress of Belaincourt, and he had sworn that no woman, after his mother died, would ever rule there again. No woman would ever bear his name as Nicolette had done. He would take a mistress when it pleased him, he had told her, as half the men in France did...but all she would ever have from him would be his body.

'At least you could have taken a man to your bed...not that young upstart.'

Her breath was ragged in his ears, her long nails digging into his back.

'I have a man now—the only man I want. Take me somewhere away from here, Alain. I am dying for want of you,' she begged.

'If we leave here, my dear, the only place I shall take you will be the Seine, and there I shall throw you in and watch you drown.'

For a moment his words did not register, and then she tried to draw back, startled by the harshness of his tone. It was too dark to see his face, but she knew something was horribly wrong by the way he held her fast against him. She could not move, and when she tried to speak his mouth silenced her—with bruising kisses that made her legs grow weak with longing, but instilled panic in her heart. What did he know? Whom had he spoken to?

He *could* not connect her with the attack on Alexandrine—why should he?

'Alain, have you been drinking? Why don't we leave and go somewhere quiet and secluded...I promise you will not be wasting your time.'

'Are you so anxious to die?' Alain's words chilled her. 'I am quite serious, Claudia...At this moment I would like very much to kill you—and Paul Boussières alongside you. Life is cheap to you both, isn't it? So cheap that you consider everyone expendable. Like the men you sent to kill the Marquise the other day, and before that the one who came to Belaincourt, the night of the ball, with murder in his mind. Two men dead, and that's not counting those I killed when I rescued Luc from the clutches of his crazy son!'

'Yes...yes, he is mad...he swore to kill me too if I didn't help him!' Claudia cried out, as his fingers numbed her wrists with an agonising grip and, too late, she realised she had betrayed herself. Her lips clamped shut as Alain drew back and shook her so hard she thought her neck would break.

'Go on...tell me more. I want to know where he finds these men. Particularly the one who escaped me that day and reported back to him that the Marquise was dead. It must have been a shock to discover otherwise.'

'He'll try again and again until he has what he wants,' Claudia whispered. 'Her dead—and his hands on his father's money. From what I hear it shouldn't be too long before the old man is dead, and then she will have everything. A simple accident will make Paul...very rich. You must do something about him, Alain. He frightens me.' As Alain frightened her. She could not see his anger, but she felt it radiating from him and sought desperately to wriggle out of the situation into which she had allowed herself to be manoeuvred. She had only herself to blame for letting Paul Boussières use her. The whole scheme had badly misfired, and now she was about to lose the only thing that meant anything to her.

'I intend to, but not until his father is dead. Luc is my friend and I'll not bring him more pain by taking the life of his son—even if he does deserve it. But when he is gone... Tell him that, Claudia. Tell him that, as soon as his father is laid to rest I shall call him out and kill him.'

'And return to the comforting arms of the grateful widow!' she flung back, and felt him stiffen. 'I thought you would tire of her... what can she offer you that I can't? A country wench accustomed to rolling in the hay with the local boys... is that the experience she brought to you? Your tastes are changing, Alain; you always used to be so particular.'

'They must have deteriorated the day I met you,' Alain said, disgust enveloping him at her total lack of control. She would say anything to extricate herself from trouble, malign anyone who came to mind if it shifted his anger from her to them. 'Don't forget to give Paul my message.'

'If I do he'll send someone after you, I know it.'

'Then that luckless person will die—as the others he used as would-be assassins. I intend to stay alive, my dear—to see the look on his face before I kill him.'

'Take me back—on your terms. I'll do anything if it can be as it was between us.' Claudia balked at the idea of conveying such a message to her new lover. But, if she did not, she felt sure Alain would ensure it reached Paul another way.

'I don't want you, Claudia. Now or ever again. If you show your face at Belaincourt I shall have you run off like the slut you are.' Before she knew what he was about he had plucked the necklace from her throat. She cried out, and tried to grab it back, but her hands were knocked aside. 'This, by the way, was taken from the Marquise by the men sent to kill her. Did you know where it had come from? Whose neck it had adorned—and more attractively, too—before Paul gave it to you?'

Claudia choked on an answer. Paul had produced it from beneath his pillow after they had made love this morning, and fastened it about her neck as she lay in bed, wondering it if had been won across the table at Versailles. It was vaguely familiar... only now did she realise it must have been Alexandrine she had seen wearing it some weeks before. He had dared... How he must have laughed at the pleasure his gift had given her. Money or jewels always pleased Claudia. She had almost ruined her husband with her extravagance. Luckily he had died before the money totally ran out, and she had sold most of his property in the country for a sum which gave her a very comfortable and elegant living at Versailles. And, of course, there were always other men who paid handsomely for the favours she bestowed on them.

She sagged back against the wall, drained of strength, as she contemplated her dilemma. She was involved in murder and theft—but if she even hinted to Paul that she wanted no more of his schemes... She shuddered, unable to contemplate his reaction. She would get rid of him as soon as possible. There were several men she could think of who would be willing to kill for her, but the choice must be made with extreme caution. She did not want to use one she could not afterwards wind around her little finger. She did not want to replace one Paul Boussières with another equally—or more—unpredictable! Or she could marry again and have the protection of a husband. No! That was too drastic a measure even to be considered. She liked her freedom too much. Perhaps her friend the Duchesse de Châteauroux could suggest something more subtle.

'You are going back—to her!' she accused, as Alain stepped back and she sensed, rather than saw, the smile which spread across his face at her chagrin, her helplessness to prevent his going to another woman—her rival.

'Am I?'

'She will not have you for long,' Claudia vowed, as he turned and the darkness swallowed him up. 'If I can't have you, Alain Ratan, neither will she!'

CHAPTER EIGHT

ALEXANDRINE was still awake when Alain's carriage
brought him back to Belaincourt. She had retired a little
after ten o'clock and become engrossed in a book of
light verse which Jeanne had left with her, written by
the plump, rosy-cheeked Abbé Pierre de Bernis, whom
she had met at the Hôtel de Gesvres where Jeanne's
soirées were usually held.

She had dismissed Francine, knowing the girl would
go directly to the cottage where Jules now slept at night
and spend several hours with him before returning to
the small ante-room which adjoined Alexandrine's
sitting-room. She would be sorry to see the girl leave her
service. There was so little difference in their ages that
she thought of her more as a friend and confidante these
days instead of a servant. But she knew she must not
allow her own feelings to enter into it if Francine wanted
to be married. Although in Alexandrine's eyes Jules was
in no way a reformed character, and she could never
think of him as becoming a model husband, for
Francine's sake she sincerely hoped he had put his old
ways behind him.

Suddenly she heard the door open, and saw a figure
shadowed behind the candle he held, looking across to
where she lay, frozen in surprise. There was a flurry of
bedclothes as she pulled them high about her unprotected shoulders before Alain advanced to the bed and
dropped something on to the cover at her fingertips.

'Do not look so alarmed, Alexa—such a show of
modesty between us is a little unnecessary, don't you
think?' he drawled wickedly. 'I am merely returning an
item of your property that was stolen from you.'

She gazed wide-eyed at the lapis-lazuli necklace, the
blue stones glinting up at her dully in the candlelight.

She had thought never to see it again. But even as questions came flooding into her mind and she managed at last to stammer, 'How? Who...?' Alain turned and left her. The sound of the door of the bedroom closing after him brought her upright in the bed.

How long she sat clutching the cold, hard stones in the palm of her hand she did not know. He had come into her room as if it was his right, had returned to her an item that had been stolen from her that day in the forest by the one man who had escaped his wrath, and then had left again without a word of explanation. Where had he found it? Who had it been passed to? Did he think she did not want to know?

Pushing her feet into the pair of leather slippers beside the bed, she pulled on an over-robe and hurried to the communicating door. As she pushed it open she realised it had not been closed properly. Was he expecting her to follow him? She hesitated for a moment only, until the need to have her curiosity satisfied outweighed the foolishness of stepping into his bedroom.

Alain stood beside the bed with his back to her, easing himself awkwardly out of his dark beige velvet coat. At the startled gasp which escaped her lips, he came wheeling about, his eyes narrowing in disbelief. At the same time the breath caught unexpectedly in his throat at the sight of her, framed in the soft, golden glow of the candlelight, which turned her hair to the colour of ripe corn and emphasised the blue flecks of the hazel eyes which were wide with alarm.

'You are bleeding again.' Hesitantly she took a step towards him. He saw she still clutched the necklace tightly in one hand. 'Let me call Selim—or Gaston.'

'No!' His authoritative tone stopped her hand from pulling on the bell rope to summon help. 'I would prefer your touch to that of the Moor. Gentle he is not—and Gaston fusses over me like a mother hen. I'm not an invalid, Alexa. Nor am I helpless—except that it's a damned awkward place to reach by myself. Am I not deserving of your help?' he chided, as she stood thunderstruck by the audacity of the suggestion.

'If you are implying I should be grateful for what you have just returned to me, yes, I am—and for that reason alone I will do as you ask.'

'There are clean towels and bandages on the wash-stand.' He indicated a marble-topped stand to her left. 'And clean water, I hope.'

She inspected it and nodded. Alain stripped off his shirt, unabashed at the slow colour rising in her cheeks, the way her eyes avoided his as she brought a basin of water and towels and set them down on the bedside table.

'I suggest you close the door. A wise precaution, don't you agree? Although I am not expecting any other visitors.'

'Were you expecting me?' she asked, as she complied with his wishes.

'Hoping, perhaps—not expecting,' came the candid reply, which did little to ease the fluttering feeling in her stomach as she began to clean the wound on his shoulder. His skin was smooth, dark brown beneath her fingers, muscles tensing as he experienced a moment of pain. 'You surprise me at times, with the unexpected. That's what makes our relationship more interesting. I dislike predictable women—and unfortunately most are.'

'We do not have...a relationship. We spent one— very short—night together, for which I am totally to blame for not screaming for help and having you thrown out of the house!' Alexandrine flared, determined to conquer the effect he was having on her. His hands moved upwards to rest lightly each side of her hips, burning her skin through the thin material of her robe. She glared at him, but he did not take them away.

'Do you think I would have allowed that?' Alain mocked, watching the embarrassed glow in her cheeks deepen to a still rosier hue. She had not changed in any way since they had met, he realised. Her skin was still petal-soft and unadorned, its natural beauty not hidden beneath layers of rouge and powders, and he had never seen her wearing any of the ridiculous black patches that were now favoured at Court. For important occasions she complied with Court etiquette and powdered her hair, but he preferred her hair as it was now, softly curling about her ears and neck...as fine as duck's down.

'Stop looking at me like that,' she said, fastening the last piece of bandage into place about his shoulder. He flexed it, and nodded approval of her skill. The intense gaze of his pale eyes was making her knees grow weak. What was she doing here in his bedroom, caring for him like a loving, dutiful wife? 'I know what you are thinking. Stop it!'

'Of course you know. It is the way I often think of you. Dripping wet, like Venus arising from the waves...and lips as sweet as nectar from the gods.'

'Oh, you are impossible!' His mood confused her. 'I shall leave.'

'Don't you want to hear where I found your necklace?' Alain murmured, relaxing back on to the bed, his arms folded behind his head in a casual pose that added to her growing agitation. He was making her feel as if it was quite natural for them to be together like this—as if she belonged in his room, at his side. She fought to control the conflicting images which flashed through her mind as she looked at him. Love and hate—which was it now? How could it be anything other than love which welled inside her at this moment, blinding her to who and what she was, to what he was, and to what could very well happen between them if she were not strong enough to deny what was in her heart? Of course she wanted to hear where he had been and who he had seen, and he knew it. Yet his manner was pleasant, almost indulging, not at all smug as she might have expected. 'Come and sit down.'

She did so, pulling her robe about her and ignoring the gleam which sprang to his eyes. Without warning he sat up, removed her hands to her lap, drew open the robe so that it rested about her shoulders and revealed the flimsy, aurelia-golden nightgown beneath. Without a word he brought the candle closer on the table so that the light fell full upon her.

'I have more beauty with me here than in all of Versailles,' he said, and Alexandrine dissolved into helpless laughter.

'Alain, you are impossible,' she repeated, barely able to contain her mirth. He had sounded so serious. Did he expect her to believe such flowery compliments, to be swayed by the mood of the moment? She was closer to it than he would ever know. To be able to laugh eased the tension tightening inside her. 'You have a different face for different people, do you not?'

'Do I?' He resumed his casual attitude, eyes closing slightly as they considered her.

'I think so, and I know why. That way no one ever gets to really know you. Aloof—untouchable—enigmatic—and never vulnerable. That's what you really fear—to be vulnerable. To discover perhaps that you still have a heart.' Did you really kill your wife? Alexandrine had to bite her tongue to stop the words from slipping out. A man of deep passions would love violently, harbour grudges, yearn for vengeance if his trust, his love was betrayed. Was he such a man? She believed so.

'You are about to spoil a magic moment with questions that should not be asked,' Alain said quietly, shaken by her perception. Her very accurate perception. Had anyone told her about the way his wife had died? Although it was common knowledge at Court, few cared to revive the memory of those unfortunate weeks that had scarred him for life, in the fear that their talk would reach his ears and they would be called to account for their loose tongues.

'No—you are,' she retorted. Her fingers began to reach for the robe to cover herself, then, as one dark eyebrow rose sardonically, she allowed them to drop back into her lap. 'Unless you tell me what I am dying to know, I shall go back to my room this instant.'

'And, if I do, will you stay?' Alain asked.

'No. Of course not.'

'Very well,' he said quickly, as she began to rise. 'Claudia had possession of the necklace. I suspect she came here today to discover how much I knew—or suspected—about her involvement in all this.'

'Perhaps she came because she cares,' Alexandrine murmured. 'I think she really does.'

'Claudia puts her own needs first. If anything, I come a bad second. She isn't important, anyway.' She inwardly winced at the way he dismissed the other woman. If Claudia honestly loved him, his cruel abandonment of her could turn that into a deep, searing hatred...to be used against him. Paul would feed on that kind of loathing. She sensed he possessed the same hatred for his father and for her.

'Paul gave it to her, of course,' Alain went on. 'What a twisted mind that young man has. He must have known one of us would recognise it. Perhaps he hoped it would be Luc, who would probably have been foolish—and proud—enough to call his own son out. Either that, or Claudia would have provided someone to staunchly defend her honour. Luc would have been killed...' Alain lifted his shoulders meaningly. 'That would leave only you...and you will forgive me when I say you are an easy target, Alexa. You seem heedless of the dangers which surround you. Did I not warn you never to ride alone? Yet you left the château—alone, without your bodyguard.'

'The poor man was dead,' she cried.

'Yes, he was, but you did not know that. You did not look for him, did you?' Mutely she shook her head, accepting his reprimand. What had happened in the forest she had brought on herself—and had almost cost Alain his life, too.

'We shall be safe at Noyen. If you think we need men to protect us there, then please find them for us. Nothing must spoil the peace Luc will have there. He has to rest...' She broke off, suddenly overcome with the realisation of what would soon take place. She thought she had accepted it as an inevitable fact, but the closer it came to the moment... Alain frowned at her, leaned forward to tilt up her chin.

'When do you leave? You shall have all the men you need.'

'As soon as the doctors have examined Luc. Possibly the first week in June. We shall spend the summer there, and . . .' She could not go on.

'And return to Paris glowing with health and vitality! Maybe even *enceinte* if Luc's health improves?' Alain suggested, without knowing why the idea had suddenly sprung to mind. Luc adored her, yet there was no sign of a child, and according to the gossip from the Hôtel Boussières the mistress always slept alone. It seemed incredible that he should not be trying to beget a son and heir. It was what every man wanted. It was what Alain had wanted, that first year of his marriage. Now he knew that if he ever took another wife it would be for that reason alone—and she would be as ugly as sin. As Alexandrine paled and her eyes failed to meet his, he asked curiously, 'Just how long has it been since Luc came to your bed, Alexa?'

'You have no right to ask that!' she gasped indignantly. She realised his hands had slipped beneath her robe . . . the thumbs were pressing upwards into her soft flesh . . . teasing the nipples through the silk. The sensation which engulfed her made her feel giddy with pleasure, induced in her a longing to sink against him, confess everything.

'How long, Alexa?' Alain drew her carefully towards him. Nor did she resist or try to pull away, although he felt her body grow rigid against his. 'Weeks? No, I suspect months. You ache to be touched—I can feel it in you.' He slid the robe from her shoulders and tossed it to the floor. Gentle hands cupped, squeezed her breasts. Searching kisses took her mouth by storm and held her poised above the dark abyss of surrender, the chasm which would swallow her up and never again let her go . . . if she . . .

'No, Alain,' she moaned, as the touch of silk scalded her from shoulder to waist, abandoning her body to his caresses. 'We—must not! It is impossible. Please do not do this to me again. I cannot fight you!'

The ring of sincerity—of desperation—in her voice might have halted him had he not already been inflamed by his own desire to have her again. She was almost his, and then it would be over... In the same moment as that thought was with him, there was another, one he refused to acknowledge and dismissed instantly from his mind. What was he seeking to prove? Was he not lying to himself? Was not this overwhelming commitment to protect her only an excuse to hide what he feared had happened to him for a second time? He was vulnerable—more vulnerable than he had ever been in his life before. The realisation was shattering!

'Nothing is impossible,' he whispered against her hair. The nagging voice within him was silenced as he pressed her down upon the coverlet, raining more kisses on her face and shoulders, down over the rounded breasts to the flat stomach. Why no child? the voice returned to ask, and again he brutally squashed it. She was his. No matter what his reasons, he could not let her walk away from him again. 'You say you don't like me, but you want me, Alexa. Need me. I do not trust you—believe in you—but I want you! Need you! You cannot deny what is between us.'

'No.' For a moment he did not believe he had heard the almost inaudible word that announced her total surrender. He drew back slightly, and looked down into eyes brimming with tears, a mouth trembling from his kisses.

'At last we are honest with each other. I knew we would be one day.' She lay in silence as he stripped off his clothes and then gathered her in his arms again, his weight pressing her deep into the feather mattress. 'The months you are away at Noyen will be long and tedious for me, but when you come back to Paris I shall be here. We shall be together again.'

Noyen! Paris! Alexandrine closed her eyes as he began to make love to her. She could think of neither at this moment. Perhaps she would not return from the country... how did she know he would be waiting for her? He cared no more for her than he did for Claudia de la Fontaine. But it did not matter. They were all that mattered until the morning. Then perhaps she would be able to think clearly again...

She awoke with the warmth of the sun on her face. The curtains had not been closed, and the room was full of brilliant yellow light that made her eyes ache until they became accustomed to it. As they did, the realisation came to her that she was not in her own room. She turned her head upon the pillow—and found Alain's dark features close to hers, the harsh lines she sometimes saw about the mouth and eyes now erased as he lay relaxed, at peace in sleep. Her nightgown lay on the floor, half covering her slippers. A few feet away was the robe. Two golden spots of colour made almost transparent as they lay bathed in the sun's rays.

She had to return to her own rooms. If someone came... Her hand began to push away the covers, and was instantly caught up in lean brown fingers.

'Where do you think you are going? It is early.'

'*You* were not tempted to linger, if I remember,' she replied, suddenly ill-at-ease beneath the gaze of his green eyes. They devoured her as they had done last night. They aroused her, as did the hands that reached out and drew her against the hard, masculine length of his body.

'I had my reasons, which are of no importance just now. One day perhaps I will unburden my soul to you, but not now, dammit!'

'Let me go, Alain, before we are discovered,' she protested.

'So it's different now, in the light of day, is it?' The lazy smile which played around his lips contrasted with the angry glint which sprang to his eyes. 'You've had what you wanted and now you will leave, is that it?'

'You did!' she flung back, not understanding the change in him. Why was he being deliberately provocative when each moment heightened the danger of them being found together? 'Why are we arguing? It is nothing that can be continued between us here and now—perhaps it never will be,' she added quickly. 'Who knows what the future holds for either of us?'

'Perhaps you should consult your friend on the Left Bank. Solange, isn't it? The fortune-teller.'

'How do you know her name?' Alexandrine asked, taken aback.

'Jeanne must have told me,' Alain returned with a shrug, but even as the words left his mouth he remembered it had not been her, but Paul. And how the devil had *he* known?

'Then she must also have told you I don't believe in her silly predictions. Let me go, Alain. Please,' she begged, as he laid his lips against a bare shoulder, and then began to move them in the direction of her breast. She was pulled down beneath him, dominated—her own knowledge being limited—by the skill of his love-making. Tiny cries were torn from her lips as he subjected her to that skill against which she was a helpless child, and which, when he drew away from her, left her lying weak and dazed beside him.

'Now you can go, Alexa—if you still want to.' She did not know he had been as ruthless with himself as with her, deliberately holding back from that final culmination until his senses swam and it descended upon them both like some devouring beast. And yet, as he watched her climb slowly from the bed and pull on her robe, he knew he would want her again before the day was out. Nothing had changed...

'Alexa, forgive me...I didn't mean to be selfishly cruel...sometimes I can't help it...when I remember...' He broke off as she turned and looked at him. She had given him so much pleasure, and now she stared at him like a lost waif, seeking guidance. What did she want from him? He had nothing to give. 'Don't ask more from me. I am what I am...accept that. I have experienced how love becomes twisted in a man's mind until he wants to kill the very thing he loves—adores with every breath in his body. It has happened to me once; I will not allow it to happen again.'

Alexandrine's hands trembled as they reached for her slippers. He stretched out a hand to her, but she ignored

it. The questioning looks she threw him were more elo-
quent than any words, and his lips tightened.

'Don't anger me...not you, too!'

'Until you want to kill the very thing you adore...'
she breathed. 'Your words. It is true, then!'

'What is true?' He prayed she would not ask, and
knew she must.

'That—that you killed her! Murdered your wife! Took
her life because she would not return to you...'

As he started up in the bed and the bedclothes were
thrown aside, she turned and ran into her sitting-room,
flinging the door closed behind her. He had been so
afraid she would want to know...and he had not denied
the accusation! He was guilty! A murderer! She felt sick
with shame and guilt that she loved such a man, yet at
the same time was seized with a mad impulse to return
to him, cradle him in her arms and tell him she believed
otherwise. Yes, he was capable of it, but he had been
driven to it by the treachery of his beautiful wife...

Excuses...she loved him enough to find a thousand
of them...

'Are you not feeling well, *madame*?' Selim's voice enquired, and the room swam giddily out of focus for a
moment before she raised horrified eyes to the black face
which confronted her. He had been waiting for her...and
behind him, her wide eyes proclaiming the distress she
felt at not being able to warn her mistress, stood
Francine. She had returned at around two in the morning
and, seeing the empty bed, had accurately guessed where
Alexandrine had gone. The soft murmur of voices, the
sounds of love-making from the room beyond had confirmed it. She had curled up on a chair to await her
mistress's return, pleased that the communicating door
had come into its own at last.

Selim's arrival had sent her into a panic. He too had
seen the empty bed before she could close the door. And,
when he had questioned her, his fierce manner had
brought the answers spilling from her lips—when all her
instincts had been to lie in the hope of protecting her
beloved mistress.

'What do you want, Selim?' Alexandrine stepped past him, gathering her robe together at the neck, fighting against the terrible fear which gripped her. He knew! She could read it in his eyes. He would tell Luc!

'I have been waiting to give you a message, *madame*. This past half-hour,' came the stony reply.

Her cheeks blanched. So long! He could have overheard her conversation with Alain . . . worse still . . .

'Very well. Deliver it, and please go. I wish to bathe.'

'You have had an unsettled night, *madame*?' the Moor enquired, moving in front of her so that he could look full into her face. Her guilt was there for all to see. She had been with Alain Ratan as he suspected. And it was not the first time. How frail these women were. In his own country she would have been stoned as an adulteress—as his own wife would be when he returned home and pronounced sentence on her for her treachery. Here, in this licentious country of France, of what importance were one or two lovers?

But was this not what Luc had hoped for—planned for? He did not condone her actions, but neither could he stand in judgement knowing how cleverly they had both been manoeuvered into this very precarious position. Selim even experienced a rare moment of compassion for the way they had been manipulated.

'No. Why should you think that?'

'Alexa, I shall not allow us to part this way. We must talk——' The doors behind her were flung open and Alain stood there, further words failing him as he stared into the ebony face of the Moor. 'I'm sorry. I did not know you were engaged.' The way he recovered his composure was admirable, Alexandrine thought. Hardly a pause elapsed before a smile crossed the suntanned features and he was inclining his head in Selim's direction. 'I shall come back later when you are free.'

'My business will take but a moment,' came the unemotional reply. 'As you are both here it will save me delivering the message separately. The Marquis wishes to return to Paris today.'

'My husband is well enough to travel?' Alexandrine's mind reeled at his words. Why the urgency? Had something happened in Paris he had not told her about? Instantly Paul came to mind.

Selim's gaze rebuked her in silence for daring to ask after the health of her husband when she had just come from the bed of another man.

'Tell my husband I am ready to leave at his convenience.' She forced the words through stiff lips. 'Francine, come and help me. We must waste no time,' she ordered, turning away, and the maid followed her into the bedroom.

'No, Monsieur le Duc, that would not be wise.' Selim blocked Alain's way as he began to follow. The two men measured each other in silence, the Moor's face expressionless, Alain's tight with anger.

'No man gives me orders in my own home. Stand aside or——'

'Or—what?' Large hands came out of the wide sleeves of the Moor's robes and hung by his sides. A challenge? Or a warning? 'I have no quarrel with you, Monsieur le Duc. Leave her alone. You do not know the hornets' nest into which you would place your hand.'

'Save your riddles for Luc; he is probably the only one who understands them,' Alain snapped, wondering which part of this man's huge frame would not break his fist if he struck out.

'Then I shall say it more plainly. Do not see the Marquise again. I shall go further. You *will not* see the Marquise alone again.'

'And who will stop me? You, my black friend?'

'I am not your friend at this moment. In some future time—perhaps. That will depend on whether or not you heed my...'

'Threat?' Alain challenged. The man could crush him with one hand, he suspected, and he was in no condition to put up much of a fight with his shoulder not fully healed. But to back down and do nothing... The ghost of a smile flitted across Selim's face as indecision raged inside the man who faced him.

'Let us call it friendly advice. The Marquis will never know what is between you if it ends now.'

'If you breathe one word, I shall be forced to kill you!'

'I do not doubt you would attempt to take my life. I underestimate neither your courage nor the extent of your friendship with Luc. Despite *this*, I still believe you are the only true friend, apart from myself, that he has ever had. I have not forgotten that you saved his life.'

'Then why do we stand here at each other's throats?' Alain demanded in puzzlement.

'Because the situation as it is cannot—will not—continue. I shall not allow it. Until he is dead, Madame la Marquise will not be alone with you—or indeed meet you for any purpose other than those which would ordinarily bring you together at the Hôtel Boussières—or at Versailles. After that, she may take a dozen lovers, for all I care. There is no more to be said, *monsieur*. Either you accept my advice—or the consequences of their rejection.' Selim bowed shortly, and left Alain standing in the middle of the room, lost for words.

Never, in all his twenty-nine years, could he remember encountering such a man. He was both annoyed at his impertinence—the astounding arrogance that decreed how he, Alain Ratan, Duc de Belaincourt, should live his life—and seized with a desire to laugh at the whole situation and dismiss it as ludicrous. What did it matter if Alexandrine returned to Paris? They would meet again very shortly at Versailles, and there no one could stop him from speaking to her, touching her, stealing her away out of sight of this man who had set himself up as her watchdog.

It was a while after he had returned to his room, and was dressing to go and bid farewell to Luc, that he found himself wondering as to the Moor's dogged insistence that his relationship with Alexandrine be ended. What was it he had overheard the first day she arrived at Belaincourt? A vivid picture of Alexandrine, casually reclining on the window-seat, bathed in sunlight, of the Moor standing at her side, of a scene of intimacy, was revived to his view... 'You stay because you want to...

It is out of love!' How clearly he recalled her words. And the reply from the Moor, 'Yes, out of love.'

The Moor loved her! Luc loved her! He had dismissed as lies Paul's attempts to make him believe that she had been interested in him too. Whom *did* she love? Was she capable of love? Dear God, these thoughts would drive him mad if he did not control them! Where was the detachment with which he had first embarked upon this game? What had he achieved? Nothing—except a continuous gnawing hunger in him to possess a woman whose image constantly changed in his mind. When she was with him, she was all he had ever wanted...he was blind to her faults. But when they were apart the nagging suspicions returned, and a different picture presented itself, of a scheming little wanton who had married an old man for his wealth and was praying for the day he died and she became rich in her own right—and free! A woman who could enchant and destroy—if he was to believe all he heard about her—and who had taken lovers under the very nose of her husband. Yet when she had lain in his arms he could have sworn she was an innocent in the ways of love; he could forget Paul's wild stories, ignore the Moor's damning words. But, when he was alone at night, old demons returned to torment him, to remind him of another woman he had loved—who had betrayed him and died under strange circumstances.

A few days after the Marquis and Marquise de Mezière returned to Paris, Alexandrine got her husband to allow himself to be examined by several doctors other than Selim—not without the necessity for a great deal of persuasion on her part. She could not believe that one of the eminent men who practised in the city could not find some remedy which would lift her husband's spirits, restore some vitality to the body that was withering before her eyes. It was as if he had given up, she thought, and was allowing the life to drain from him without a fight. He was cheerful enough in himself whenever she was with him, but he did not leave his room now and spent long hours in bed. As if he had accepted that death was

close, and was awaiting the arrival of the grim reaper
without resistance. This was not the Luc she knew.

Waving aside her protests, he was insisting she resumed
the social whirl of activities that had occupied her at
times before, insisting she returned to Versailles as soon
as possible. Versailles meant Alain Ratan, and watchful
eyes following every move they made. When she showed
no enthusiasm he became almost angry, chiding her for
neglecting the duties he himself could no longer carry
out. To please him she began to ride every morning in
the Bois, her usual routine before she had left Paris. She
accepted invitations to the theatre and soirées and frequented the places where she was expected to be seen—
but to Versailles she did not yet have the courage to
return.

She rode early in the Bois, preferring it without the
throng of people who paraded through it in their finery
with wives and mistresses later in the day. Always, following her at a distance, was one of the men who had
accompanied them back to Paris from Belaincourt. Six
in all, chosen by the Duc de Belaincourt to act as
bodyguards.

Alexandrine had not seen Alain since leaving his
beautiful home. The separation had given her time to
prepare herself for their next meeting, when she would
tell him firmly and unemotionally that they must never
be alone together again! Never give way to the wildness
which had consumed them on two separate occasions!
Never betray the trust of the man they both loved! He
had to listen to her. *She* had to be the strong one.

This was the morning that Luc was to receive his visitors, and so she lingered longer than usual in the Bois,
praying that one of them would bring Luc hope. But in
her heart she knew her husband was dying and that
nothing could save him. She felt so helpless and inad-
equate. As she slowly turned her horse about, she found
her way barred by a horseman who came out of the trees
ahead without warning. Fear gripped her: she swung
around to look for her escort—and then at the same time
recognition of the dark face dawned, and she realised

the latter would not intervene, for the very man who now faced her was the same who had hired him to protect her.

Alain inclined his head towards her with a polite, tight smile, his eyes lingering on the wide-brimmed, pastel-coloured straw hat set upon her head, its dark green ribbons streaming past her shoulders, matching perfectly the colour of her gown.

'Good morning, Alexa. Luc told me I might find you here. Are you savouring a little of the freedom to come?' came the mocking taunt.

'I don't understand you.' Their first meeting since Belaincourt and he was insulting her! She had not expected a joyous reunion, but not this—contempt!

'Should a loving wife not be at the bedside of her husband when sentence of death is being pronounced upon him?' Alain flung back. 'Come now, don't be so indignant. He is dying—we both know that. Was it your idea?' His tone became harsh, and the pale green eyes deepened to an emerald hue, so chillingly cold they made her inwardly shudder.

'Yes. Why should I not be concerned for him?' Alexandrine returned, thinking he meant the gathering of doctors at the house. 'As his friend, do *you* not hope something miraculous may happen?'

Alain looked startled at her words, then angry.

'Dammit! We are alone, you don't have to play the innocent with me now. I'm talking about my leaving Paris. After the usual *coucher* at around one-thirty this morning—after a boring evening when the King was preoccupied and everyone else stood around afraid to voice what was on their minds—the King slipped out of the palace and left to join the army. I received a message requesting my immediate presence at Lille.'

'Requesting,' Alexandrine echoed. She did not know whether she was dismayed or relieved at the news. He was going away! She was safe! Yet it gave her no pleasure. 'Then you don't have to go—if you don't want to.'

'A request from the King is the same thing as an order,' Alain replied, his gaze devouring her face. She had to know, yet he could have sworn his words had startled her. 'The Moor doesn't have the power to intervene with the King, even though he had the damned audacity to tell me never to see you again.' He gave a short laugh. 'Who was it? Your friend Jeanne? Did she whisper in the royal ear that the attentions of the Duc de Belaincourt were annoying the Marquise de Mezière... or perhaps she was too subtle to mention a name? That would never do, would it? Not that it matters. The result has been the same. I have been ordered to join my men at Lille, and I am leaving at once. I shall not forget this, Alexa. When I return, you and I will settle this score.'

'I have no idea what you are talking about. Selim... you say he threatened you? I can't believe it.' Yes—she believed it. She had seen the contempt in the Moor's eyes when Alain had come into her room barely moments after she had stepped from his. Selim knew of their relationship and would do anything to prevent it from reaching Luc's ears. As she would.

'I am not afraid of his threats. I can handle him if he ever dares to do so again, and the next time my sword arm will not be incapacitated. You are a liar, Alexa. It had to be you.' He kneed his horse closer to hers, and, when she gathered up the reins to move back, a hand snaked out and caught her wrist in a paralysing grip. His expression was as black as the thoughts pounding at his brain. 'You shall not escape me this easily! What is mine I keep.'

'I am not yours!' she gasped.

'You can take as many lovers as you like while I am away, but I warn you: if I discover you have, and I learn their names, I shall call them out and kill each and every one of them. You are mine,' he repeated, tight-lipped.

'I belong to my husband—or have you forgotten I am married?' Her tone was scathing. A couple walking past cast curious glances in their direction, and she watched the woman smile and hide her face behind a fluttering fan as she turned to whisper to her companion. And then, in that moment, she knew how to keep Alain from her when he returned to Paris. To drive home a dagger as deep and wounding as the one which had been used on him in the Forest of Sénart. The eyes which were raised to meet his challenged his right to tell her to do anything, and the pride which blazed out of her lovely face started the blood pounding in his veins.

'You are—and always have been—correct in assuming there have been men other than my husband. How could there not be? Luc is so much older than I am. And, in particular, one man I was fond of, more than of the others.' The lean fingers tightened about her wrist until she wanted to cry out with the pain, but she knew that if she gave way she might well be unable to continue with her hideous lie. 'However, Selim has threatened not only you but also me, and I believe him capable of anything. I . . . I shall not see this man again. What we had is over—as it is over between us.'

'Until Luc is dead and you are free to go whoring again.' Alain's voice was murderous. 'You bitch!'

Had he struck her she would have welcomed it. Instead, however, he dragged her against him, totally oblivious to the other occupants of the Bois. His mouth crushed hers, bruising, hurting, wounding. And that long-drawn-out, shattering kiss lasted until she sank against his chest, drained and helpless to hold back an answer. The moment her lips softened, she heard an oath, and he flung her away from him so violently that she had to grab at the pommel of the saddle to steady herself.

'That will ensure you do not forget me, Alexa!' Alain could not trust himself to remain a moment longer. She sat weakly, watching him as he rode his horse like a man possessed, and it was some considerable while before she had gathered sufficient composure to leave the Bois herself.

It was done—over!

CHAPTER NINE

ALEXANDRINE took a warm bath upon returning to the house. Luc had been sleeping when she had looked in on him, and she knew that meant she would have the whole of the afternoon to herself. She needed the time desperately, to compose herself after the encounter with Alain. He had kissed her with contempt in his eyes—hatred in his heart—yet had she only imagined how his lips had answered hers a moment before he had torn himself away? The memory of their parting would haunt her in the days to come. How she wished she had not sent him away believing such a terrible lie! Yet, even believing she had taken other lovers, he still proclaimed his intention of returning to claim her. Out of revenge—not love—and that was what cut her the deepest!

Francine asked her permission to visit old friends across the river. Now that she could not meet Jules as easily as she had done at Belaincourt he had taken to accidentally bumping into her in the market-place or when she accompanied Alexandrine to a fitting at Madame Héloise. Alexandrine suspected he would be waiting for Francine tonight at the house of Solange, with all the latest news. It was one way to follow Alain's activities without anyone knowing why, she realised.

The day had been unusually humid and an unpleasant heat had not eased with the coming of darkness. Alexandrine pushed aside most of the covers and lay with only a sheet over her. Damp curls clung to her cheeks and the nape of her neck as she moved uncomfortably on the pillows. The distant sound of thunder began to grow closer, and she felt herself growing tense. How silly she was to allow a simple thing like a storm to upset her! But, with her nerves still on edge, it was impossible to relax, to accept it was growing worse as it passed overhead, but would soon diminish, after which she could sleep for as long as she wished without interruption.

At last sleep came, but nightmares plagued her rest. She dreamed of Alain upon the battlefield, and the hands he held out to her were covered in blood! And then Luc appeared to challenge him for consorting with his wife—and they fought. But Alain threw down his sword and would not fight his friend. Selim appeared, a huge scimitar upraised, and struck at the younger man—and Alain fell mortally wounded to the ground...

Alexandrine awoke with a start. It was not the return of the thunder reverberating above the rooftops that brought her upright in bed, a shrill cry of fear escaping her lips, but the figure who stood watching her—long, bony fingers stretched like talons towards her face. She flinched away, terrified...

Luc's face, illuminated as lightning invaded the room, was hideous to see. Saliva was running down his chin, and his eyes were wide and staring, like nothing she had ever seen before. The skin was drawn back tightly over the thin cheekbones, like a leather mask. A death mask! As his fingers touched her cheek, she screamed and reeled backwards, falling from the bed in a panic, to cringe against a far wall as he came slowly towards her—she was mesmerised with terror.

'Luc! What do you want from me?' Her words fell on deaf ears. She realised he not only did not hear her—but did not seem to know her identity.

As she threw up her arms to ward him off, the door flew open. She had a brief glimpse of Selim's pinning Luc's arms to his sides and propelling him away, as she fell half-fainting into the arms of a maid.

She fought against the blackness threatening to overcome her as she was helped back to the bed and lowered gently into it.

'Water...please.' Was the quavering little voice hers? 'Francine, where is Francine? Find her.'

'She is not here, *madame*. She went out hours ago.'

'Yes . . . yes, I had forgotten.' Alexandrine fell back amid the pillows, her hands covering her face, trembling.

'Madame la Marquise . . .' Selim stood at the bedside. The maid had gone and they were alone. Her eyes flew to the bloody graze on his forehead. 'It is nothing. The Marquis has the strength of a young bull when one of these attacks consume him. He is calm now. I regret you were so badly frightened, but he has eluded me for over two hours. I went to search for him in the grounds, but he must have been hiding upstairs and came to you the moment I left the house.'

'Eluded you,' Alexandrine echoed, drawing herself upright. 'You make Luc sound like a dangerous prisoner, to be guarded at all times.'

'Which is exactly what he is—now. He has kept the truth from you; I will not. It is too late for that. He is too dangerous. God knows what he would have done had I not found him in time.'

'He would have—killed me . . . I saw it in his eyes. Why? He knows about Alain, is that it? Have you told him? I thought you were his friend, and yet you bring him only pain!' she cried.

'Calm yourself. I have said nothing to him. Your secret is safe with me. He has suffered enough as it is. What I tell you now is between us. No one else must know. But it is time that you fully understand what has been happening these past months. Together we shall—we must—protect the Marquis's name from those who would profit from this—and from his death.' He stared long and hard at Alexandrine. There was no way to soften the blow he was about to deal her. She would have to be strong and deal with it as best she could. 'He wanted to keep it from you, but tonight has made that impossible. He did not tell you the whole truth about his illness.'

'What more is there?' Alexandrine whispered. Did she not know? Had she not seen it in Luc's eyes for herself?

'The real reason I have kept him so heavily sedated: to prevent such incidents as that which has just occurred from taking place. I had forgotten the cunning with which he can deceive—as he did tonight. For a long while now my powders have lessened the devastating effect of the madness which now controls his brain. To increase the dosage will surely kill him.'

'Madness!' Alexandrine shuddered as she repeated the dreaded word. That look on Luc's face. Now she understood.

Selim nodded. 'Tonight the final thread of sanity has snapped. He has lost all reason.'

'What do you want me to do?' she asked.

'Protect his name. He has given you everything. Soon—if you still desire it—you will have the man of your choice. But until the Marquis is dead—and that will be soon, very soon, *madame*—you will pretend to the outside world that there is nothing wrong. His illness is being treated as best possible. That is all they need to know.'

'The—the doctors who came to examine him...' Alexandrine began.

'He threw them out. Charlatans, all of them. They can do no more for him than I do—less, in fact. They do not care for him as I do. How deeply do you care, *madame*? Enough to return to Versailles alone? When Paul Boussières learns his father has refused the help of some of the most learned doctors in Paris, life will not be easy for you. He will make the most of such news to wage a vindictive campaign against you.'

'I owe Luc much more than mere gratitude,' Alexandrine replied. 'And, whether you believe me or not, I care for him very deeply. No one will slander his name, I promise. And no one will ever call him "poor mad Luc". Isn't that what you are afraid of? It will never happen to such a wonderful man.'

'It may be days before he recognises you again. If I can rely on you to deal with matters outside the house, then I need not leave his side.'

'Yes, Selim. You can rely on me.'

Selim returned to attend Luc, but when he was gone Alexandrine shivered and rose from the bed, hugging her arms about her as she began to pace the bedroom.

She felt unable to sleep. The storm had abated, but the violence which had erupted during the night made the thunder unimportant.

Luc—mad! How everything now fell into place. His desire to have a bride, but never to make her his wife. His lack of interest in having a family. Paul! Already she had seen the tainted blood beginning to show itself in his unpredictable actions. This, then, was the inheritance Luc had passed on to his son. Slow, lingering madness until the day he was no longer in control of what he said or did. It was horrible!

She agreed with Selim that no one else should be told. Luc, she decided, would once again become ill enough to be confined to his bed—allowed no visitors. Somehow she would deal with the situation until the end came. How soon would that be? Another week—a month? Every day he would be suffering and she could offer no consolation...no hope. But he would die with dignity, with the respect of friends and acquaintances. She would spare him the final humiliation, no matter what it cost her.

The arrival of the handsome monarch of France amid his soldiers in West Flanders had the same effect as if the army had suddenly received a god into their midst— which, to many a poor, ordinary foot-soldier, he was. Immediately he fell to planning new campaigns with the old Maréchal Duc de Noailles, who had replaced Fleury as the King's mentor. Fleury had once had the confidence of Louis XIV and advised his grandson on similar policies. Of one rule he reminded his sovereign over and over again: favourites had never ruled the Court of the Sun King—nor must they rule his. In the face of the awesome power exercised over Louis by the Duchesse de Châteauroux, the advice was rarely heeded.

The people of Paris waited expectantly for news. At Versailles the Queen held her court as usual, ate too much and waited with an infinite patience for a communication from her husband. At her home at Plaisance with her sister, the Duchesse de Châteauroux waited for the next messenger who would bring word of her royal lover.

Menin fell to the French, followed shortly by the capture of Ypres, despite the strong English forces which had swelled the ranks of the Austrian enemy. Paris went wild with delight. There was rejoicing in the streets, where poverty and hunger were forgotten in the splendour of the French victories. The presence of the King had brought about a miracle!

The Queen and the Court rejoiced and prayed for the war to soon be over. Only one person grew more ill-at-ease as the days slipped by. Marie-Anne, Duchesse de Châteauroux, had begun to notice how some people now clamoured for the company of the dull Queen, as if believing that when the King returned it would be to her he first went and not to the woman who had ruled his heart—and, very often, his throne. There was only one thing for her to do, and that was to follow him to Lille and reassert her authority over him.

He had been gone now for over a month. She could wait no longer. She would show those simpering Court fools who was really the first lady of France. It was comforting to know Madame d'Etoiles was so big with child that she could not move outside her *hôtel* in the rue Croix-des-Petits-Champs, or she too might have taken it into her silly head to follow the King and offer him solace so far away from home.

This was the perfect opportunity for her, the Duchesse decided, to strengthen her hold over the King and ensure once and for all that the little *bourgeoise* was never in his thoughts again.

'Have you heard about the Duchesse, *madame*?' Now she had finished with Alexandrine's fitting, Madame Héloïse was able to resort to her favourite pastime—gossip. 'She presented herself at Court and asked permission of the Queen to go to Lille. To the King's side! Can you imagine the nerve of the woman! If anyone should be at his side it should be his wife—not her!'

Alexandrine could not envisage the Queen dragging herself from the comfort of Versailles and the staid little élite that surrounded her, to join a man who had long ago ceased to love her and treated her as little more than an object. Except for State occasions they were rarely seen together. She had her life and he his.

Alexandrine was not looking forward to returning to Versailles, but she had promised Selim and she had every intention of making a grand entrance to confound her critics and, she hoped, keep questions at bay—for a little while, at least. Her new gown was of white satin and brocade, the apron of the skirt divided to reveal an underskirt of tiered lace into which were woven hundreds of tiny diamonds, which would shimmer in the candle-light at Versailles like the iridescent wings of a dragonfly.

The gown had cost far more than anything else she owned, but she shrugged off a moment of guilt as she stepped out of it. Money was of no importance. If she had to spend every sou Luc had in order to keep his secret safe from his son and those who would destroy him, then she would—and without a single regret. He had given her everything she had. What she was doing now was a small thing in return.

He was recovering slowly from the last devastating attack which had left him in a semi-conscious state for several days. He had known her when she had looked in on him before leaving the house, and Selim had told her he was pleased with his progress, that in a day or two Luc would be able to get out of bed and sit in a chair. But Alexandrine had seen the phials of powder and the pitcher of water on the side-table, and the glass where a milky substance still lingered, and the look in Selim's eyes as she had bent to kiss Luc's cheek had told her nothing had changed. As she had stood for a moment in the corridor to regain her composure before going out, she had heard the bolt being pushed home on the door behind her. Luc was nothing more than a prisoner now, and Selim was his gaoler—yet also his salvation. Now she too must play the role thrust upon her until her poor, tormented husband was released from his suffering.

'My dear Madame Boussières, how good to see you here again. I was wondering if you would return, with your husband's health as it is.' Madame de Mailly was one of the first to approach Alexandrine when she arrived. There was nothing this woman did not hear, Alexandrine thought. 'I hope he is improving. Did his stay at Belaincourt not bring about any change? The Duc is such a wonderful host, or at least he was until that wife of his caused such an uproar and scandal with her untimely death that he closed the house to visitors. I do believe you are the first people he has had there since her death. A little womanly persuasion on your part, perhaps?'

'I am sure you know the Duc well enough to know no woman could make him do anything against his will,' Alexandrine returned. She wanted to ask if there was more news from the front, but dared not. Too many pointed questions would be like an admission of her interest in the absent Duc de Belaincourt.

'How right you are, *madame*. And with men of his kind at the front we shall soon win this wretched war. Men like Alain Ratan—and the King, bless them—are leading our soldiers to victory.' She did not think it necessary to include anyone from the lower ranks of the army in her praise. They were, after all, fighting for the honour and glory of their beloved France; that was sufficient. 'I do hope the Duc will not be hurt. One hears such terrible stories of soldiers dying like flies. But I am being morbid. He comes from a long line of fighting men. Brilliant soldiers, all of them. There was never a Ratan man who did not distinguish himself in times of war. But we were discussing your husband, Madame Boussières, not a healthy young scoundrel like Alain. Do you know the rogue did not even say goodbye to Mademoiselle de Morrière? And the two of them almost betrothed. She is devastated!'

'My husband's health has given cause for concern these past few days.' Alexandrine chose her words with care, knowing that even though this woman was a friend they would be repeated. 'He must have caught a slight chill after returning home. But he is having the best attention possible and only this morning his physician informed me he is recovering.'

'My dear—a word of advice.' Madame de Mailly cast a quick look about her before drawing closer. 'There is talk—unwarranted, mark you, but nevertheless beginning to arouse some considerable interest—about this Moor that attends the Marquis.'

'Selim is also a close family friend. He has been with my husband many years. We both,' she laid heavy emphasis on the words, 'have complete confidence in his skills.'

'Monsieur Boussières, the Marquis's son, is hinting at a more—sinister reason for the relationship. Some addle-brained idea that your husband is being kept drugged—a prisoner in his own house! A preposterous idea, but, remembering the trouble he has caused you in the past, I advise caution, *madame* . . . in everything you do—and say.'

'I shall remember, *madame*, and I thank you for your concern.'

'Whether you believe it or not, my dear, I do care what happens to you. It is not often one sees such unspoilt beauty at Versailles,' Madame de Mailly said quietly, patting Alexandrine's hand as she moved away.

Alexandrine sought out Henri, Duc de Blas, on the pretext of seeking information about Alain for her husband, who, she told him, was most anxious as to his friend's whereabouts and health.

'Alain? Probably getting drunk with the King,' came the disconcerting answer. 'Everyone in the army will be celebrating our victories and they will be no exceptions. I have not heard from him for over a week, but I am not worried. We spoke before he left and he did me the honour of making me executor of his estate, should anything happen to him. He left several sealed envelopes with me and other instructions, but, of course, I shall not have to act on any of it for he will soon be back, winning again at cards, with me still needing to write out my note.'

'My—husband was somewhat surprised that the Duc took himself off so suddenly.' Alexandrine said carefully. 'He was hoping to return the hospitality he had shown us at Belaincourt.'

'Ah—that . . . yes, his departure was sudden, but there was nothing he could do about it. An order from the King, you understand.' For which she had been blamed, Alexandrine thought, waiting patiently in the hope he would enlighten her further. After a moment and a cautious look behind him to ensure no one was standing close to them, Henri continued. 'It has been suggested . . . whispered in certain quarters . . . that his absence from Court was contrived.'

'For what reason? I don't understand. He is not the most popular of men, I know, but he is the least offensive I can think of.'

'The suggestion is that a certain lady of his acquaintance bears him a grudge. There was quite a scene here one night before the King left. Alain and this lady were outside—and after he had left she was found to be in a most distressed condition . . . She even went so far as to say he had actually threatened her life! Can you imagine that? Unfortunately, that aroused a few memories, of his dead wife, you know, and that began the ugly talk all over again. At first I thought he might have thought it a wise move to leave France for a while, but then, when I heard of this lady's continued malice against him . . . I began to wonder. You see, she has a friend in rather a high position here at Court, who might be willing to do her a favour. Why not? She would receive something in return. That one always does.'

'Claudia de la Fontaine and the King's mistress,' Alexandrine breathed and Henri lifted a hand in warning.

'No names, I beg of you. I share your belief that those two have plotted against Alain, and I have written to warn him what to expect when he returns. He knows how to deal with women like that. Assure the Marquis he is well, and convey my own wishes for a speedy recovery to him.'

'Thank you, Monsieur le Duc, I shall do that.'

Claudia and the Duchesse de Châteauroux plotting together against Alain. There could only be one reason.

Something had taken place between Claudia and her ex-lover when he had retrieved the stolen necklace, something that he had not conveyed to Alexandrine, and now Claudia was seeking some way to pay him back. Had he really threatened her? Alexandrine dared not dwell on that question too long, for it brought to mind the suspicions surrounding the death of his wife. He had not denied killing her...so perhaps it was possible.

No! She would never believe it of him. There had to be another explanation. But it was obvious he had frightened Claudia into desperate action. At least Henri's letter would let him know his accusations against Alexandrine had been groundless. It had not been Alexandrine who had brought about his departure, although she doubted if the news would count for much. And he was safe and unharmed. Suddenly the evening, despite the lack of its usual gaiety and of the King took on a gayer atmosphere for her.

Before the evening was over, the Duchesse de Châteauroux left Versailles and with her went Claudia de la Fontaine. If one mistress could go to the aide of the man she loved, why not another? she had laughingly remarked to a close friend, not known for her ability to keep secrets. Within the hour the whole Court knew where she had gone and why. A few speculative looks were cast in the direction of a figure seated at one of the tables, but Alexandrine gave no sign she had become aware of them or that she was the least interested in the departure of either woman. But her concentration had been shattered—and she lost heavily...

With the coming of summer, heat once again invaded the city, driving many of the wealthier families to the country as plagues of flies made life unbearable, and in the poorer parts there were, again, outbreaks of sickness. As Alexandrine sat at Luc's bedside, sometimes reading from one of his favourite books but never knowing if he understood a word she said or not, it was possible to shut Alain Ratan from her mind, to pretend they had never shared a tender moment or the thrill of unbridled passion. But at Versailles or in one of the many salons she frequented, or in the company of Jeanne d'Etoiles who was as well informed as to what was going on everywhere as Madame de Mailly herself, it was not so easy to forget him.

News filtered back to Paris of the army advancing— of casualties! For days she could not shut out the memories which crowded in on her... and her sleep was disturbed by the same recurring dream.

Together with a bevy of jewelled, glittering, lavishly dressed friends and attendants, Claudia de la Fontaine no doubt among them, the Duchesse de Châteauroux had arrived in Lille to the unexpected anger of both soldiers and townspeople alike, who had taken instant offence at her presence in their midst. She was subjected to rude comments wherever she showed her face, and ribald songs were sung about her in the taverns and around the camp-fires. Alexandrine heard that when the news was whispered to the Queen of her rival's discomfort she was seen to smile broadly, and that evening ate more heartily that she usually did.

At the beginning of August the King moved on to Metz and the Duchesse followed, to be jeered at in the streets and generally abused wherever she went.

Yet, undaunted, she moved into apartments in the Abbey of St Arnauld adjacent to those of her royal lover, who—on the pretext of having erected a closed gallery through which he might pass unseen to attend Mass— was able to visit her privately. Such a secret was not kept for long, however, and it served to increase the anger of the people against the favourite.

When the envoy of Frederick of Prussia arrived, Louis threw a sumptuous banquet. The latter hoped to persuade the King into an alliance against the Empress Maria-Theresa, which would serve to shorten the lengthy conflict now in progress. La Châteauroux sat on the King's right hand, nodding approval to the suggestion. It could only benefit France, after all.

It was said that the King drank too much and ate some contaminated food, for by the following morning he had developed a high temperature and his skin was clammy

to the touch. Panic spread like wildfire through the army
and the King's retinue. The King was ill! Word reached
Paris. The King was dying! There was pandemonium at
Versailles!

The Duchesse and her sister arrived to take charge of
the sick-room, but her authority was challenged by the
Princes of the Blood accompanying the King, who insisted that his chaplain, the Bishop of Soissons, be sent
for immediately. She protested, to no avail, that the
malady which afflicted him was not serious and would
soon pass, but in the end was forced to give way. No
sooner had the Bishop seen Louis than he voiced his
opinion that Père Pèrusseau, the King's confessor,
should be sent for. Again the Duchesse was forced to
give way, and it became clear to her that there was a
conspiracy to send her from the King's side. They told
her Louis was dying. She did not believe it! To do so
would mean she must also accept her power over him
was ending—that she must give up all she had built over
the years as his mistress.

Père Pèrusseau had a problem. Either he had to send
the favourite away, so that he might absolve the sins of
the King—a thing not possible with her still at Metz—
before he died, or he had to let her remain!

The King had been ill before, and had looked little
different then. What if he was not dying? The anger and
retribution of the Duchesse would ruin the confessor's
position. She would have his head!

There were many who waited eagerly to see her dismissed and sent back to Paris. The First Gentleman of
the Bedchamber, the Duc de Richelieu, found support
not only for his niece but for himself gradually slipping
away. The Duc de Châtillon openly applauded the ex-
pulsion of the Duchesse. His hatred of her was as great
as that of the young Dauphin to whom he was tutor.

In the streets and taverns of Metz the people waited,
hoping, praying the focal point of their hatred would be
driven from the city without delay.

In one of the local taverns, where he had taken
lodgings, forsaking more comfortable surroundings for

an atmosphere he preferred, Alain Ratan was a silent witness to the insurgence of bad feeling which swept the people. The Duchesse de Châteauroux had become as potent, as lethal as a virulent disease in their minds. He did not like the woman and considered her power over the King a dangerous weapon, which she would not hesitate to use to further her own ambitions and those of her friends, but he did not wish upon her the violence and mayhem those about him did. If she were to be found alone in the streets, he mused, as he finished a tankard of ale and called for another, she would be torn to pieces by a mob. They would have no mercy on her. They thought of her as a blot on the fair name of France—the shining honour of their god-like King. To have followed him like a common camp woman—and to have taken the place of his wife at his side!

Alain had been surprised to receive a summons from the Duc de Chartres that morning, and upon arriving at the King's abode had been shown immediately into his presence and left alone. Even the Duc de Richelieu had not been allowed to remain, and Alain had discovered why when Louis, pale, weak and barely able to speak, had beckoned him to the bedside. It had been necessary to lay his ear against Louis's mouth to fully understand his words. They had so taken him aback he could but nod his acquiescence. If the King were to die, he was to deliver a message to a certain lady whom they both knew, upon his return to Paris. To convey to her the undying gratitude of the King of France for the many hours they had spent in pleasant conversation together. Would that they could have been repeated...

So ill, yet it was not Marie-Anne, the favourite, in his thoughts, but Jeanne d'Etoiles, the prize he had not yet captured and, perhaps, now never would.

Alain stared into his ale and then swallowed it without appreciation. His company of men were made up of the men who worked on his estates and their relatives, with a few odd Parisians thrown in. A rough lot, but good fighting men and he trained them well...and hard. They had distinguished themselves in the field and, so far, there had been only two casualties. A fact he was proud of.

It was impossible not to think of Paris... of the Hôtel Boussières—of her. A fierce expletive broke under his breath as he found her image in his mind yet again, remembered the softness, the warmth of her against him that last night before she left Belaincourt. Whose arms held her now? he wondered, and the thought incensed him. Henri, Duc de Blas kept him informed of what was going on at Versailles and had undertaken the task of managing his estates, if anything happened to him. He was young in years, but with a good head on his shoulders—and fast becoming a close and trusted friend. Alexandrine was back at Versailles, showing little concern for her bedridden husband, and even asking about himself on the pretext that it was her husband's concern which prompted her questions. Hoping he would draw his last breath the next time they engaged the enemy, no doubt, he thought humourlessly.

A pretty serving-girl replaced his empty glass without his ordering and he nodded appreciation. She lingered by the table, an open invitation in her eyes. With her perhaps he could forget for a few hours, Alain thought, as he rose and followed her upstairs.

On an early morning visit to the house of Jeanne d'Etoiles, Alexandrine encountered Henri, Duc de Blas. She paused on the steps when he excused himself from his friends and made his way across to her. As always these days, the first topic of conversation was the King's illness.

'The Queen received word late last night that the King is worse. Tomorrow she will leave to join him at Metz. It is her intention to be near him at the end. It is expected of her, naturally.'

'To share his bedside with the Duchesse de Châteauroux?' Alexandrine said in amazement, and the young man shook his head.

'Have you not heard? It was in Alain's latest letter.' Alexandrine said nothing, but it was obvious from the strange look he gave her that he imagined she and Alain were in constant communication. 'La Châteauroux was forced to leave Metz. The townspeople were becoming so incensed by her presence that she feared for her life should she remain. She slipped out of the town at night in a closed carriage belonging to the Maréchal de Belle-Isle, who apparently took pity on her. He will not be too popular, I can tell you.'

'I have no affection for that lady, but to be assaulted in the streets... It is a horrible thought.'

'You are too soft, Madame la Marquise, although Alain too agrees that had he witnessed such an occurrence he would have been forced to intervene on her behalf. And he has no reason to love the Duchesse, has he?'

'Indeed he has not,' Alexandrine returned.

'By the way, he wishes to be remembered to you.'

'I shall tell my husband. He will be relieved to learn the Duc is in good health.' As she was!

'Do that, *madame*, but that was not my message. He wished to be remembered to you—alone,' Henri replied with a slight smile.

Alexandrine found, in the hours that followed, that she had little time to dwell on the astonishing words relayed to her, for she discovered that the news of the King's illness had sent Jeanne into a near panic. Like the Duchesse de Châteauroux, she saw her dreams disintegrating before her eyes. All indications were that Louis was going to die. If he was not very seriously ill, would the Queen go to Metz when one of her daughters, little Therêse-Felicité, aged only six, had just died?

She wept and clung to Alexandrine's hand, and the latter found it impossible to calm her. As the pains grew worse, she too became convinced she was about to die. Alexandrine prayed it would be an easy time for her and that the child would be healthy, even though she had not carried it to the full term. It horrified her that she should suffer so much pain in order to bring a new life into the world. Yet, when the midwife presented the exhausted Jeanne with her new daughter, the contented smile on the face of the proud mother was proof enough that it had all been worth it.

'She has my eyes,' Jeanne whispered with a wan smile, as she handed the infant to Alexandrine. 'She shall have the education fit for a princess. And I shall call her Alexandrine.' She stared thoughtfully into the face of her friend. 'Solange told me I would have a girl. And you, she predicts, will have a boy. He must have a strong name—like his father.'

Her eyes closed, and Alexandrine handed the baby to the wet-nurse and tiptoed from the room, knowing Jeanne had not been referring to Luc when she uttered the words.

Selim was bending over the bed when Alexandrine came quietly into her husband's sick-room. He held Luc's wrist for a moment longer, then laid it back on the coverlet and looked up at her.

'He is sleeping peacefully.'

'He looks so relaxed, Selim. I never thought to see him this way again,' she whispered. In sleep her husband's face was wiped clean of the pain and torment which had ravaged it for so many months. 'You have worked a miracle.'

'No, *madame*, I have given him peace—as was asked of me,' the Moor returned, beginning to gather up the phials from the table. 'I hope Madame d'Etoiles is well?'

'She has the most adorable baby girl.'

'And you envy her.'

'Do I? Yes, perhaps, just a little. When I held the tiny thing in my arms...' She broke off, her cheeks firing with colour. 'I realise for me it is not possible. I have accepted it.'

'Anything is possible, *madame*...in time. You look tired. May I suggest you rest for a while? There is nothing you can do here.'

'For an hour only. Perhaps Luc will want me to read for him when he awakes.'

She was aware of the odd smile which flitted across the ebony face as she closed the door behind her. Selim had never welcomed the presence of anyone else in the sick-room, watching over his patient with the protective jealousy of a lioness with a new-born cub, but did he have to make her feel so useless at this time?

Attired in a loose robe, she stretched out across the bed, but she found it impossible to relax. At first she blamed it on the excitement of the morning...and the strange message from Henri that Alain wished to be remembered to her—as if he could ever be forgotten! But then she realised it was neither: it was something Selim had said to her—something that brought her starting up, heading for the door...

'I have given him peace—as was asked of me.' He had been gathering up the precious phials containing the powders which kept Luc sedated—as if they were no longer needed. Peace! What kind of peace?

She knew the answer even before she flung open the door and stood on the threshold, staring into the now darkened room. The only pale glow of light came from the two candles, one placed on either side of the bed where her husband lay motionless. Something moved in the shadows beyond the bed, and Selim materialised to face her, arms folded over his massive chest. His presence dominated the room, yet she realised she was no longer afraid of him. He was human, after all, with feelings like everyone else. Had he not proved it by what he had done?

'I was not sure you understood. You do understand?' She nodded, lost for words. 'It was agreed between us a long time ago that when Luc was no longer in control, when he became dangerous to himself and those he loved—I would set him free. Last night he asked it of me. You will tell everyone he died in his sleep while you were visiting Madame d'Etoiles. That way, should there be questions——'

'Questions,' Alexandrine echoed. She forced herself to the bedside, touched the limp hand that lay upon the silken covers. Still warm, as if he was only sleeping, after all. Bright tears filled her eyes, spilled unnoticed down ashen cheeks as she dropped to her knees and rested her cheek against the leathery skin. 'Questions, Selim? My husband died in his sleep, as you said. That is all anyone needs to know. We shall keep his secret, you and I. No one will ever know the truth.'

Watching her as she wept silently at the side of a man she had never truly known, who had used her as an object of pleasure, without giving her the satisfaction of being a fulfilled woman, Selim wondered if he would ever understand the mind of a woman. Yet he accepted that, as Luc had loved her in his way, so she too had loved him. Because of that and the name she still bore—and most of all the promise he had made—he would protect her until another, more capable and more acceptable, returned to do so.

CHAPTER TEN

ALEXANDRINE felt a touch on her arm. She allowed the
dry earth between her fingers to fall gently upon the polished casket in the hole at her feet, before lifting her eyes
to Selim's guarded features. The past two days since
Luc's death were taking their toll, stretching her nerves
to breaking point, sapping her strength until she felt like
a rag doll. Without him at her side, she knew she would
never have survived the final ordeal—the funeral of her
husband. Now it was over! Now she could leave Paris.
She had no reason to stay, and she did not intend to
allow herself to become the centre of more speculation
and malicious rumours.

Somehow she had struggled through that long day
when Luc's friends and colleagues had come to the house
to pay their respects. Most came out of morbid curiosity, she knew, only half listening to the murmured
condolences, uttered parrot-fashion time and time again
without one iota of feeling in the voices. Only Henri,
one of the last to arrive, had, she believed, genuinely
regretted the passing of the Marquis de Mezière. He stood
a few feet away from her now, often glancing in her
direction. She sensed an almost protective air about him,
although they only ever encountered each other at
Versailles and he was more the friend of Alain than of
her.

Alain! He would receive her brief letter soon. She had
simply written that his dear friend Luc had died peacefully in his sleep. What else was there to say? She
expected no reply from him. He would believe she now
had all she wanted. Money, position, a respected name.
He would not come to her as he threatened, for that
would mean he cared—and that was too impossible to
believe.

'Madame la Marquise...prepare yourself.' Selim's words, too low to carry beyond the two of them, made her stiffen in apprehension. Thrusting his way through the crowd of mourners waiting for Alexandrine to turn away from the graveside, Paul Boussières halted on the other side of the yawning chasm which housed his father, and stared long and hard at her. Gone was the foppishly dressed individual she had always known.

Not only was he attired in the most sober clothes, but a dark handkerchief was pressed to wet cheeks. She could only stare back at him in sheer disbelief. He looked so ridiculous that, in other circumstances, she could have laughed aloud. She was thankful for the heavy veil which covered her features. It hid the fear in her eyes as she watched the looks exchanged around him. How could anyone believe he was a grieving son? Yet they did! As easily as they would suspect the worst of her! Her stomach fluttered uneasily.

'Father...Father...that she should have brought you to this!' The onlookers gasped at the words, watched open-mouthed as he fell to his knees beside the hole. Paul Boussières grovelling in the dirt! Had he truly loved the man who had fathered him after all? Was he in truth the one maligned, and not the slim woman covered from head to toe in black?

If there were some who were convinced too easily Henri, Duc de Blas was not one of them. As he stared at the other man he was relieved he had sent an urgent note to Alain by special messenger. The rumours he had heard were without foundation, of that he was sure, but ugly enough to cause pain and embarrassment to the widowed Marquise. She was vulnerable now, with no one to stand at her side save for the ebony-faced Moor—and his presence did little to refute what was being said. Indeed, his manner, when they were seen together, was fuel for the fire.

'Murderess!'

Alexandrine recoiled from the word flung at her, from the hatred on the face of Paul, as he scrambled to his feet and stood swaying unsteadily on the brink of the grave.

'You—and him!' A trembling finger was thrust out towards Selim. 'You killed him—poisoned him—for her!'

And you are mad, like your father! she wanted to scream back. Selim's hand closed over her arm. She cared not who saw her cling to it for support. She could say nothing—do nothing, without revealing to everyone the terrible truth.

'You are overwrought, *monsieur*. I wish I could believe it is over the loss of your father and not of his fortune. How dare you appear like some repentant sinner clothed in sackcloth and ashes, and perpetrate this—this ghastly charade to a ready-made audience, most of whom are only here out of curiosity, anyway? May God forgive you, for I never shall.' Alexandrine could hardly contain her anger. She was afraid of his warped mind and the vengeance she believed he would try to exact for his being disinherited—and the next time there would be no Alain Ratan to come to her aid. To leave Paris now would condemn her in the eyes of many people, but she had no choice. If she stayed, she would be murdered. She had no doubt of it.

The hem of her black gown swirled in the dust as she turned about, looking neither to the left nor the right as she walked proudly to where the carriage waited. Some mourners followed. Others remained to see what Paul Boussières would do now. She had publicly insulted him! Henri fell into step beside her, uncomfortable at the look Selim gave him. Someone should warn her about his manner. His closeness to the Marquis had been well known and accepted by most, but to expect them to overlook the possessiveness he was now showing for the new widow was asking too much.

'Madame la Marquise, if you ever need a friend...' he said quietly, sincerely, and Alexandrine smiled at him gratefully as he assisted her into the carriage.

'You are very kind, *monsieur*, and your offer is appreciated, but I am not remaining in Paris to become the object of ridicule.'

'You are leaving? But, *madame*...should you not refute this ghastly accusation?' Henri protested. 'While I understand your desire to seek peace at such a time after your loss, your absence will only make the tongues wag more. And think what Paul Boussières will have to say about it.'

'There is no way I can prove my innocence,' Alexandrine returned. 'I must rely on the loyalty of those who know me. Do *you* think me a murderess, *monsieur*?'

'Good heavens, no!' de Blas gasped, colouring profusely at her bluntness. 'But if you would only allow the Marquis's body to be examined...now, before it is too late. It would prove to everyone how vindictive this man is towards you. He would never trouble you again.'

That was what she had thought when Jules had killed the man Paul had sent to assassinate her. When Alain had rescued her from a terrifying night with Paul and his friends, and she had discovered what it was to have him hate her. Nothing daunted him. His hatred was too great. He did not know fear, only the desire to destroy.

She glanced into Selim's impassive features, and heard again the words Luc had said to her one day, so far away now, as he was handed a glass of pale, milky liquid. 'One day this concoction will be the death of me.' It had! And if she allowed Luc's body to be examined, Selim would be accused of murder, and she would stand at his side as an accomplice, if not the instigator of the heinous crime.

'Thank you for the advice, *monsieur*. I know it is meant well. But I shall allow no one, for any reason, to disturb the blessed peace in which my husband now dwells.'

'Then, I can only say again—if you ever need a friend...'

It had begun, Alexandrine thought, as the carriage moved slowly away from Saint Paul's, the churchyard where only the nobility were buried. She had been warned

how Paul would react after the death of his father. He
had lost no time! 'Rumours now, accusations later,'
Jeanne had hinted. Had Madame de Mailly not been
afraid of the same thing? That Paul would continue with
the accusation that she had kept Luc a prisoner in his
own home, to be slowly poisoned by the man responsible for his welfare. Alexandrine would be branded as
the greedy wife, patiently biding her time to become a
rich widow . . . and there was nothing she could do about
it. The scandal would no doubt follow her to Noyen,
but there she was known and loved. No one would believe ill of her and, with time, she prayed she would be
allowed to live a quiet, uncomplicated life.

Alain was forced to wait for over an hour before he was
admitted to the King's presence. If Louis did not grant
his request, then he would have no alternative other than
to slip away as soon as it was dark and risk incurring
his sovereign's displeasure.

He stood patiently in front of the table where Louis
was studying several large maps spread out before him.
Soon winter would be upon them, making further campaigns impossible. He wondered if the King was relieved
that he would soon be able to return to Paris and the
arms of his mistress.

'Your message implied this is a personal matter,
monsieur.' At last the King relaxed back into his chair
and looked at the man before him. Alain Ratan asked
favours from no one. That made the request not only
personal—but urgent!

'Yes, sire. I wish permission to return to Paris immediately. I received word two days ago that the Marquis
de Mezière is dead.'

That had been the first communication from Henri,
which had reached him even before Alexandrine's briefly
worded announcement of her husband's death. The news
plunged him into a black mood which even a night of
drinking did not dispel, and in the morning, when his
head began to clear, he found himself thinking more and
more of Paul Boussières. Alexandrine was alone and unprotected against his hatred. He had tried to kill her once;

would he be driven to do so again? She had Selim, he reasoned, but it was not enough to ease the apprehension mounting inside him. And he *had* made Luc a promise that he would protect her.

And then close on the heels of these letters, had come another from Henri, brought by a messenger who had ridden his horse into the ground in his haste to deliver it. Paul Boussières had accused Alexandrine of poisoning her husband—and before a crowd of mourners, at the graveside. Was the man a lunatic? How far was he prepared to go to turn opinion against her?

It took Alain another full day of wrestling with the feelings he found he could no longer ignore before he capitulated and accepted that it had happened to him again. He did not trust her, but he loved her! She had blatantly confessed to having other men in her life, yet he knew he would want only her in his. If she was in danger, then he would protect her—kill for her if necessary. What happened after that—if anything—was in the hands of fate itself.

'He had been ill for some time, had he not?' Alain nodded. 'I liked the Marquis. A man of considerable learning. I have often spoken of him with—a friend.'

Jeanne d'Etoiles immediately sprang to Alain's mind. The message he was to have delivered to her if the King had died proved they had become more than acquaintances. Fate was intervening in all their lives!

'I am concerned for the welfare of the Marquise, his widow.' Alain chose his words with care. Even so he saw a slight smile touch the corners of Louis's mouth. 'I promised the Marquis I would protect her, should it become necessary when she was alone.'

'And you consider her in need of protection now? I was given to understand she is a most popular young woman, extremely sought-after—for her company, of course. Madame de Mailly speaks most highly of her.'

Alain knew he could hold nothing back. Sparing few details, he told of the attempts on the life of Luc and Alexandrine, the threats Paul had made against them. The hatred which was eating at his heart, driving him to destroy the woman who stood in the way of his inheriting his father's wealth . . . who was depriving him of the money desperately needed to pay off his mound of debts. Louis's dark brows rose in surprise as the Duc de Belaincourt, who had evaded the clutches of some of the most beautiful, available women at Versailles, stood before him and confessed he was in love. The thought of him playing a chivalric role, racing to the rescue of a damsel in distress, touched the romantic in him. Madame d'Etoiles had been right. In love, but not knowing it until the woman he loved was threatened with danger. Louis longed suddenly for Paris and the quiet atmosphere of Jeanne's salon, where they could be closeted together for hours without being disturbed. How could he, so delighted with the new love in his life, deny another man the pleasure he had found?

'You have my permission to leave immediately, *monsieur*. When you arrive in Paris, you will make it known that the Marquise de Mezière has the protection of the King of France, and that you have been chosen by me to ensure her well-being until I return.'

'You have some news for me?' Paul Boussières looked up at the slim youth who was shown into his presence. From a chair close by Claudia rose to leave, but he waved her back to her seat, a smile hovering about his thin lips. She did not like it when he smiled at her that way. Three days had passed since he had unexpectedly attended the funeral of his father, and for those three days she had been waiting for some explosion of anger—threats made against the woman who had not only his father's name, but also his fortune. Yet none came. That worried her even more than the outbursts of temper she had grown used to—and now feared—over the past months.

She knew the newcomer by sight—a rogue from the Left Bank, as were most of the men Paul hired to do work for him these days. A thief perhaps, or worse. He looked harmless enough, but there was something in his eyes that deterred Claudia from flirting with him and, for all his youth, it was always he whom Paul summoned to his presence—always he who went back to the

others and gave them their orders. Young and dangerous, she had decided—and better left alone.

'The woman is stubborn, but I am making progress.
She has admitted that the Marquise de Mezière visited
her establishment last year in the company of another
woman—Madame d'Etoiles.'

'My clerk is taking down her every word?'

'Exactly as she tells it . . . well——' the youth's face
dimpled into a boyish grin '—he has an imagination
which will aid you well in your desires.'

'An imagination fired by the prospect of gold,' Paul
sneered. He would never be rich, of course. Paul had
already decided that anyone connected with him at this
time would be disposed of when he had succeeded in his
aim, including the man before him. The fools! Did they
think he would allow them to go on living, to bleed him
dry in the future? That would leave only Claudia to deal
with. And he could buy a dozen of her . . . 'Do not make
me wait too long. I need proof my father was poisoned
and I want it quickly. As to the other matter, is that in
hand?'

'Tonight my men will bring you what you want if you
wish.'

'Good.' Paul relaxed back in his chair, and reached
for the glass of brandy at his fingertips. Claudia's eyes
followed his every move. He could feel the fear in her,
and the knowledge heightened the tremendous sensation
of power which had been growing in him since his carefully laid plans began to reach fruition. 'I think our
special guest should be here to participate in all of this,
don't you agree? Take her at the first opportunity—leave
no witnesses.'

'Have I ever?' The young man caught the purse tossed
his way, wondering how much Paul Boussières would
inherit once his stepmother was out of the way. Enough
to keep him and his friends in luxury for the rest of their
lives, that was sure.

'The last time I sent you after her, you failed me,'
Paul said as he turned towards the door. 'I will not tol-

erate a second mistake. I want her here tonight!
Understood?'

'Perfectly, *monsieur*. She will be at your disposal by
midnight,' came the chilling reply, which made Claudia
suddenly sit upright in her chair.

She was beginning to put two and two together, and
she did not like what it was adding up to. All these
strange comings and goings at the dead of night. Rough,
uncouth men, who looked as if they would cut your
throat for a sou, loitering about the house . . . her house!
Whatever was being planned, Paul would make her a
part of it!

'What are you up to?' She crossed to the decanter of
wine and poured herself a liberal measure, feeling her
composure deteriorating fast beneath the pale eyes which
followed her. How they unnerved her! And she had once
considered this man a nonentity—a fool! Her fool! She
was the fool, and if she did not extricate herself very
quickly from him and his mad schemes she would be
brought down with him. She would lose everything! 'I
will not have my house used in this manner. You make
it impossible for me to bring my friends here any more.
And this act of yours—of pretending to be in mourning
for your father—makes it impossible for you to attend
Versailles. I shall have to go alone.'

'If you leave this house without my permission, my
dear, I shall have you brought back—and the men I send
to do it may not be to your liking. I almost have what
I want here—in the palm of my hand—and no one,
especially an empty-headed little whore like you, is going
to deprive me of it. Be nice to me, Claudia. How long
you continue breathing depends on how co-operative you
are.' Paul chuckled as she fell into a chair, ashen-faced.
'I am glad you at last realise you are dealing with a man.'

'A madman!' she flung back, and cried out as Paul
came out of his seat like an unleashed animal. One hand
sent the glass spinning from her grasp, the other seized
her by the throat. His fingers were thin and wiry, the
strength in them beyond belief. Her eyes bulged as he
thrust her back into the velvet chair. She was a woman

of some considerable strength herself, but she was helpless. A vision of the night she had been confronted by Alain flashed through her mind, the memory of his hands at her throat also. He had been angry beyond words, but in her heart she now felt sure he would never have killed her, despite his threats. Paul was different. He would kill—or have her killed—slowly, would watch her agony and enjoy every moment. He was mad! Could no one else see it?

'Then take great care, my dear Claudia, not to upset me again. Be grateful I am in a good mood. I think you need a lesson in obedience. Tonight I shall show you what happens to those who think they can oppose me. You shall join me for the entertainment downstairs. If you behave yourself, I may even allow you to use one of the irons on our special guest. You must have guessed who it is by now...'

'Al...Alexandrine!' Claudia gasped in air as his grip began to relax. As he drew back, she knew that if the threat became reality and Alexandrine, Marquise de Mezière, was brought to the house, she would never be seen alive again!

'Come in, Selim. I have finished here now.' Alexandrine sat back in her chair with a deep sigh and motioned the Moor to come closer. Before her on the bureau were sheaves of neatly stacked papers. She pushed one towards him. 'All this is of no consequence. Burn everything. And these...' Her fingers lingered on the largest pile. 'These are of a very personal nature. For my husband's sake, I think they should go into the fire. The others are bills which I shall deal with before I leave for Noyen.'

She had spent a whole day and most of the evening carefully sifting through all of Luc's correspondence. She wanted nothing incriminating to fall into the wrong hands. Once she had left the house, she had no doubt that Paul would invade it, searching for the proof he needed to confirm his bizarre claims. She had given the servants instructions not to obstruct him in any way, and she would leave word with the lawyer that, should he wish to do so, Paul could take up residence in the Hôtel

Boussières with her permission. She would never live there again!

'You are still determined to leave Paris and go to Noyen?' Selim asked quietly. 'A departure so soon after the death of your husband will provide his son with more ammunition to use against you.'

'And what could I do if I stayed, Selim? Prove my innocence and yours by having Luc's body pulled from the ground and examined? Or perhaps I should return to Versailles, and flutter my eyelashes coyly at a few prominent men and persuade them to stand by me in my hour of need? You know I will do neither. When I am out of reach I pray everyone will get bored with Paul's constant accusations. I do have friends at Court, Madame de Mailly and the Countess Vostock. And Henri, Duc de Blas...'

Selim noticed how she stopped short of the name of the man she needed most in her life at this moment. Was he bitter enough still to stay away and allow her to fight this battle alone, or would he be drawn yet again to her side, unable to deny what was in his heart?

'I shall visit Madame d'Etoiles tomorrow afternoon and start for Noyen the morning after. I shall travel light. The heavy baggage can follow later. And you, Selim, what will you do now?'

'I am free, *madame*. I shall return home. There are many things there I left unfinished,' came the answer which sent a momentary chill of fear through her. After all this time with Luc, he was still going to go back and seek out the wife who had betrayed him, the brother who had left him to die in the desert. She knew he would kill both without a qualm. Yet, since that awful day he had discovered her coming out of Alain's room at Belaincourt, he had said nothing to her! Sensing her un-asked question, the Moor reached into his robes and produced a leather-bound book which he held out to her.

'There is much you do not understand. This will answer all questions and set your mind at rest. You were in no way to blame for what has happened, *madame*.

You were carefully manipulated by a man with a brilliant brain, who, realising he could not have what he most desired in life, set out to create a new fantasy for himself—this time with a happy ending. And he has succeeded, believe me. With this in your possession and shown to the right people—who no doubt could be persuaded to make its contents known to the King—Paul Boussières will be silenced forever, and you will be able to enjoy the happiness Luc intended you should have.'

Alexandrine's fingers trembled as they closed around the well-worn leather.

'You talk in riddles, Selim. What is this?'

'A diary of many years' standing. Luc's diary. It contains his innermost thoughts about everything—and everyone. He has bared his soul to the world, *madame*. Spared no details of his madness, nor the consequences of his unhappy marriage and the unfortunate inheritance he has left to his son.'

'And you would have me make this public!' she gasped. 'I could not! Neither of us want the world to know he—he was...'

'A madman!' Selim gave a strange smile. 'If you do not clear yourself, *madame*, it will all have been for nothing.'

'Only as a last resort will I use it,' Alexandrine replied. Luc's diary—his most intimate thoughts. She was almost afraid to open it and see what he had written!

Francine closed the lid of yet another trunk and sighed in relief when she looked about her and saw there were very few clothes to be put away. Although the majority of Alexandrine's things would be despatched to Noyen in a week or two, she had no intention of allowing other hands to touch such finery, or envy the array of exquisite jewels her mistress possessed. She was still unsure of the decision she had herself made—to remain in Paris and marry Jules. She felt her place was with her mistress, for a short while at least. She was grieving deeply over the loss of her aged husband. Francine did not understand the solemnity of her mood—nay, the strangeness of it since she had come into the room two hours before and seated herself in a chair to read the book she had brought with her.

She had loved the Marquis—as well as a beautiful young thing of her age could love an old man—and she had cared for him, made him proud of her. Yet now she was free, she did not seem happy. The sadness in her eyes was like one who had lost everything! Why had she not sent for the Duc de Belaincourt? He would not only be able to console her, and perhaps bring a smile again to those pale cheeks, but he would stand at her side against those who meant to do her harm. Paris had something new to gossip about. Even the market that morning had been full of giggling women who plied her with stupid questions. She had slapped one grinning face. How could anyone believe her mistress capable of murder! She had crossed the river without delay, to seek help from Solange, but the woman was not at home and had not been seen for a day or so. She, of all people, could have given the Marquise reassurance. She would go again tomorrow, before the departure for Noyen.

'Shall I bring you some refreshment, *madame*?' She stood at Alexandrine's shoulder, curiously gazing down at the open pages and the large, scrawling words spread across them.

'No. I shall call if I need anything.' Alexandrine did not even look up, and the maid returned to the packing more intrigued than before.

Alexandrine was mesmerised by what she read, torn apart by some of the heart-rending rhetoric. It was an epic—the soul of a man laid bare. A man seeking, through his travels to other worlds, to escape that which he feared most—the world of reality in which he would some day lose his reason. He had spared himself nothing. His childhood, and later the discovery of the taint his mother had passed on to her son. The years of seeking medical help wherever he could find it—the gradual acceptance that he was doomed to madness. The wild years of carousing throughout the world, seeking new experiences, new friends, new places of interest until, all avenues of hope exhausted, he returned to France—to Paris and the son in whom, every day, he saw more of himself.

She felt tears prick the corners of her eyes as she closed the diary. The last pages she had read time and time again. Luc had planned everything. It seemed unbelievable, but it was true. For some reason, soon after their marriage, he had decided he must find a man who would care for Alexandrine when he was dead...and he had chosen Alain Ratan, Duc de Belaincourt, as her new husband. With foresight—and great deviousness— he had deliberately thrown them together. The chance meetings, the visits to the Hôtel Boussières—even the visit to Belaincourt had been planned. In turn he had manipulated them all. Even Selim? she wondered, as she rose to her feet and swayed towards the door.

'*Madame*, are you all right...?'

She did not hear Francine's anxious voice behind her, was conscious of nothing until she entered Luc's room and confronted the Moor. He was sitting in front of her husband's desk, lost in his own thoughts. Several times she had found him this way. He had rarely left these rooms since Luc's death, she remembered, and wondered if he found it as difficult as she did to erase him from his thoughts.

One look into her face was sufficient to tell the Moor she had read the diary from beginning to end. He stood up and his presence, as always, seemed to dominate the room, reminding her of the power he had wielded over both Luc and herself. Yet even he, a Prince in his own country, would be nothing more than a common criminal if she allowed the book in her possession to be made public.

'Have you come to stand in judgement on him?'

'No, how can you think that? I have come to tell you I think we should destroy the diary,' Alexandrine said quietly, avoiding looking at the large, empty bed to one side of her.

'Have you considered the alternative? Paul Boussières will destroy you! Use the book as Luc intended—clear yourself.'

'And you, Selim. Dear God, I don't know what to do. How can I allow you to be accused of this foul crime when you are innocent—as innocent as me? It was Luc's wish—he has written it here—when the time came, if he were too weak to take the—the poison himself, you would keep your promise to free him from his misery. Who can I trust to read his innermost thoughts, and not revel in the havoc they can cause by revealing the truth? There would always be questions...'

'Which could be silenced by one powerful enough,' Selim interrupted. 'Who would dare question the King of France if *he* declared us innocent?'

'The King...but how? Jeanne! She was fond of Luc. She will keep his secret. I know of no other, and she might be able to speak to the King. She must, Selim! She is our only hope. I shall go to her first thing in the morning,' Alexandrine declared, faint hope rising in her. 'Forgive my faint heart...whether you believe it or not, I shall do nothing to injure Luc in any way...no matter what happens to me.' As the ebony features broke into a smile, she gave a gasp. 'You *wanted* me to go to Jeanne. You knew I would not show it to anyone else!'

'It is not written that you should leave this world yet. Luc was quite impressed with the woman Solange when we visited her and she told him you were not meant for him and never had been.'

'You—he visited Solange!' Alexandrine exclaimed. 'Did—did you follow me that day?'

'Do you think I would have allowed you to go off alone with the Duc, even, as you planned, to the dressmaker? Even when Luc had already planned for you? It was too soon to be bold, *madame*. Luc was curious to learn what you had been told. Afterwards, when we returned to the house he said, "*Inshal'lah*. I cannot change what is written for her in the stars. She has always belonged to another. I but interrupted her upon the journey to reach him. Now I shall remedy that." Do not let all his efforts be in vain.'

'I cannot speak for the Duc de Belaincourt,' Alexandrine said, clutching the diary close against her

heart. How could she show him this, reveal that what
had happened between them had been because Luc had
wished it to be so? And he had thought *he* was chasing
her! Using her!

'A pity. You have need of a man at this moment. I
shall accompany you to Noyen and remain until we hear
from Madame d'Etoiles. I have waited many years to
return home,' he added as Alexandrine opened her
mouth to question the unexpected decision, 'and I have
learned patience. You must do the same. It may take
some time for the diary to reach the right hands. Impress
upon her the urgency of a reply—and the delicacy of
the situation.'

'Believe me, she will be most discreet,' he was assured. 'Her own position is somewhat delicate, is it not?'

'*Mon Dieu*, my poor Alexandrine! I did not realise what
a bizarre life you had been leading. I was not foolish
enough to believe all those tales of a blissful, contented
marriage, although you told them at times most con-
vincingly, but this... I am speechless.'

Speechless was something Jeanne had not been from
the moment Alexandrine arrived at the house and they
were closeted together in the small parlour at the back
of the house. The instant she began to peruse the diary
there were frowns, gasps, exclamations of amazement...

'It was not as terrible as you think,' Alexandrine protested. 'But you can see my dilemma. I cannot let just
anyone see this! Luc would be the laughing-stock of
Paris, and I could not bear that.'

'You have not considered the other thing that could
happen.' Jeanne's expression was suddenly grave. 'This
diary, in Luc's own handwriting, proclaims that when
he died he was not in full command of his senses. True,
it clears both you and Selim of murder—but... don't
you understand? You will give Paul Boussières just what
he wants—proof that his father was incapable of making
decisions. The last will could be revoked. You would
have nothing; it would all go to him.'

'I don't care about that... but everyone would know
about Luc as well. Oh, Jeanne, how stupid of me. I

didn't think of that at all. Then even the King cannot see the diary...'

'The King counted the Marquis de Mezière among his friends, as did his father before him. I shall despatch this to him this afternoon by a trusted messenger. It will be given into his hands alone, together with a letter which I shall write as soon as you have gone. I promise you I will lose no time, Alexandrine.'

'Tomorrow Selim and I are leaving for Noyen. Don't worry, we still have the men Alain provided for us. We shall be well guarded. We shall wait there until we hear from you.'

'You will return to Paris in triumph,' Jeanne promised. 'I shall ask the King to extend a personal invitation for you to attend Versailles the moment he returns home.'

'You—you have that much influence over him?' Alexandrine said, awed by the new dimension her friend had achieved.

'It is a small favour—asked of a friend—for a friend.' Jeanne laughed softly. 'Go home now, and don't worry. I shall see you soon—when you return to Paris.'

There were tears in Alexandrine's eyes as she climbed into the waiting carriage, for she did not have the courage to tell Jeanne she would not be coming back. Paris meant Belaincourt and Alain—and the love she knew she must deny herself. She would not be used again by any man!

The attack on the carriage was swift and merciless. Alexandrine had ordered the drive back to the Hôtel Boussières to use a route through the Bois, so that she could take a last look at the place where she had enjoyed so many early morning rides. Totally engrossed in her thoughts, she did not hear the muffled cry of pain which was all the unfortunate coachman could utter before his life was abruptly ended and his body was tossed callously into thick bushes. Her first indication that anything was wrong was when something dark plunged past the window, and the carriage began to pick up speed.

Startled, she glanced out of the window and, realising they were heading out of the Bois, in the opposite direction to the house, she leaned out, the wind whipping her hair and bringing tears to her eyes, so fast was the carriage now being driven.

The face which turned in her direction was not one she recognised. There was no sign of the coachman or her bodyguard. She pulled back, a hand against her mouth. She was being abducted and there was nothing she could do about it. They were heading away from Paris—but where? As a cluster of small cottages came into view she leaned out of the window and screamed for help—but in vain. A man and a small boy working in a field alongside them stared for a moment at the distressed features of the beautiful young woman, before shrugging their shoulders and returning to their work. It was not wise to show interest in how the nobility chose to amuse themselves.

Alexandrine was seized with the wild idea of throwing open the door and hurling herself into the road. She would be hurt—perhaps knocked unconscious—and would gain nothing from such desperation, but what other choice had she? But even as the idea entered her brain a thin man clambered through the curtained window. The jolting of the carriage threw him on to her and, before she could recover her wits, he had thrust an evil-smelling piece of cloth about her mouth. A knee in the small of her back forced her face down on to the seat, and her hands were secured behind her back with rope that bit painfully into her soft skin. The swiftness with which she was bound, the ease with which her assailant overcame her, told her she had encountered this kind of man before—in the Forest of Sénart, the day an attack had been made on her life. And those men had been sent to kill her by Paul Boussières. These were his men too! Bound, helpless, half senseless with fear, she fought back the tears as the carriage continued at its horrendous pace away from the city. Taking her she knew not where. At the end of the journey would there be death at the hands of these cold-hearted men? Or would Paul be waiting to exact his revenge on her? What difference was there? Only death awaited her when the carriage stopped...

When the carriage came to an abrupt halt she was thrown violently to the floor where she lay with swimming senses, barely conscious. She was aware of being dragged out into fresh air, but the blow to the head she had sustained had so dazed her that she could not ascertain where she was as she was propelled at a fast pace towards a large house. That it was a fashionable house was all she was able to see before her knees buckled, and she slumped, half fainting, against her kidnapper. The man swore at her, tried to jerk her to her feet and then, seeing it was no use, he picked her up as if she were a sack of vegetables, tossed her over one hard shoulder and strode on. The last remaining breath knocked from her body by his roughness, Alexandrine's senses faded...

She became aware of intense heat on her face. A stifling heat, accompanied by the putrid smell of something burning. Dear God! Were they going to burn her alive? Her eyes took some little while to focus upon her new surroundings. The scene which revealed itself to her brought her upright with a shrill scream of horror—only to find her hands were shackled above her head to a large iron ring, embedded in the damp stone wall against which she had been placed.

She was in a large cellar filled with an array of torture instruments which would have made the blood of the bravest man turn to ice—and at that moment Alexandrine was feeling far from brave. No one knew where she was! Selim would not think her absence anything to be concerned about perhaps until it grew dark...and Jeanne did not know of her detour through the Bois...

A man moved into her line of vision to heap more coals on to the red-hot brazier. He was stripped to the waist—sweat gleaming on his half-naked torso as he turned and stared in her direction. He would enjoy applying the irons to her—it was written all over his squat, ape-like features. He took a pace towards her, a hand reaching out to rip away her bodice, but a shadow moved off to one side of Alexandrine. A voice she knew well, dreaded to hear again, chuckled softly.

'You are too impatient, Leonard. You are an insensitive oaf. Perhaps the lady will co-operate with us and save herself a great deal of pain.'

Paul stepped in front of his helpless captive and studied her terrified face for a long moment. The last time, before Christmas, that he had had her at his mercy his amusement had been interrupted by Alain Ratan. What a comforting thought it was that the man was at Metz with the King, unable to rush to the aid of his mistress! He had no doubt they were lovers. As once before, a woman he desired preferred the Duc de Belaincourt to him! And her other champion, the Moor, was miles away in Paris and would never know what had happened to her. Perhaps, as a gesture of kindness, Paul decided, he would tell him before he had him, too, disposed of. There would be no one left to oppose him when he challenged his father's latest will—and he would be able to present proof that Alexandrine had not only taken a lover, but had conspired to have her husband done away with. Everything was so nearly in his grasp.

You are mad, like your father...the same words that had come to Alexandrine's lips at the graveside came now as she looked into his smiling features, but they were not uttered. As then, she knew the futility of unleashing on him the terrible secret carried within her. With his mode of life, he would begin to suspect soon enough...or others would... Dear God, allow her to live to see that day, she prayed. She feared she would be dead, her body disposed of somewhere where she might not be found for years—if ever at all—and, even after Jeanne had shown the King the diary, it would be of no help to her. Alain would know the truth—that she was not the frivolous adventuress he believed—but the thought at that moment brought her no comfort. Only the sight of him could have done that...

Paul came closer. The stench of perfume about him made her stomach heave. His face was more heavily powdered and rouged than usual, and the handkerchief waved beneath her nose reeked of musk. He laughed as she flinched back to avoid the fingers which caressed her bruised cheek.

'Be nice to me, Alexandrine. I am all that stands between you and a very slow, painful, lingering death. Give me what I want, and I shall have Leonard end it quickly for him—he has already had enough fun with the gypsy woman. To excess, as always, I fear. She will be of no use to me again. No matter, I have what I want from her. From you, I need confirmation of her story...'

'Solange...' Alexandrine's voice was barely audible. That terrible smell of burning...

And then against the opposite wall she saw something that no longer resembled a human being. Once it had been an attractive woman who had told her fortune, made her amused by the speculation she would take a lover and be happy. Solange! Was that creature, half-naked, the flesh branded on every visible part—face, legs, breasts, stomach—was it possible? She closed her eyes until the waves of nausea subsided, but upon opening them was unable to drag her gaze from the hideous sight. Was this what Paul had planned for her if she did not do all he asked of her?

'Why? She never harmed you! You did not even know her.'

'But you did, my dear, and my father also visited her for a consultation, did he not? She has been extremely useful to me. I would have had to get rid of her anyway, so her death is of no importance,' Paul added with a shrug. 'As I shall rid myself of anyone who stands in my way.'

'I am going upstairs, Paul. I cannot stay here a moment longer.' Claudia, silent until now, hidden in the shadows beyond the blazing fire, could contain her repugnance of the whole scene no longer. Paul had forced her to accompany him to the cellar and watch the torture of the gypsy woman. That had been bad enough, watching him excited by her screams, urging Leonard on and on to extract more information, berating him when his brutality failed to produce it—cackling glee-

fully when his methods were successful. Now
Alexandrine was to be the focal point of his entertainment. He would make her suffer, whatever she said
to save herself, she suspected. And then on whom would
he turn? Her! Anyone who stood in his way—anyone
who knew too much. She could almost feel the searing
hot irons upon her breast! She shivered and turned to
the door, ignoring the jibe from behind.

'I thought perhaps you would like to apply the first
iron to your rival's soft skin, Claudia.'

'You will enjoy it much more than me. I shall wait
for you upstairs.'

'My dear, this is far more entertaining than you could
ever imagine. More than you are.'

She knew that to run from him would have aroused
his anger, made him send someone after her... but the
moment the door of the cellar closed behind her she
picked up her skirts and fled upstairs. To the servant
who came in answer to her summons she gave a hastily
penned letter.

'Give this into the hands of Selim the Moor at the
Hôtel Boussières—and no other. Take care you are not
followed. There is madness afoot this night, and if you
are caught—you will pay for your mistake with your life!'

'Now, my dear, we are alone and can continue with
our business uninterrupted. Claudia has no stomach for
this—and I do not blame her.' Paul ran ringed fingers
over Alexandrine's bruised cheek as if concerned by the
sight of it, then without warning viciously pinched it.
He broke into peals of laughter as she cried out and
jerked back her head. 'That is nothing to the pain you
shall feel if you are uncooperative. Let me explain how
delicate is your position. When you understand what will
be done to that lovely body of yours by Leonard here,
I think you will prefer to do as I ask, and then I shall
be kind and allow him merely to cut your throat. There
is a well here...' He indicated a ringed flagstone set in
the floor near her feet. 'It has been of great use to me
in the past. It is not bottomless, as everyone believes,
but will take whatever descends into it into the Seine.

By the time you are found, Alexandrine, I doubt if you will be recognised. You will end up in some pauper's grave, unknown, unclaimed...a fitting reward for such as you.'

'Selim will know...' Alexandrine gasped through dry lips, as the man Leonard pushed several ugly-looking irons into the flaming brazier.

'He will not be difficult to deal with. Without your protection—and with the incriminating document I shall produce, signed by you, naturally, which will describe how you and he planned to kill my poor father, and how the Moor even persuaded dear Papa, against his will, to marry the little orphan and bring her to Paris, at your instigation—I shall probably be able to have him stoned in the streets.' Paul studied the ashen face which still bore traces of defiance in the tightly closed mouth, the loathing and contempt in the eyes which held his. She was going to be stubborn. How wonderful. The evening would not be dull after all!

A snap of his fingers brought his clerk from the table behind him with a chair for him to seat himself.

'The gypsy's confession,' he snapped. 'It is time the Marquise heard the evidence I shall produce against her.'

Alexandrine fought against the waves of faintness which threatened to drag her down into the black abyss of unconsciousness. It would be a blessed relief to give way, but the respite would be brief. She had no doubt that whatever she said Paul was going to have her reduced to the same terrible, grotesque, mutilated heap of flesh that hung on the opposite wall. Nothing could save her. And then what was left of her would be disposed of in the well, to float perhaps for days in the dirty waters of the Seine. Hopelessness engulfed her. Her legs buckled and she sagged weakly against the damp stones behind her, held only by the iron cuffs about her wrists. It was a moment only before the pain of them biting agonisingly into her soft skin was sufficient to drag her back to reality, and she heard the mocking voice, like something out of a nightmare, reading from one of the papers he held.

'My dear *Madame*, I am sending you a small token of my gratitude for assuring me of a bright future…and with the man I love. Is that not what every woman dreams of…?'

Her head jerked up, eyes widened in surprise, then horror. It was part of the letter she had sent to Solange when the gypsy woman had returned her fan and with it a prediction of her future. Those words were like a curse upon her head now. 'There will be two men in your life.' Luc and Alain! 'You will love only one'— Alain!

'A note of thanks for a silly fortune-telling.' She flung the words at him disdainfully. 'No one can make anything of that.'

'I can, my dear Alexandrine. This,' another piece of paper was waved before her tortured gaze, 'is the proof, signed by the gypsy woman herself, that you were supplied with certain—powders, for which she is also very well known—powders which, administered slowly, carefully, will *kill*! The death of my father has, of course, assured you of a bright future with the man you love. Alain Ratan. Did you think I didn't know? I've watched you together, seen the way you look at each other…'

'If we are so besotted with each other, why has he not come to me when I need him most?' Alexandrine cried. 'We are not lovers!'

'How noble a gesture, but you do not have to protect him. I shall deprive him of you—that will be sufficient. And should he prove troublesome, I might begin to hint at *his* involvement in my father's demise. If you could persuade an ugly swine like the Moor to do your bidding, Alain would have stood little chance. And there is still the matter of the new will, is there not? The driver of the *fiacre* that took you to Belaincourt that day was most helpful. He left you there, alone with Alain. And you, who professed to be a loving wife—such behaviour when your husband had been kidnapped—his very life threatened.'

'By his own son.' Alexandrine could hear the fear creeping into her voice, but she could not hide it. She knew only too well how easily people—especially the vain people at Court—could be swayed, with pretty words, promises, bribes! Many had believed the worst of her from the beginning, a pretence Paul had kept alive with his innuendoes. It would not be difficult for him to persuade others she was a murderess as well as an adulteress.

'A contrite son who has done penance for his mistake,' Paul chuckled. 'Claudia's money—and her faith in me—has done a great deal to convert those who were at first sceptical that I was a reformed character. Now, let us see what we have so far against you, Madame la Marquise de Mezière. That will be the last time you hear that title from anyone's lips. First, we have an unknown little country wench, with good looks—and ambition—who marries a man older than her own father. A man who gives her everything—money, clothes, jewels—and introduces her to the nobility of Paris. She finds her life with an old man boring, and longs for the excitement she finds at Court. She hungers like the wanton she is for the company—nay, more than the company—of younger men to satisfy her lustful nature. Her husband's close friend is also his physician, a most useful person, knowledgeable in the art of healing—or, in this case, the diabolical art of administering slow death. She enlists the aid of this man—to what end? To dispose of the unwanted and now unnecessary husband. By what means she persuaded him to this one can only guess...and I, naturally, will be on hand to remind everyone how beautiful you are—*were...*.' Alexandrine flinched visibly as he corrected himself. A red-hot iron was withdrawn from the brazier. Leonard approached with it held at arm's length, until she could feel the heat of it against her bare shoulder. 'Let her feel it—just a little,' Paul murmured, his eyes intent on Alexandrine's terrified features. 'Caress that lovely skin—oh, so carefully—if you touch it, you oaf, I'll have you in her place next.'

Alexandrine could not escape the menacing iron. She shrank back against the wall, but it came closer—closer. To move more would thrust her shoulder against it. She closed her eyes, biting her lip to hold back a scream as the intense heat seared the unprotected skin...but did not touch it...and after a moment was withdrawn. Her shoulder throbbed and a large area had become bright red.

Without warning hooked fingers fastened themselves in the front of her gown and ripped the bodice open to the waist. The protective shift beneath followed, baring her breasts to all in the room. Paul leaned forward in his chair—for an instant she was reminded of Luc as he wiped a hand across his mouth. Luc had looked at her in that strange way too, when the madness was coming upon him. She realised now how desperately he had fought against not only that, but his own needs. His tremendous will-power had made it possible for him to hold back the dreaded malady longer than most men— Paul did not possess his strength. With her death Paul would have everything he had ever wanted. His father's money and title, his house...and the affliction, which would soon—very soon, she suspected—make itself known to him. Earlier, she knew she would have done no good to herself, or others, by revealing the insanity inside him, but now what did it matter? Jeanne would show the King the diary. The secret would go no further. It was her only comforting thought. As for Paul Boussières—before she died, she would tell him the dreaded secret that had been kept from him since childhood.

'The iron,' Paul snapped, incensed by her silence. He wanted her to beg for mercy, for otherwise there would be no enjoyment in it for him. Damn the woman, why was she not grovelling before him? She was helpless and facing a most agonising death, which would break the bravest of men, yet defiance still lingered on her pale face. He would soon change that.

He leaned forward in his chair, his eyes riveted on the red-hot iron approaching Alexandrine's cheek. So intense was the heat that a lock of hair curling towards her aching shoulder began to singe. The scream which broke from her lips brought a smile of satisfaction to

Paul's expectant features. He signalled Leonard to draw back as her eyes closed and she sank fainting against the wall. He did not mind waiting now. When she recovered her senses, they would begin in earnest.

Alexandrine's senses were slow to return. How long she drifted in and out of that strange state which was neither consciousness nor unconsciousness, she did not know. Always when she opened her eyes, the flames of the brazier seared them until the tears ran. The smell of burning remained in her nostrils to remind her how close she had come to being disfigured. Paul was playing with her, trying to break her spirit—and he was succeeding. The fear of the iron being laid against her body—as she knew it soon would be—could no longer be contained. If begging for clemency—appealing to the better nature of this man determined to destroy her—would have raised one iota of pity in him, then she would have done so. Anything! Anything to save herself, but she knew how futile the gesture would be.

Her wrists felt as if they were breaking and it took a tremendous effort on her part, to will strength down into her trembling legs so that they supported her again and eased the pain the chains were causing her.

'Give our guest some refreshment; it may help loosen her tongue,' she heard Paul order, and the next moment the clerk appeared before her swimming vision and put a glass to her lips.

'Drink, lady, and then tell him what he wants to hear. Sign his wretched confession. Save yourself,' the man whispered as she drank thirstily of the wine, hoping it would dull her senses still more against what was to come.

You fool! she almost cried, as he moved away and she saw the way Paul's gaze followed him. You will be next. No one who has witnessed what happens here tonight will be allowed to live.

'And now, my dear Alexandrine, we shall proceed. Your confession is ready for you to sign.'

'I shall sign nothing. Even if I do, you will still kill me. Without my signature, you have nothing.'

'Do you not think so? When you disappear without trace, what do you think people will make of that? There will be a sum of money missing—and all your jewels—and so the only conclusion they will draw is that you were guilty of adultery, guilty of the murder of my father, and have fled the country to avoid arrest and certain death. My father's estates will revert to me. I really have thought of everything, you know. I am not am amateur. When I wish to be rid of someone, I do a very good job.'

'You—you have killed before...?' Alexandrine forced the words through stiff lips. 'In cold blood? Planned to take a life?'

'Why do you look so surprised? In cold blood...hardly that. But in the past there have been those who—annoyed me to a point where I could not bear their presence any longer. Women, particularly, seem to come into that category.'

'I don't believe you!' she flung back, seizing on the wild idea that if she could keep him talking long enough—no matter how distasteful the subject—it might delay her own unpleasant demise. 'No one can disappear without questions being asked—an investigation by friends or relatives.'

'But of course there were questions, in all the cases. They were all answered. The widow LeClerc took her own life because an unknown admirer had jilted her. She drank a quantity of poison which should have been used to destroy the garden weeds. It was more useful when she took it.' Paul gave her a lopsided grin and a nerve twitched violently in one cheek. 'She took a long time to die, the old bitch—so did Nicolette... You know who I mean, don't you? I am enjoying this, do you know that? It's not often I can have a captive audience...' He chuckled at the pun. 'I can tell you about it because you will never repeat what you hear. What a pity you cannot run to Alain and tell him of the great favour I did for him.'

'You—killed Alain's wife! It was an accident...'

'A cleverly contrived accident. She should not have laughed at me. She signed her own death warrant when she did.' A sly look crept across his face as he pondered on his own cleverness. 'I was not good enough for the trollop. She hated Alain, but she said even he satisfied her more than I did. She should not have said such a terrible thing to me. But I paid her back. It took her hours to die, too, but when she was found back in the forest where she'd been hunting, later that afternoon, no one could tell quite whether the damage to her body was caused by being dragged by a bolting horse through a dense forest—or whether something more—unusual— had happened to her. Unfortunate, wasn't it, that a stone should hit her horse just as she fell momentarily behind her companions . . . and such a—*coincidence*—that my men happened to be near by . . .' He chuckled at his own cleverness. 'I did Alain a favour.'

'You caused him unbelievable pain,' Alexandrine cried. Innocent, and he would never know the truth of it.

'As I hope I shall again, for he will never know what happened to you, will he? He will always wonder if he made a fool of himself again by falling in love with a woman whose morals were as low as those of his dead wife. Why should he always get what he wants, just because he is good-looking and wealthy?'

'Because he is a man.' Alexandrine forgot the pain in her wrists and shoulder as blue fire leapt across the space separating them. If a look could kill, Paul should have shrivelled in his chair. And he hated her even more for this last show of strength—of revulsion. She had looked at Alain Ratan, like other women he had wanted, and after that, he was unimportant. He hated her for being close to the father who had always rejected a close bond between them, hated her for being so beautiful and so aloof from him! Hated her for giving herself to another man when she could have had *him* as a lover. Most of all he hated her for that. Now, she too would pay for her foolishness.

'I have lost patience with you, Alexandrine. I have no more time to waste with pleasantries. Leonard, apply the iron—properly this time. It will be interesting to see how long she can last. The gypsy woman managed to hang on for two days...I don't think this little, wilting flower will endure more than a few hours. But they will be entertaining hours.'

'You are mad—just like Luc!' Alexandrine screamed the words at him, and the cellar was suddenly still. Leonard, a fresh iron just withdrawn from the fire, froze, his gaze on Paul Boussières. The clerk behind him dropped the sheaf of papers he held, but made no move to pick them up, his eyes also riveted on the man in the chair, whose knuckles had grown white as they tightly closed about the glass in one hand. She had put into words what they already suspected, she realised. No one could act as he did and be sane.

The stem of the crystal glass snapped in two. What remained was hurled to one side to smash against the wall.

'Luc was mad when he died...as his mother was before him. As you will be—are! You can do nothing to stop what is happening to you—it's the truth. Ask Selim. Why do you think he was so protective with your father? He kept him sedated to try and hold back the terrible malady...but in the end it was impossible...'

'You lie. You bitch!' Eyes blazing, Paul leapt from his chair to deal her a savage blow across the face. 'You are like all the rest of them, but I'll show you...' Wheeling around, he snatched the iron from Leonard and thrust it before her face. 'Scream, damn you! Confess!'

Alexandrine's senses began to leave her again. The nauseating smell of burning became stronger. Any moment she expected to feel the torturing pain of the branding-iron upon her skin. Dear God, take me now, she prayed. Do not force me to endure any more. She screamed, but the sound seemed to come from a long way off...yet was there not another sound too...?

Voices! Loud, angry voices which were making themselves heard above the curses Paul was raining in her ears. A scream . . . not from her lips . . . of agony . . . more shouting . . . and then an arm about her waist . . . her wrists unshackled . . . and she sank against whoever held her, not knowing who—or how—only that she had somehow miraculously been spared Paul's demented revenge.

She opened her eyes on to Selim's coal-black features, and tears flooded down over her cheeks as he examined the places where the white-hot iron had threatened.

'I have salve to take away the pain and something to make you sleep for a day and a night. When you awake this will be no more than a dream . . . You are safe, *madame*.'

'Safe?' Alexandrine shuddered, her mind reeling with questions. 'How did you find me? I was kidnapped in the Bois . . . he wanted me to confess to Luc's murder . . . Solange . . .' She clung to him, reassuring herself with the solidness beneath her fingers, that she was indeed safe.

'Hush, my love, do not talk now.'

It was impossible. It was not Selim holding her now, but Alain, his face bruised, his shirt ripped and one sleeve blackened by the heat of the iron Leonard had thrown at him before he died on Alain's blade. She could say nothing, only look at him in disbelief—in wonder, until he could stand it no more and gathered her against his chest, laying his lips against the place where Paul had struck her, burying his mouth into the mass of blonde curls singed about her neck. He had ridden like a devil to reach Paris, only to find Alexandrine had not returned to the Hôtel Boussières after her visit to Jeanne d'Etoiles. The Moor had not seemed surprised by his appearance, or by his desire to find Alexandrine and take her directly to the safety of Belaincourt, and had not hesitated to accompany him to Jeanne's house. To learn that the woman he loved had left there hours before had heightened Alain's suspicions that she was in grave danger.

As once before when he was in need of good fighting men, he had sent Jules to enlist the aid of men who would ask no questions for a full purse of money. He did not care what he had to do to secure Alexandrine's release from wherever she was being held. Selim he sent to fetch Henri, Duc de Blas and two others, both connected by marriage to the royal family, who would, he knew, respect Louis's command that Alexandrine should be placed under his protection...and would act as witnesses to whatever took place.

He did not have time to read much of the diary Jeanne had thrust into his hands, her young face pale with concern as she ordered him to read and come to know the woman he had in the past maligned with his suspicions, but he saw enough, in Luc's familiar hand, to know what was written was the truth.

He could not find the words to tell Alexandrine now, but later, when the horror of it all had faded a little, he would tell her of the rage which consumed him at his own blind stupidity. The time he had wasted hating, suspecting, instead of accepting and loving her as he knew he always had from the first moment he had seen her.

'Who—who are those men?' Alexandrine became aware of three figures standing on the cellar steps. Henri she recognised, but, although the other faces seemed to be familiar, she could put no names to them.

'Witnesses to all Paul has tried to do. We overheard everything, Alexa, and on the way here we encountered a messenger sent by Claudia to warn Selim of your danger. At the last, she too has realised what she was dealing with. As a result of her confession, as well as our testimony, Paul will spend the rest of his days in the Bastille—or a madhouse.'

'You heard everything?' Alexandrine whispered. 'Nicolette...'

'Yes, that too. God rest her soul, I no longer loved her, but to die like that...' Alain's voice broke, and he held her close again. Only as his fingers brushed her exposed breast did Alexandrine become aware of her nakedness and draw together her ripped bodice as best possible. At once, as he saw the mounting embarrassment in her face, he drew off his jacket and wrapped it firmly about her. 'It is time to take you away from this place of death.'

'No!' From across the room Paul scrambled to his feet and screamed at her. 'No—she must die! She killed my father . . . gave herself to him so that he would do her bidding. The gypsy said so . . .' He flung a quivering hand out towards first Selim and then Solange. To all who watched, it was clear he was totally losing control. Laughing and crying at the same time. Tears streaming down his cheeks, streaking the heavy powder and rouge he wore, until his face became a grotesque mask. Alexandrine shivered and felt Alain's grasp tighten. Even though she knew she would be protected from this man for the rest of her life, she found herself wondering if a day would go by when she did not remember this night, or hear his voice in her sleep, feel his cold fingers touching her skin. While he lived, would she ever know peace?

'There is someone upstairs who will give us the truth, *messieurs*,' Alain said coldly. 'As will that unfortunate man cowering in the shadows, who has doubtless witnessed all that has taken place. To save his skin he will talk.'

'Yes, yes. Anything. Ask me anything.' The clerk fell to his knees, trembling. 'What I have written is not the truth—he made me . . .'

With an enraged cry, Paul flung himself at the man, but, even as his hands closed about his neck, Selim was upon him, prising them free, throwing him backwards with such force that he could not recover his balance. He gave one hideous scream as he teetered on the edge of the yawning hole behind him, opened in readiness to receive Alexandrine when he had finished with her, and disappeared from sight. After what seemed to everyone an eternity, there came a faint splash from the bowels of the earth, and then the only sound was that of Alexandrine sobbing in Alain's arms.

'Now it is truly over, my love. It was an accident. Selim is not to blame, any more than he shall be held responsible for Luc's death. Or you.' He raised his head, and pale green eyes gleamed a warning as they stared at the two men beside his friend Henri. 'Whatever was overheard here, gentlemen, you will report in private to the King. Not one word will be revealed to another living soul. I demand that in his name. Do I have your word?'

'You do, Monsieur le Duc. For the King's ears only.'

'And mine, *monsieur*.'

'Thank you,' Alexandrine whispered weakly. She was drained of strength. She wanted to hold him, let her lips tell him the depth of her love, but she was too weak and exhausted. Alain smoothed the loose hair from her face, and gently pressed his mouth against hers.

'Let us be gone from here. I want you to myself without these eyes on us. We shall be together as was meant to be...'

'Jeanne has shown you Luc's diary...oh, no, Alain...I want your love—not your pity!'

'You little fool, you have always had my love. I was coming to you long before I knew what Luc had planned for us. I was afraid for you.'

'Where are you taking me...?' She raised her head from his shoulder, as she was lifted and carried away from the stench of death and the threatening brazier and the sight of Solange. Her head began to reel, and she replaced it against the comforting silk of his shirt and the warmth of his skin that revived so many wonderful memories.

'To Belaincourt.'

'Alain, you cannot! People will talk...oh, think what they will say...' Why was she protesting, as if she did not want it, too?

'I am empowered by the King to protect you and see to your welfare until such time as he returns. Have no fear. You will be vindicated—and Selim. Once Jeanne has shown the King the diary, and you are received back at Court, there will not be one word said against you.'

'But Belaincourt...'

'I shall have that scatterbrain little maid brought to look after you. That will please Jules, and if there should be gossip——' He looked down at her, a wicked grin on his face. She was his. His! He felt as if he was walking on air. Heady, as he might feel after a bottle of Luc's best wine. 'Then I shall have to prevail upon the King's grace to allow us to marry before the mourning period is over, will I not, my love? I am not going to allow you out of my sight ever again.'

ROMANCING THE PHONE

Win the romantic holiday of a lifetime for two at the exclusive Couples Hotel in Ocho Rios on Jamaica's north coast with the Mills & Boon and British Telecom's novel competition, 'Romancing the Phone'.

This exciting competition looks at the importance the telephone call plays in romance. All you have to do is write a story or extract about a romance involving the phone which lasts approximately two minutes when read aloud.

The winner will not only receive the holiday in Jamaica, but the entry will also be heard by millions of people when it is included in a selection of extracts from a short list of entries on British Telecom's 'Romance Line'. Regional winners and runners up will receive British Telecom telephones, answer machines and Mills & Boon books.

For an entry leaflet and further details all you have to do is call 01 400 5359, or write to 'Romancing the Phone', 22 Endell Street, London WC2H 9AD.

You may be mailed with other offers as a result of this application.

TASTY FOOD COMPETITION!

How would you like a years supply of Mills & Boon Romances ABSOLUTELY FREE? Well, you can win them! All you have to do is complete the word puzzle below and send it in to us by March. 31st. 1990. The first 5 correct entries picked out of the bag after that date will win **a years supply of Mills & Boon Romances** (*ten books every month - worth £162*) What could be easier?

```
H O L L A N D A I S E R
E Y E G G O W H A O H A
R S E E C L A I R U C T
B T K K A E T S I F I A
E E T I S M A L C F U T
U R C M T L H E E L Q O
G S I U T F O N O E D U
N H L S O T O N E F M I
I S R S O M A C W A A L
R I A E E T I R J A E L
E F G L L P T O T V R E
M O U S S E E O D O C P
```

CLAM	**HOLLANDAISE**	**OYSTERS**	**SPICE**
COD	**JAM**	**PRAWN**	**STEAK**
CREAM	**LEEK**	**QUICHE**	**TART**
ECLAIR	**LEMON**	**RATATOUILLE**	
EGG	**MELON**	**RICE**	
FISH	**MERINGUE**	**RISOTTO**	
GARLIC	**MOUSSE**	**SALT**	
HERB	**MUSSELS**	**SOUFFLE**	

PLEASE TURN OVER FOR DETAILS ON HOW TO ENTER

HOW TO ENTER

All the words listed overleaf, below the word puzzle, are hidden in the grid. You can find them by reading the letters forward, backwards, up or down, or diagonally. When you find a word, circle it or put a line through it, the remaining letters (which you can read from left to right, from the top of the puzzle through to the bottom) will ask a romantic question.

After you have filled in all the words, don't forget to fill in your name and address in the space provided and pop this page in an envelope (you don't need a stamp) and post it today. Hurry - competition ends March 31st 1990.

**Mills & Boon Competition,
FREEPOST,**
P.O. Box 236,
Croydon,
Surrey. CR9 9EL
Only one entry per household

Hidden Question _____

_____

Name _____

Address _____

_____

_____

_____ Postcode _____

COMP 8